Taunting the

BIKER

CASSIE ALEXANDRA

Taunting the Biker

<u>BOOKS BY AUTHOR</u>

RESISTING THE BIKER
SURVIVING THE BIKER
FEARING THE BIKER
BREAKING THE BIKER
TAMING THE BIKER
LOVING THE BIKER
LURING THE BIKER
DESTROYING THE BIKER
TAUNTING THE BIKER

PHOENIX RISING

THE BURN
SWEET TREATS

<u>PARANORMAL FANTASY</u>

ALPHA

<u>OTHER BOOKS WRITTEN UNDER
PEN NAME KRISTEN MIDDLETON/K.L.
MIDDLETON</u>

TANGLED BEAUTY
TANGLED MESS
TANGLED FURY
SHARP EDGES

BLUR
SHIVER

Taunting the Biker

VENGEANCE
ILLUSIONS

VENOM
SLADE
TOXIC
CLAIMED BY THE LYCAN

JEZEBEL
DEVIANT

ZOMBIE GAMES
PAXTON VS THE UNDEAD
WITCHES OF BAYPORT
PLANET Z
THE COMPLEX

SEARCHING FOR FAITH
LOOKING FOR LAINEY
FORGET ME NOT
HEAR THEM SCREAM

ONE

CHARLIE

Buffalo, NY
Friday, July 22

I STARED OPEN-MOUTHED at my cell phone, still in shock at what had just happened. My fiancé had just sent me a text message, breaking off our engagement. Breaking off our entire *relationship*.

In… a… fucking… text….

"Who does that?" I said out loud, shaking in anger.

Not even a call. Just a stupid message telling me that he was confused and needed space. As far as I was concerned, he had more than he needed in his head and I was better off without him.

"Did you say something?" my father, Tony, asked behind me.

I swore under my breath. I really didn't need this right now. I knew if he found out Cody had just broken up with me, he'd gloat and then throw a damn celebration party. My father had been against our relationship from the very beginning. Even worse, if he knew how Cody had done it, he'd dive right into the "I-told-you-so" speech. I wasn't in the mood.

I turned around and made up something about getting a telemarketing call.

His eyes searched mine. Fortunately, I was too angry for tears. "You look like you're ready to bust someone's balls," he said with a slow smile. "Don't let them get to you, Charlotte. In fact, stop answering calls from numbers you don't recognize. It's a waste of time."

"Yeah. I know." I turned around and started walking away. "I'm going upstairs."

"Wait. What do you think of the new pool and landscaping in the back? Nice, huh?"

My father, a wealthy real estate investor and entrepreneur, had just spent over one million dollars for an in-ground swimming pool. It was surrounded by natural rock, had two beautiful stone waterfalls, a private grotto, and a slide. At night, the entire thing lit up, which made it even more impressive.

"It's gorgeous," I admitted.

"I'm glad you approve. I spent a small fortune trying to get it right." His smile fell and he stared at me with concern. "You look stressed out. Why don't you take something for it and go relax outside by the pool? It's such a beautiful day."

"I know. I just got back from playing tennis with Abby," I reminded him.

Abby was my father's "assistant" and very beautiful. Blonde, curvy, and always dressed to the nines. Even on the tennis court. She was also only a few years older than me and we got along fairly well. Sometimes, I could tell she was trying a little too hard to be my friend, which was amusing. In reality, I knew she was *more* than just my father's assistant. Everyone did. Even my mother, Bianca, who was currently living in Paris. My parents were still married, just living separate lives. Mom claimed it was because of her business—she was a former model-turned-purse designer. I also knew that she couldn't stand some of my father's business associates, who were always afoot and sometimes very annoying to me as well. Of course, she also had her own "assistants", including a very hot gardener named Phillipe, and her pool guy, Ferol. It was definitely a strange relationship between my parents. I had to believe that they both knew about the affairs, too, considering the little time they spent together. My father would visit my mother once every couple of months or she'd come here. But then again, he was a very possessive man, so it was hard to imagine that if he actually did know, he was fine with it. I'd learned over the years to not ask questions, however. Neither of them ever gave me any straight answers.

"Oh. Where is Abby?"

"She went home to shower and change. She said she'd call you later."

He looked pleased again. "Perfect. Well, I'm going back to my office. I'll be there if you need anything."

"Okay."

I went upstairs to my room, took a shower, and called my best friend, Jackie, and told her about Cody.

She gasped. "You've got to be kidding me?"

"I wish I was. He didn't even have the nerve to call me," I said, pacing in my room.

"That's total bullshit. You must be fuming."

"Yeah. You could say that."

She sighed. "Well, at least you learned what an asshole he is before marrying the turd."

I agreed.

"You seem to be taking this pretty good, considering."

She was right. In fact, I felt more angry than heartbroken. I just wasn't sure which made me more upset—the fact that Cody had broken up with me, or that my father had been right about him.

"I'm too pissed-off to be heartbroken right now," I replied, although I'd shed a few tears on the shower. Mostly because I'd spent so much time preparing for the wedding. We'd planned a big, expensive one, too, with all of the bells and whistles, courtesy of my father. Even though he'd been unimpressed with Cody, he'd opened up his wallet to help pay for everything, which had been a miracle in itself.

"I get it. Not to mention you're stuck living at home longer," she said.

There was definitely that.

I was tired of living with my dad. Yes, I had everything I wanted and needed at my fingertips, but it came with a suffocating price. My overprotective father still treated me like a teenager and it drove me crazy. Just the week before, I'd been at the mall with Jackie, and had caught two of his security guys following us. Right away, I called my father to complain. Of course, he'd brushed it off.

"Believe me, I didn't send them. They're probably there on their own time," he'd stated. "Don't be so paranoid, Charlotte."

Right.

The goons ended up following us around the mall for over an hour, trying to act inconspicuous. It had been comical, especially when we walked into Victoria's Secret and spent twenty minutes inside. At one point, the two must have thought we'd slipped out because they entered the store and then left quickly after spotting us. Eventually, I confronted them directly and asked what in the hell they were doing. They made up some excuse about shopping for their girlfriends and then finally disappeared.

"I can't keep living here," I said, walking out onto my balcony, which overlooked the swimming pool below. Although it looked like paradise, I wanted to be as far away from it as possible. I knew it was just one more ploy my father had construed to try and get me to stay. In fact, I'd begged and begged for a pool when I was a child. His excuse was the cost, although I would have settled on anything. I just loved the water. It wasn't until I told him about getting married to Cody that he suddenly decided it was time to have one in the backyard. "Maybe I should go away to college?"

"Hell yeah, you should. Isn't that what I've been telling you for the last five years? You have to stop letting your father dictate your life."

"Easier said than done," I murmured.

"What's he going to do if you enroll? Lock you up in your bedroom like Rapunzel?"

"True," I replied, walking back into my bedroom. I closed the sliding glass door, headed over to my vanity table, and sat down. "And, Lord knows I need to get away from this place. Not just this house, but maybe even New York."

I thought about the last conversation I'd had with him about college. I'd just turned twenty.

"I told you before that you don't need to go to college," he'd scoffed. "Your grandfather left you the kind of inheritance that will keep you living lavishly for the rest of your life. If you go off to school, some bum will sweep you off of your feet and end up controlling that fortune someday."

I'd argued back that I wasn't a damn fool, but my stubborn and headstrong father wouldn't listen. As usual. He also insisted that I live with him, at least until I received my inheritance at twenty-five. Being young and easily manipulated, I'd given in. Now that I was older, I wanted my independence and was willing to do almost anything for it.

Maybe even marriage.

The truth was, I'd been having my own doubts about spending the rest of my life with Cody, whom I'd only known for eight months. In the beginning of our relationship, he'd seemed so confident and smart. Not to mention handsome, attentive, and sweet. But, after we started making plans for the wedding, I'd noticed that he could also sometimes be a whiny, self-centered snob.

"For sure. You don't want to be stuck under your father's thumb for the next two years. I hate to say this, but maybe you should have taken that modeling agent up on that offer last year?"

"Yes." Sighing, I stared at my reflection in the mirror. I looked a lot like my mother, with my strawberry-blonde hair and green eyes. She been a runway model when my father had met her during a fashion show after-party in Milan. He used to tell me that he'd saved her life by making her give up her career.

"Modeling leads to eating disorders, drugs, and suicide," he used to say. "Your mother was lucky when she met me. She was living on saltwater and cucumbers at the time. Her roommates were heroin addicts. The path she was on would have eventually killed her if I hadn't gotten Bianca out of that scene."

Of course, her version of the past had been quite a bit different. She'd talked about traveling, parties, and meeting famous celebrities.

"I stopped modeling for him, which was a mistake," she once told me. "Never give up what you love for anyone. You'll one day end up regretting it."

"I'm serious, Charlie," Jackie said, returning me to the present. "You should really start thinking about applying to some colleges for the fall."

11

I was currently working as a hostess at my uncle's restaurant, *Wine Garden*, and had often thought about taking a few cooking classes. I enjoyed experimenting with foods, although I didn't get much of a chance to cook because Dad employed a chef to prepare all of our meals. Now that I didn't have much to hold me back, besides my overbearing father, I decided that the food service industry was definitely worth taking a closer look at. I told Jackie about it.

"That's a great idea. Just make sure you enroll in one that's nowhere near Buffalo," she said. "Maybe you can shoot for France or Italy."

I laughed. "Right. Wouldn't that be insane, though? My mother would be ecstatic if I moved to Europe."

"I'm sure she would. Watch, your father will probably buy a house near the school you choose," she mused.

My smile fell. He had the money and was an investor. With my luck, he probably would. "Don't jinx me."

"Sorry. You should seriously think about going finding a culinary school, though. It would be good for you."

"I think I will."

"Good. Oh crap. I have to go. I'm meeting Brian for a late lunch and wasn't watching the time."

Brian and Jackie had been seeing each other on and off for the past year. He seemed like a nice enough guy, although I had a feeling that their relationship was starting to fizzle out. She mentioned that he was getting to be a little too clingy and needy, which annoyed her.

"Oh. No problem. How's your mom, by the way?"

"The same as usual."

"Tell her I said 'Hi' the next time you see her."

"Will do. Keep me in the loop about your college plans."

"For sure."

"See you later, Gater."

"After while, Dile," I replied, almost forgetting our old familiar, parting mantra.

A SHORT TIME later, I pulled out my laptop and started researching culinary schools. Of course, there were so many to choose from and I didn't exactly know where to begin. Unfortunately, many of the top schools were in New York, which was definitely still off of my list. As I continued scouting for other ones that looked interesting, my cell phone rang. I checked the screen but didn't recognize the number. Curious, I answered it anyway.

"Hello?" I said.

"Cody Sanders accepted a bribe to break up with you," a man replied in a gravelly voice. "From your old man."

My stomach clenched up. "What? Who is this?"

"Fifty-thousand dollars. *Cash*. Apparently, that's all you were worth to him." He hung up.

I stared at my phone in horror.

Was it true?

His dumping *had* been damn sudden.

I dialed Cody's phone number. Of course, he didn't answer the phone so I left him a message.

"Call me. I need to ask you something."

I hung up and then tried calling back the mysterious caller. He didn't answer, either. There wasn't an option to leave a voicemail either. Frustrated, I tried looking up the phone number on the Internet, but couldn't find anything to help me distinguish who'd called. Frustrated, I called the number back again. This time, someone *did* answer. A woman.

"Excuse me, I just received a call from this number," I said, pacing again. "It had to do with Cody Sanders?"

"This is a pay-phone," the woman said tersely. "I don't know anything about a Cody Sanders."

"Oh. Sorry." I hung up my phone and it immediately began to ring.

It was Cody.

"Did my father pay you to stop seeing me?" I demanded angrily into the phone.

There was a long pause, and then he replied. "I don't know what you're talking about."

I would have much rather heard a firm "No" than that response.

My stomach tightened with anger.

Cody wasn't rich. He sold motorcycles for a living. I'd kept the news about my inheritance from him, because I never wanted our relationship to be about money. Of course, he knew who my father was and that we were extremely well off.

"So, is that all I was worth?" I said sharply. "Fifty-fucking-thousand?"

"You're not making any sense. I gotta go," he said and hung up on me.

As much as I didn't want to believe it, his responses had been weak, making me livid. I stormed out of my bedroom and went to my father's office. He was on the phone, but must have noticed how angry I was because he hung up.

"Did you pay Cody to stop seeing me?" I snapped.

"What?" He gave me a puzzled look. "You two broke up?"

If it was one thing that I knew about my father—he could look anyone in the eye and lie his ass off without

14

blinking. He sometimes did it during his business dealings and had bragged about his money-making poker-face.

I sat down across from him with my hands clenched, trying to keep my anger under control. "Someone called and told me that you paid Cody fifty-thousand dollars to break it off with me."

His eyes narrowed and his jaw tightened. "Who?"

"I have no idea. They called from a pay-phone."

"Do you have the number?"

His answer told me all I needed to hear. Tony was more concerned with who'd called than actually denying their claims. It made me sick to my stomach.

"Dad, *did* you pay him off?"

He looked at me like I was crazy. "No. Of course not. I'm footing the bill for your wedding. Why would I try and sabotage everything?"

"Because you never liked him. Don't deny it. You told me that on several occasions."

"Well, now I like him even less because he's putting you through all of this," Dad replied. "I didn't bribe Cody. Did he actually say that I did?"

I stood up. The walls felt like they were closing in on me. I needed to get out of there. "No. He denied it as well."

This time, my father's poker-face failed him. I could see a flash of relief in his eyes. He sat back in his chair and crossed his arms, looking much more comfortable. "I don't know who is spreading these rumors about me, but they're lying. Are you sure it was a pay-phone?"

I went over the conversation I'd had with the woman.

"Let me see your cell. I want the number."

"If it's a lie, then why does it even matter?"

His face darkened. "Because nobody fucks with Tony Armati and his family. Get me the number. *Now.*"

I glared at him. "And you wonder why I want to move out?"

His expressions and voice softened. He smiled sheepishly. "I'm sorry, Charlotte. I'm just so outraged that people are playing games."

I stared at him hard. "You and me both."

Tony let out a sigh. "Please. May I have your phone?"

"It's in my room. I'll be right back."

As I left the office, I was still reeling. I didn't want to believe that Tony would stoop to such a low level. I also didn't want to believe that Cody would end our relationship for money. But, something told me that they were both capable of what was being accused, and I felt nauseous.

After returning to his office, and giving my father my phone, he called the number and someone answered.

"I understand this is a pay-phone," he said to the person on the other end. "Where exactly is it located?"

I watched him write down the information and noticed it was on Tuffler Street. Not the nicest of neighborhoods and on the other side of the city.

"Thank you," he said and then hung up.

"So, you have a location. How is that going to help?"

He set his pen down and sighed wearily. "Look, I didn't do this, okay? I swear."

"On your mother's grave?"

"Charlotte, you're not a child anymore. Adults don't swear on people's graves."

I frowned.

"You're right, though, I thought Cody was unsuitable for you. The truth is, even though this is costing me a lot of dough—"

I raised my eyebrows. "Really?"

"I'm talking about the deposits I've made on the wedding that are non-refundable," he explained with a pained look. "Anyway, I'm glad you're free of him. Now you can meet someone who will take good care of you. A man who will have your best interests in mind."

God, he was so old fashioned.

"That's just it, I don't need anyone to take care of me. In fact…" I told him about my plans to go to culinary school.

He brushed it off again, just like I knew he would. "If you want to learn to cook, I'm sure Berta can teach you what you need."

"It's not the same thing and you know it."

We went round-and-round with the discussion. In the end I stormed away, furious at my chauvinistic father who was so damn narrow-minded; I knew he'd never give me his blessings for anything other than what he wanted. Which, once again, had me wondering about the call from earlier. I knew there was only one way to find the truth.

Determined to do just that, I called Jackie again. Fortunately, she answered. I told her about my conversation with my father and how I'd decided to confront Cody, face-to-face.

"Tony might be an award-winning fibber, but Cody couldn't lie to save his life."

"True. So, you're really going to do this?"

As much as I didn't want to see him, I knew it was the only way. "Yes. I need to know for sure."

"Alright. I'll tag along for moral support," she said. "When do you want to do it?"

"The sooner the better. Tonight he has a meeting with some clients at Murphy's. I'd like to catch him when he's least expecting it."

She groaned. "Murphy's? Yuck. Really?"

"Yeah. Sorry."

Murphy's was a dive bar if ever there was one. But, Cody was a cheapskate and most of his clients were sketchy.

"I should have known. Well, we'd better spray ourselves with Lysol before entering that shit-hole," she mused.

Knowing what a neat-freak she was, I pictured her sliding a small can of it into her purse. "You can wait in the car. I'll go in myself."

"Oh, hell no. I want to see his reaction when you confront him. I'm driving, by the way, so I'll pick you up. What time is good for you?"

"I'm not sure. Should we have dinner first?"

"Yeah. Sounds good. I'll need a couple of drinks to get me into Murphy's."

I smiled. "Okay, How about seven? If you're driving, I'm buying."

"Sounds good."

TWO

MADDOX

Murphy's
8:55 pm

"YOU CAN WRITE me a check now and I'll ship 'em to you as soon as they arrive in our warehouse," Cody Renner said.

"I'm not buying anything sight-unseen," Tank replied, looking frustrated. "Even at that price."

"I understand. Again, I apologize for this mess. I know it's an inconvenience. Hell, it is for us, too."

Tank frowned. "Not as much as it is for the two of us. When are they supposed to be arriving?"

"Monday morning," he replied.

Monday-fucking-morning?

"You've got to be shitting me," I muttered, trying not to explode.

Tank glanced my way. "I know, Brother. I know."

I reached for my missing cigarette packet, wishing I'd waited until New Years to try and quit smoking. It had been three weeks since my last drag and I thought I'd been doing pretty good, considering.

And now this shit.

As the two men next to me went back-and-forth about the motorcycles we'd put deposits on, my thought returned to earlier. The morning had started off shitty and had only got worse. First, I received a call from my five-year-old daughter's mother, Kathy, telling me that Aubrey needed to get her tonsils out and her insurance wasn't covering it. That was followed by a flat tire on the Tahoe we'd rented for the trip to New York. Then, just a short time ago, some asshole had tried picking a fight with me after I offered to buy his girlfriend a drink. It wasn't my fault she'd sat down next to me at the bar and flashed me her tits. In my world, that was an invitation if I'd ever seen one. The least I could do was offer her a drink.

Anyway, maybe that part wasn't all that bad, I thought, thinking back to when she'd approached me.

"I just got them," she said, lowering her top quickly when the bartender gave her a warning look. "What did you think?"

They'd been the size of cantaloupes, and definitely looked fake. But, I was a red-blooded, horny bastard and already picturing them jiggling as she bounced around on my cock.

I raised my beer. "Well worth it. Boner approved."

Giggling, she glanced down at my bulge, which re-emphasized my point. "I guess so."

"How long you have 'em?" I asked, enjoying the conversation.

"About two months. They're finally healing up." She reached up and squeezed them. "Is it weird that I can't stop touching my boobs?" she whispered.

I groaned inwardly. The chick was teasing the hell out of me. I wondered if she was a stripper. She definitely had the body for it, with or without the implants.

I smiled. "It would be less weird if you let me do it."

She laughed and sat back in the stool. "At least buy me a drink before asking."

"Bartender," I called. "Get this little lady here whatever she wants. Put it on my tab."

That's when her yuppie boyfriend approached.

"The fuck if you're buying her anything, asshole," he said, looking wired.

I swiveled my stool around and faced him. With his slicked back hair and monkey-suit, he was obviously in the wrong bar. Not to

21

mention that he looked like he was strung out on something, probably coke, causing him to make some poor choices.

"Excuse me?" I replied.

"You heard what I said." He puffed out his chest, his poor attempt at looking intimidating.

"Oh, for heaven's sake. He was just being nice, Wendell," the girl said, scowling at him.

I smiled coldly. "Yeah, Wendell."

"Go to hell," he snapped, glaring at me.

Instead of breaking his face, which I'd reluctantly talked myself out of, I stood up and gave him a better idea of who the fuck he was dealing with—an ornery sonofabitch who made this guy's six-foot frame look dinkier than what I had tucked in my boxers. Curiously enough, the tension in the air only made my boner harder.

Yeah, I'm twisted like that.

Realizing his mistake, Wendell took a step back. "Fuck it. It's not worth getting kicked out of here."

I stared him down until he backed away farther.

"Come on, Cindy," he said, looking at her, his face red. "Let's go somewhere else. This place is a dump."

"But, I'm hungry and the burgers here are supposed to be amazing," she protested.

"I wouldn't eat at this shithole if you paid me," he muttered. "I'll meet you by the door."

Cindy sighed. "Fine."

"Bye, Wendell," I said, smirking.

He ignored me.

Amused, Cindy got to her feet and looked up at me. "How tall are you, anyway?"

"Six-five," I replied, sitting back down on the stool. I towered over most of the guys I knew, except for Tank—the president of the Gold Vipers. The club I was now a member of. I'd recently relocated to

Iowa, where Aubrey's mom was also now living. She was caring for her mother, who'd been diagnosed with cancer. Wanting to see my daughter as much as possible, I followed her. Fortunately, I'd known Tank since we were kids and the transition had gone pretty smoothly. My old man, Bastard, had actually founded the Gold Vipers, and so our families had some history together.

"Damn, you are one tall drink of water," she murmured, eyeing me up and down.

I was about to offer her a taste when Wendell hollered for her from the doorway.

"See you around," she said, pulling the strap of her purse over her shoulder.

"Take care."

I watched her leave the bar, hips swaying. I knew that as pretty as she was, the chick had some heavy baggage. Especially if she was flashing her tits around other men, even with a douchebag boyfriend like Wendell. Personally, I preferred traveling lightly, anyway.

"Monday isn't going to work," Tank was saying, bringing me back to the present. "We'll be gone by then." He nodded toward me. "Mad Dog's starting his new job and I gotta get back to take care of some club business. I thought you said we could take a look at these Hogs tonight?"

"I thought so, too. They were supposed to arrive this afternoon. Unfortunately, there was a mix-up with the delivery company," he explained.

"This sounds like a whole lot of bullshit," I griped, not liking the shifty salesman. Something wasn't settling right with me. "I sold my fucking ride. Not to mention all of the bullshit we went through with our rental. The only reason we were giving you our business was a friend recommended you and we thought the ride back would be fun. If we can't get this done this weekend, I'm taking my money elsewhere."

Cody started apologizing again.

"I'm not interested in excuses," I said, cutting him off. I looked at Tank. "I'm sorry, brother, but I need a bike now. I don't care what kind of deal he's pushing."

"Hold up," Cody said. "Let me call my old man and see if we can come up with another solution."

I looked at him. "You do that."

Cody took out his phone and walked away.

"This guy is really pissing me off," I said to Tank. "He knew how badly we needed the bikes and swore they'd be here."

"I know. It's bullshit. If he wasn't giving us such a sweet deal, I'd walk out right now. Hopefully, he'll figure something out."

"Yeah. We'll see."

Tank chuckled.

"What?"

"You've toned it down, brother. Back in the day you'd have stormed out of here, not looking back."

"Yeah, well, Aubrey's taught me patience," I replied, thinking about my daughter. She was the only thing that really mattered to me, besides the club.

"I hear you. Being a father tests your every limit. Even more than being a husband. Speaking of which, what's going on with you and Kathy?"

"Nothing. We tried to make it work, but she refuses to tolerate club life. The woman used to nag me constantly about stepping away."

"I'm surprised since she knows it's part of who you are."

"Which she tried to change. Anyway, I don't think marriage is for me, anyway. I'm happy the way things are."

"You sound like I used to."

"Not everyone finds themselves the perfect woman like Raina," I replied, although everyone knew she was a handful. But, Tank was happy and that's all that mattered.

"True. Don't give up hope, though. There's a woman out there for you."

"There's a *lot* of women out there for me. Doesn't mean I have to settle for just one," I said, smiling.

"Spoken like many before you who are now dragging around the old ball-and-chain."

"This talk is making me even thirstier."

He chuckled.

I called for the bartender and ordered us a couple of shots. As we were finishing them up, Cody walked over with a smile on his face.

"Good news. My father called the shipping company and raised some hell. We're getting them in by noon tomorrow."

"So, we're stuck here overnight," I grumbled to Tank, although I was relieved. We'd planned on sticking around until Saturday evening, anyway. "Fuck."

"Guess so," Tank muttered.

"I'll cover your overnight expenses," Cody said, pulling out his wallet. He took out two hundred dollar bills and handed them to Tank.

"What about my expenses?" I said, scowling. "We're not sharing a room. Hell, maybe something will finally go right today and I'll actually end up with a piece of ass to keep my mind off of this mess."

"Lucky you," Tank replied, rolling his gold wedding band around his ring finger and staring down at it. "I won't be so lucky, unless Raina miraculously shows up."

"I can find you some chicks," Cody said, pulling out two more hundred-dollar bills. He handed me the money. "My treat."

"I don't need help in that department," I said, looking around the bar. "Although, there's not much to choose from here."

"Too bad that chick with fake titties left," Tank said with an amused grin.

"No shit." I stuffed the money into my wallet. "So, what time tomorrow?"

"I'll call you, but it should be before twelve," Cody replied, pulling his phone out. "You guys like strippers? There's a place up the road. Bambi's. I'll give you a ride, pay for some drinks, and drop you off at a hotel."

"What about our Tahoe?" I asked.

"It'll be safe here. I know the owner. I'll let him know you're going to keep it overnight," he replied.

"Sounds good," I said. "Tank?"

"Yeah. Let's do it," he replied, looking around. "A little eye-candy never hurt anyone."

"Obviously you've never been slapped around by some Double Gs," I replied, thinking back to my twenty-first birthday. My old man had bought me a lap dance and the chick had left me black-and-blue.

"I used to own a strip joint, remember?" Tank replied.

"Lucky you," Cody said. "What happened to it?"

He held up his ring finger. "I got married. That's what happened to it."

"Another reason I'm not falling into that trap," I said. I didn't need anyone else influencing my life besides my daughter.

"Me neither," Cody said. "I barely dodged the bullet myself."

"You were engaged?" Tank asked.

He nodded.

"What happened?" replied Tank.

Cody scratched his head and smiled grimly. "More shit than I can talk about. Anyway, you two ready?"

We finished our beers and followed him out.

THREE

CHARLIE

A S WE WERE pulling up to Murphy's, we saw Cody walk out of the bar with two scary-looking bikers.
"Wait. Don't let him see us." I pointed toward the back of the lot. "Pull over there."

She did what I asked and then we watched the three get into Cody's Mercedes.

"Where do you think he's bringing them?" Jackie asked.

"I don't know. Let's follow them and find out."

"Okay."

We watched as Cody drove out of the parking lot and then we tailed them to a strip club up the road.

"Figures," Jackie said dryly. "Cody is such a pig."

I was burning up inside and could barely talk. He obviously didn't give two shits about me. Not to mention that if he really *did* get paid to break up with me, he was about to spend some of it on strippers. "Let's park."

She gave me a curious look. "What are you going to do?"

"What we came out here for. To confront the prick."

"Yeah but… in *there?*"

"Sure. Why not? I'll ruin his night at the strip joint by making a fool out of him. What could be better?"

Jackie grinned. "This should be good."

We waited in the car for fifteen minutes and then walked inside.

"You work here?" the bouncer asked, eyeing me up and down as we entered the building.

"No," I replied, not sure whether to feel flattered or offended. I had on a pair of white shorts and a silky short-sleeved black shirt that tied at my waist. Underneath the top,

I wore a pushup bra, but you could only see a little bit of cleavage. I'd also taken extra care with my hair and makeup, to show Cody what he was missing.

"Then, there's a cover-charge," he replied.

Jackie started to complain.

"I got it," I said, pulling out my wallet. "How much?"

"Ten dollars each. Pay the lady in the booth," he said, pointing toward the attendant.

After we paid, we walked down a long hallway and into the club. It was dark, loud, and smelled like perfume and some kind of incense.

"Let's go over there," I hollered to Jackie over the song they had playing, *Shakin' Hands* by Nickelback.

She gave me a thumbs-up and followed me over to table in the back. It was in the shadows and far enough from the stage to be out of sight from Cody and his clients, who were now seated close to it. As soon as we sat down, a young woman approached us wearing peach lingerie.

"Can I get you two a drink?" she asked, smiling.

"Sure," I replied.

We both ordered rum and Cokes.

"Checking out the competition?" the waitress asked me.

I raised my eyebrow. "Excuse me?"

"You don't work at Dreams?" she replied, tilting her head.

"No. What's that?" I asked.

"A gentleman's club. A little more upscale than this place," she replied. "I thought you looked like someone who worked there. I'm sorry."

"No problem," I replied, relaxing.

She looked at my top. "Are you here for Amateur Night?"

"I'm not a stripper," I said, a little sharper than I'd intended.

The waitress's face turned red. "I'm sorry. Oh, God, I feel like an idiot. You're just so pretty." She looked at Jackie. "You both are. Anyway, I meant it as a compliment. Not to mention that we don't get many women in here, anyway. Unless—" she smiled weakly—"it's Amateur Night."

"It's okay. I didn't mean to sound like a bitch either. It's just been a bad day for me," I replied. "I'm sorry."

"Don't apologize," she said. "We all have those."

"So, it must be Amateur Night tonight?" Jackie cut in.

She nodded. "Yes. The winner gets five-hundred dollars in cash and keeps the tips she makes."

"That's pretty good," I replied.

"Last week, this woman walked out with two thousand dollars total. She did two dances and made out like a bandit," the waitress replied.

"Holy shit," Jackie said and looked at me.

I chuckled. "Crazy Money."

"No kidding. I'm too shy to take everything off," the waitress said, looking down at her teddy. "Otherwise, I'd be pulling in a lot more money. This place looks like a dump, but we get a lot of business."

"I bet," I said, noticing a large group of guys walk in. One of them had on a crown and looked hammered.

"Bachelor party," the waitress said. "This should be interesting. I'll get your drinks. Sorry again."

"It's fine. I'm flattered, actually," I replied, trying to make her feel better.

She smiled and left.

Jackie grinned and shook her head. "See, I always told you that you should have been an exotic dancer. Think how pissed off your old man would have been."

"No shit," I replied, looking toward the stage. There was a stripper with breasts the size of watermelons sliding up and down the pole. "Honestly, I doubt I could ever be that hard up for cash."

Not that I had didn't have experience taking my clothes off and getting paid for it. I once modeled for an art class. It had been my ex-boyfriend, Monty's, idea. I'd been nineteen at the time and he'd been a few years older. He'd also taught the class. I'd been self-conscious the first time, but after seeing some of the portraits the students had created of me, I ended up doing it a few more times. By the last class, I'd lost all modesty. I actually still had one of the portraits Monty had done of me, hiding somewhere in my closet at home. I wore nothing but a sheer, red scarf and heels. Even I had to admit, it was an amazing piece. Fortunately, my father had never found out about it. He would have blown a gasket.

"Me neither. Check out the size of those guys with Cody. I wonder if he's hired bodyguards now," Jackie joked. "Maybe he heard you were looking for him."

I chuckled. Both were muscular and had tattoos. I couldn't see their faces because their backs were turned toward me, but I imagined them both to be mean-looking.

"I'm sure those are buyers and he's showing them a good time," I replied as the waitress returned with our drinks.

"How long are we staying here?" Jackie asked.

"I don't know," I replied.

The stripper left the stage and the DJ announced that they were going to be starting the amateur contest soon.

"You sure you don't want to win some money?" Jackie asked with a smirk. "Apply it toward culinary school?"

Smiling back, I took a drink of my cocktail. "Could you imagine the look on Cody's face if he saw me walk out on stage?"

"It would be *hilarious*. Too bad you don't have the balls to do it."

"Excuse me? Did you forget who you're talking to?"

She'd dared me to do many things throughout the years, and I'd met the challenges head-on. Like, flashing my boobs to a cop we'd both thought had been hot. Another time she'd dared me to moon our high school football team. Of course, I did, although I'd worn a hoodie and sunglasses so nobody knew it had been me.

Jackie stared at me in disbelief. "You wouldn't."

"No. You're right. I wouldn't. But, I'd love to see his reaction if I actually did. Could you imagine?"

"He'd probably try and fuck you one last time."

"I'm not letting him touch me with a ten-foot pole. Or, his little four-inch one."

She laughed. "Was he really that small?"

"No," I admitted. "He's hung, but could never last. I guess he's been a disappointment in every way."

"Exactly."

THREE COCKTAILS LATER, I was incredibly tipsy and was having second thoughts about getting on stage. Especially after watching Cody act like some kind of a bigshot with the strippers. I wanted so badly to throw him off of his game.

"Gee, I wonder where he got all of that money?" Jackie said dryly as we watched Cody pull out his wallet again.

I shook my head in disgust.

She looked at me. "Do you really think Tony would stoop that low?"

"Honestly, it's possible," I replied, not wanting to admit it. I wasn't an idiot. Many times, I'd heard my father on the phone with some of his business associates; he was definitely a shrewd and intimidating man when he wanted to be. The guys who worked for him were menacing, too. I had a feeling that if they were paid enough, they wouldn't think twice about 'whacking' someone or burying a man alive while discussing the weather. I once said as much to my father, who laughed afterward. He told me that I had a wild imagination and watched too much television. It was followed by "Don't believe any rumors you might hear about me, Charlotte. A lot of people are envious of my success and will say and do anything to slander our family's good name."

"I don't understand how guys can blow so much money on girls who secretly hate them. The strippers all probably think of them as dogs. Especially, the ones who've been doing it for a while. I know I do after watching that bachelor party. If only the fiancée could see her hubby-to-be right now. He's making a fool out of himself."

I looked over at the bachelor, who was being so loud and obnoxious, even the bouncers were giving him warnings.

"I know."

One of the strippers walked up to Cody's table and I watched as he stood up and began following her into the back, which we learned was where they did private lap dances.

"Fucking asshole," I said, steaming.

The waitress returned. "Are you ready for another one?"

"No," Jackie said. "I'm good. I won't be able to drive if I drink anymore."

Half-drunk, and feeling an urge to do something outrageous, I asked the waitress about getting into the contest.

"Charlie," gasped Jackie, laughing. "What the hell?"

"You should enter," the waitress said, glancing around the bar. "None of the other girls have anything on you. You'll put them to shame."

"That's so sweet. Thank you," I replied.

"I'm just telling it like it is. You're sure to win," she added.

Her words gave me even more confidence. Especially after seeing some of the other women who'd preformed on stage. There'd only been a few, but they'd been impressive. I thanked her for the compliment.

"What would you wear up there?" Jackie asked, still looking shocked that I was even considering it.

I laughed. "Nothing. Isn't that the point?"

"You know what I mean," she replied. "Before you wear 'nothing'."

I stood up. "I'll just wear this," I said, looking down at my outfit.

"No. That won't work," Jackie said. "You-know-*who* will notice you right away. Too bad you couldn't wear a costume so he wouldn't recognize you."

She was right. That was the point anyway. To surprise Cody.

"We have an array of costumes and lingerie in back," said the waitress.

Jackie wrinkled her nose.

"Don't worry. Everything is clean," the waitress added with a smirk. "We have a washer and dryer in back. The costumes are also dry-cleaned frequently."

"Okay." I looked up on stage again and noticed a woman wearing a Little Bo Peep outfit dancing around the pole. "Do you have something that would hide my face?"

She nodded. "We have masks of all shapes and sizes."

I grinned.

Perfect.

"Panties can stay on?" I asked, although I didn't think I'd get to that point. I just wanted to remove a couple of things before telling Cody to kiss my ass.

"It's your choice. Most first-timers definitely keep them on," she said.

I looked at Jackie. "That's it. I'm doing it."

She gave me a funny look. "Are you sure? As your best friend, I should probably try and talk you out of it."

"You can't. I'm all in," I replied and then gave her a hug. "Don't worry. I know what I'm doing."

Jackie didn't look convinced. "Says the girl who's had a couple of drinks."

"Three. But, who's counting?" I replied and laughed.

Liquid courage was an evil thing. Had I been sober, I would have *never* considered doing something so crazy. My only thought was to get up on stage in front of my ex, show him what he'd given up, and then walk out of his life with dignity.

At the time, it made total sense. Even the dignity part.

The waitress took me into the back and I had to fill out some kind of a waiver. I then picked out a Little Red Riding Hood costume along with a small black mask to hide the top part of my face.

After I was dressed, my sensible side tried to make a come-back.

"I don't know if I can do this," I told one of the strippers, a girl named Randi who also worked there as a dancer. She was helping the amateurs prepare before getting on stage.

"Sure you can. You look awesome, too," she replied, looking at my chest. "Are those real?"

"Yeah." I looked down at my cleavage, which was testing the confines of the tight costume. The dress was super-short and made of red velvet. It had a low scoop neckline and the hem was trimmed with black lace. They'd also found me a clean pair of thigh-high stockings and tall, black suede boots, which were a little big, but doable.

"Lucky you. I had to pay ten grand for mine. You want a shot?" she asked. "To take the edge off?"

"I don't know," I replied, peeking through the side curtains. The guys surrounding the stage were hooting and hollering as the dancer removed her bra. All except for Cody's friends, who were sitting quietly. By now, he was back with them and looking pleased with himself.

"Randi, it happened again," I heard a woman say, sounding amused.

"What?" asked Randi.

I turned around and saw the girl Cody had paid to give him a lap dance.

"My last customer pulled out a wad of cash and asked me to blow him," she replied.

"The guy with the blond hair and long sideburns?" I asked.

She looked at me. "Yeah. How did you know?"

I felt sick to my stomach. "Lucky guess."

"Did you?" one of the other contestants asked, a woman around my age. She had streaks of purple in her hair and tattoos of skulls everywhere.

"No. Although," she sighed, "he just got back from Iraq and found out his fiancée cheated on him. If anyone deserves a BJ it's Cody. I mean, what a bitch, huh?"

I felt like someone had punched me in the gut. "He said that?"

She looked at me. "Yeah. He said her name was Charlie or something."

"Motherfucker," I growled.

"Do you know him?" she asked.

I told them about Cody's lie and how he'd texted me earlier. The other three women stared at me in horror.

"My ex-husband cheated on me," Randi said, walking over to the closet. She opened the door and pulled out a baseball bat. "He did it with my best friend. They actually had sex right here in the parking lot while I was making money to help pay for his college loans. I gave his Chevy a makeover that night with this. What kind of car does Cody drive?"

"A Mercedes," I replied, so livid I was shaking.

"Is he even in the military?" Candi asked.

I shook my head.

"Wow." She held the bat out to me. "If anyone deserves to be taught a lesson, it's that douchebag."

FOUR

MADDOX

IT WAS AMATEUR Night at the strip club, which I usually enjoyed, but for some reason, I just wasn't feeling it. I had my mind on other things, like Aubrey's tonsils and how much it was going to cost. I did get one lap dance, but was actually relieved when it was over. She was a blonde who smelled of gardenias, which I wasn't a fan of. The overpowering flowery perfume reminded me too much of my great aunt Tillie, who used to bathe in the scent.

"I need to get some fresh air," I said to Cody, who'd been trying to persuade Tank into getting a lap dance. I looked toward the men's room, which was where he'd disappeared to. "Let Tank know I'll be back in a few minutes."

"No problem," Cody said, eyeballing another stripper working the tables. He pulled out a twenty-dollar bill from his wallet. "Hey, beautiful! Come on over here!"

I headed outside and breathed in the fresh air. It had been a long day and my head was starting to ache. Not to mention, I was getting hungry, and not for anything being served inside.

I pulled out my phone to start searching for nearby diners and that was when I heard a loud noise coming from the parking lot. I jerked my head up and saw a woman dressed up like Little Red Riding Hood smashing a bat against Cody's Mercedes. At first I was so stunned, I thought I was imagining it. But then I heard the loud shattering of headlight and it woke me up.

"Hey!" I hollered, racing over to her.

Ignoring me, she swung it again and again, denting the hood of his car in several places.

What the fuck?

When I reached the chick, she turned toward me, holding the bat as if I was next.

"Hey, now. Put that thing down," I said calmly, raising my hands in the air. "Before someone gets hurt."

"Mind your own business before that someone is you," she replied breathlessly, her chest rising and falling quickly.

Talk about a vision of hotness. I don't know where they'd been hiding her, but she was drop-dead gorgeous. She had legs up to the clouds, with strawberry-blonde hair, green eyes, and a cleavage that a guy could get lost in for years.

"This *is* my business. The car you're vandalizing belongs to a friend of mine," I replied.

She laughed harshly. "You need new friends. Cody is a piece of shit who deserves to have his legs broken, not just his fucking car."

"So, this isn't just random?" I said, relaxing a bit.

"Hell no," she replied. "This is intentional."

"Are you two dating?"

"We are nothing. Not anymore."

I couldn't believe a woman like her had ever wasted time with a bum like him.

I smiled and shook my head. "Wow."

"Wow, what?"

"I'm just surprised you're letting him get to you. You obviously deserve better."

"I know I do. The question is—why do you think so? For all you know, I'm just some crazy, dangerous, half-naked bitch who's having a nervous breakdown."

I liked her feistiness. "Are you?"

"I'm still trying to decide on the 'nervous breakdown' part. The rest is pretty fucking accurate." She turned toward the car again and brought the bat up. "Are we done here?" she asked, hesitating. Her eyes narrowed. "Or are you going to run back into the bar and tell on me?"

"Aren't you doing this for attention, anyway?" I countered.

"I'm doing it for… revenge." She hit the car again with a loud thud, her breasts bouncing from the movement and giving me a boner. She straightened up and looked at me. "Plus, I have to admit—destroying his shit is very satisfying. Therapeutic even, if I do say so myself."

I crossed my arms over my chest and smiled. "Then, please. Carry on."

FIVE

CHARLIE

INSTEAD OF LEAVING, he stood there quietly and watched me swing the bat a few more times. Unfortunately, I was already starting to sober up and feeling a little foolish. Here I was, in the middle of the night, half-naked and acting like a crazy, scorned woman over a dickhead like Cody.

If that wasn't bad enough, I was beginning to feel some attraction between myself and the stranger. With his silvery blue eyes, fierce angular face, and sexy smile, it was hard not to.

"You done?" he asked when I finally lowered the bat. "You missed a few spots."

I examined my work. The Mercedes looked like it had been through a tornado. "Funny." I began walking back toward the club, grateful that a cop hadn't showed up and arrested me.

"Hold up, now," the biker said, catching up to me. "What's your name?"

"It's Little Red Riding Hood," I said dryly.

"Fine, *Red* it is," he replied, giving me a crooked smile.

"Call me that and you'll be spitting red."

He chuckled. "Makes sense, considering you're spitting bullets."

I grinned.

"That's better," he said, staring down at me. "You have a nice smile. Beautiful one, actually. I'm not flirting, by the way. That would be tacky, considering the circumstances."

"Agreed." I tried walking faster, but he stayed in step with me.

45

"You know, I'm still trying to figure out why you'd go out with such a dipshit like Cody, anyway. You're way out of his league."

"You sound like my dad."

"We fathers have to stick together. Besides, he's right. You're better off without that sleazy piece of shit. I've only just met the guy, and I can tell he's a waste of space. And that was hours before I met you."

"You're right about that."

"I'm usually right about first impressions."

"Okay, I'll bite. What's the first one you had of me? Crazy, lunatic?"

"Pissed off and dangerous."

"You were halfway there. I'm all of the above right now."

"Been there. Believe me."

"So, you have children?" I asked as we headed toward the back of the club.

"Yep," he said. "A little girl. Tell you one thing, if she ever dates a bozo like Cody, I'll shoot myself in the fucking head."

"Just don't tell her *not* to date him," I replied, thinking about all of the guys I'd went out with. Most my dad hadn't liked. "It'll only make her want to go out with him even more."

"Is that why you went out with Cody?"

The truth was, he'd been charming when we first started dating. Then things had gotten comfortable and I'd even gotten a little bored. But, when he asked me to marry him, and my father went ape-shit upon finding out, I ended up saying yes. I knew now that agreeing to marry him had never been for the right reasons.

"I went out with him because he'd fooled me into believing he was a nice guy who cared about me. I was wrong."

"Think of it this way—now that you know, you're not going to waste any more precious time with the numb-nuts. Life is too short to be with someone who doesn't deserve you."

He was definitely laying it on too thick. I smiled coolly. "You're right. He doesn't deserve me and I'm going to be a lot more careful about who I get involved with in the future. Or where I meet guys."

"So, you're saying you wouldn't consider me for a rebound guy?" he asked with a devilish grin. "I'm in town until tomorrow. I could try and help drive all thoughts of Cody from your brain."

"My, that's subtle," I replied when we reached the back exit. I turned around and noticed he was so close that I had to take a step back. "So, are you going to tell him about me?" I asked, my back now against the metal door.

"Do you want me to?"

"As much as I'd love to take direct credit for it, I'd almost like to keep him guessing. Payback, you know?"

"Payback, huh? He must have really fucked you over."

"I used to think so. Now, I'm not so sure. Maybe in the end, he just did me a favor," I said, looking into his eyes.

"Or me." He reached over and tugged playfully on one of my curls. "You know, my silence is going to cost you."

My eyes narrowed.

"Before you go swinging that bat again, let me finish," he murmured with a twinkle in his eyes.

I waited, not sure where this was going now. He definitely looked like he was going to kiss me. Part of me almost hoped he would.

He licked his lips. "I just want to know your name."

"Charlie."

"Charlie?" he repeated, raising an eyebrow.

"Yeah. As in Charlotte. Only, my father calls me that and I don't like it," I replied, immediately regretting it. I sounded like a two-year-old.

"Personally, I like Charlotte. So, everyone else but your dad calls you Charlie, huh?"

I nodded.

"What if I don't want to be like everyone else? What if I called you Red?"

"I would hate it."

"What about Chuck?"

I was suddenly disturbed by the raw power of my attraction toward him. I blamed it on the alcohol.

"I'm not a shoe. Nor am I a little bald boy with a beagle."

He laughed.

"Look you can call me whatever you want. I doubt we'll see each other again, anyway," I said.

He gave me a pouty look. "You're cruel."

"I'm a lot of things. Including Italian."

"That explains a lot," he replied, looking at the bat.

"Hey, when somebody fucks with me, I'm not going to take it lightly."

"I feel you. I'm Irish. Unfortunately, I tend to bite before I bark. Which is probably the real reason why my brothers call me Mad Dog."

"Mad Dog?"

"My real name is Maddox."

"Oh. So, what you're saying is that you're dangerous and unpredictable?"

"Only to my enemies," he said softly, staring into my eyes. "If we're tight, then I have your back for life."

"Um, why do you smell like flowers?" I asked, noticing it suddenly. "What is that? Gardenia?"

He sighed. "I think so. Don't ask."

I touched the doorknob behind me. "I should go. My friend is probably going crazy with worry."

His eyes dipped lower, caressing my body with lusting, invisible fingers. "So, do you work here or just around for Amateur Night?"

"I'm neither," I replied. "Now that I've sobered up."

"Too bad," he replied. "You're sexy as fuck."

Hunger crawled through me. The kind that could eat a man. "You… you're not so bad yourself," I replied, finding it hard to breathe as a powerful force passed between us, a raw, sexual heat.

His blue eyes turned dark with desire. He leaned forward to kiss me. Unfortunately, the door opened up behind me and I stumbled backward.

SIX

MADDOX

A WOMAN STANDING behind Chuck grabbed her arm before I could, breaking her fall. She was tall and thin with long black hair and large brown eyes. She reminded me of a younger version of Cher.

"What in the hell is going on?" the woman asked angrily. "Do you know how fucking worried I've been, Charlie?" The woman then looked at me and her eyes widened in surprise.

"Sorry, Jackie," Charlie replied, looking embarrassed. "I'm a fucking idiot. Big time. Oh, this is Maddox, by the way. Er… Mad Dog."

"Isn't he one of Cody's friends?" she replied, staring at me like I was the devil.

Charlie nodded.

"For the record, we're *not* friends. He's just selling us some motorcycles," I explained.

"Got it." Jackie looked at Charlie again. "We should go."

"I know," she replied and looked at me. "Sorry. You can't come in this way."

"I figured as much." I stepped back. "It was nice meeting you, Chuck."

She sighed. "Good grief. We're back to that?"

I laughed. "I thought you said it didn't matter. Since, we won't be seeing each other again?"

"True."

Before I could say anything else, she shut the door between us.

"YOU FEELING BETTER?" Tank asked after I walked back into the bar.

I nodded.

"We should get going," he said, looking at his phone. "I'm bored and hungry."

"Me, too. Where's Cody?" I asked, looking around the club.

"Getting another lap dance. He's going through a shitload of money tonight. Horny bastard."

"No shit. Speaking of which, I need to fill you in on something," I said, knowing Tank wouldn't squeal when he learned what had happened in the parking lot

"What's up?"

I told him about Charlie.

"No shit?" he replied, looking amused. "I wonder if she's related to Raina."

Tank's wife's temper was legendary, especially for such a tiny woman. He liked to call her his little firecracker with a big bang. Fortunately, she had a long fuse so it took a lot to get her riled up. But, when she did get angry, the entire club went into crisis mode.

"She has about the same size balls," I said with a smirk.

"Oh, hell. Well, he did it to himself. Tell you what, though, I can't wait to see his reaction when we walk out to the parking lot," Tank said. "I know that's shitty, but he's been getting on my nerves all night. Mr. big shot. Another reason why I want to get the fuck out of Dodge."

A door opening in the back of the bar caught my attention. Charlie stepped out cautiously, obviously trying to keep a low profile. It wasn't exactly possible when you looked like her. Even in her street clothes, which consisted of white shorts and a black silk shirt, she was still as sexy as hell. Behind her was Jackie, who looked our way.

I waved.

Ignoring me, the two headed quickly toward the front exit.

"That's her," I said, nudging Tank.

"Whoa. Why would anyone fuck something up with her? Either she has a lot of baggage or Cody is a complete moron."

It was possible. Normally, baggage had me running the opposite way, but sometimes crazy was worth it. Of course, my dick was the one doing the reasoning at that particular moment.

I watched as the two women walked out of the bar, feeling disappointed that I'd failed to get her phone number. A chick like her was worth another visit to New York.

"Hey, here comes Cody," Tank said, nodding toward the private rooms. "He doesn't look happy, does he?"

Cody was heading in our direction with a scowl on his face. The stripper looked almost as angry.

"Neither does she; maybe he ran out of money."

Tank chuckled.

Cody arrived at the table and finished his cocktail. "You guys ready?"

"Yeah, everything okay?" Tank asked.

He nodded.

"How was the private dance?" I asked.

He grunted. "That chick was psycho. She freaked out after I accidentally touched her ass."

"Accidentally, huh?" Tank asked with a sly grin. "You mean when you 'accidentally' got caught."

He smirked.

"I thought so. Let's blow this place," Tank said. "Did you get our rooms reserved?"

He nodded. "Yeah. The hotel isn't far from here either. There's a diner across the street, too. Maybe we can catch a bite to eat?"

"Sounds good," Tank replied. "We're both hungry."

We followed Cody out into the parking lot and when saw his Mercedes, he lost it.

"What in the fuck?" he hollered, racing toward it.

"Jesus, she play for the Yankees or something?" Tank murmured. "She obviously has one hell of a swing."

"No shit. You should have seen her in action."

"You should have filmed it for me."

"I wish I would have. She might have gone after me next though," I said as we approached Cody, who was already pulling his phone out to call the police.

He looked at us. "Can you believe this shit?"

Suddenly, a white BMW pulled up next to us. In the passenger seat sat Charlie.

"Wow, what happened here?" she asked with wide eyes.

Cody stared at her in shock, his mouth wide open. "Are you... did you do this?" he asked in disbelief.

"What was the answer you gave me earlier? Oh, yeah. No. No, I didn't." She smiled coolly.

"Are you fucking serious, Charlie?" He looked at his car again and ran his hands through his hair. "I can't believe you did this."

"She didn't do anything," Jackie said, looking over at him. "Maybe it was your *other* fiancée who did it? The one who cheated on you while you were overseas, fighting for our country?"

His face lost all its color.

"You never mentioned that you were in the military," I said to him.

Cody looked at me and shook his head.

"Anyway, why would anyone want to marry you?" Jackie asked. "You're a lying piece of shit and so desperate for money, you'd give up the only good thing in your life. Frankly, it's your loss and her gain."

"Not to mention he lies to strippers so they'll give him pity BJs," Charlie added. "That's pretty sick."

"Fuck you," Cody said. "I'm calling the cops. I'm sure there are cameras around here and everything was caught on tape."

"You sure you want to do that, Cody?" Jackie replied. "You forgetting who her father is and how much he paid you to stay away from Charlie?"

He went silent.

"My dad was right about you all the time. You really are nothing but a fucking loser," Charlie said quietly. "Let's go, Jackie."

The BMW took off, leaving the three of us.

Tank cleared his throat. "So, I take it we should walk back to the other bar and grab the Tahoe?"

SEVEN

CHARLIE

"SO, IT WAS obviously true," Jackie said as she drove me home. "Did you see the way he clammed up when I mentioned Tony?"

"Yes," I muttered, staring out the window.

I felt like I was in a bad dream. That it was all a lie. But it wasn't and I wanted to throttle my dad. What other lengths would he go to in order to get his way? This was too much. The thought of being in the same house with him made my stomach turn.

"Stop there," I said as we approached a Holiday Inn.

"Why?" she asked, slowing the car down.

"The hell if I'm going home tonight. I might burn the place down with my father inside."

She smiled. "I wouldn't blame you. You can stay at my place."

"No. You said Brian was staying the night. I'll never get any sleep with you two going at it."

"He doesn't have to," she protested. "He'd totally understand if I told him not to come over."

"I appreciate the offer but, honestly, I think I just want to be alone tonight. You know, pamper myself and take a long, hot bath?" Drink myself to sleep. I hoped they had more than a mini bar because it probably wouldn't be enough for what I was planning.

"Pamper yourself? It's the Holiday Inn. Wouldn't you rather stay at the Ritz or Hyatt?" she said, pulling into the parking lot.

"Nah. This will be fine. I'll book the presidential suite. Dickhead and I stayed at one a couple of months ago. They're really not that bad."

"Okay. You sure about this?" she asked, approaching the lobby entrance.

I nodded. "Very."

THE PRESIDENTIAL SUITE wasn't available, but the Honeymoon was.

"I'll take it," I said to the front desk attendant, pulling out my credit card.

Five minutes later, I was in the elevator and heading to the top floor. Once inside the room, I kicked off my shoes and grabbed the menu, intending to order room service. Unfortunately, the restaurant in the hotel had stopped serving dinner and the store was closed.

"There's a diner across the street," the attendant told me. "They serve alcohol and food around the clock."

"Is it any good?" I asked, wanting comfort food. Although Jackie and I had gone to dinner a couple of hours before, I'd barely eaten. My appetite was back now and I was hungry enough to eat White Castle hamburgers, which usually did a number on me.

"Yeah. They have awesome omelets and burgers."

"Sounds good." I replied. "Do they deliver?"

"Not at this time of night, but you can order things to go."

"Okay." I thanked the woman and then looked up the diner's menu on the Internet. Unfortunately, they didn't even have a website.

"Jesus, get with the times," I muttered, not wanting to have to sit in the restaurant for too long. It was getting late and I still wanted to soak in the tub, drink a bottle of wine, and forget the fucked up day I'd had.

Ten minutes later, I was inside of the diner and looking through the menu when I heard a familiar voice enter the place. Whipping my head around, I saw Maddox and his other biker friend. Thankfully, the two appeared to have lost Cody.

"Are you following me?" Maddox asked with a cocky grin.

"I was here first, so, technically, you're following me," I replied, thinking back to our moment behind the club. When he'd almost kissed me.

He laughed and then introduced me to Tank.

"Nice to meet you," I said. "So, have you two eaten here before?"

They told me they hadn't and that Cody had rented them a couple of rooms at the Holiday Inn.

"Where's Jackie?" Maddox asked.

"She went home."

"So, you're here by yourself?" he replied, his eyes lighting up.

"Yeah. Don't get too excited. I'm not staying," I said. "I'm getting my food *to go.*"

"You're killing me, Chuck," he pouted.

"My feet are killing me," I said, bending down to rub the top of my foot.

"Did I mention I give great foot massages?" he said.

"Afraid not," I replied, imagining that his hands would feel pretty damn anywhere on my body.

Tank grinned. "Brother, you never mentioned that to me either. Have you been holdin' out?"

"You just keep those dogs away from me," Maddox replied, looking down at Tank's boots.

He laughed. "I have to use the bathroom. It was nice meeting you, Charlie."

"You, too," I said.

Tank left us while singing *Who Left The Dogs Out*, which turned a few heads as he strolled toward the bathroom.

I chuckled. "He's a riot."

"Hell yeah, he is. You sure you don't want to stay and join us for breakfast?" Maddox asked.

I had to admit, now that I'd run into him again, I wasn't exactly ready to walk away. Especially with the sexual tension between us, which was still there.

Before I could reply, he added, "I'm buying."

For me, it didn't matter one way or another. My father usually picked up the tab on everything I purchased. I'd never even seen a credit card statement. But, I'd already decided to join them anyway, so I agreed.

"Sure. Why not?" I replied, closing the menu.

Maddox grinned.

The waitress seated us and a few seconds later, Tank joined us at the table.

"He talked you into it, huh?" Tank asked with an amused smile.

"She couldn't resist my charms," Maddox said before I could reply.

"He told me he was buying," I explained.

"I should have known he'd try bribing you," Tank said, laughing.

His words reminded me of why I was there and suddenly put a damper on the moment.

"Speaking of bribery," Maddox said. "What did you and Jackie mean about your old man paying off Cody?"

I sighed.

"If you don't want to talk about it, we'll understand," he added.

I decided to tell them about the deal between Cody and my dad.

"What your old man did was shitty," Maddox said. "But, in the end it paid off. Now you know what kind of an asshole Cody really is."

"I know, but I'm still pissed at my father. Not only did he stoop to something so underhanded, but he lied about it to my face."

"Are you going to confront him about it?" Tank asked.

"Hell, yeah. Just not tonight, which is what I'd do if I went home," I replied as the waitress brought us some water.

"Would you like anything else to drink?" the woman asked, looking a little anxious.

"Water is fine," Tank said.

"I'm good," Maddox added.

I ordered a bottle of wine and then looked at Maddox, who was sitting across from me. "After the shitty day I've had, I should be ordering two."

He looked up at the waitress. "Get her one to go, too. Put everything on my tab."

She smiled at him. "You got it."

"Thanks," I said after she left.

"No problem. So, what was going on with you wearing that costume earlier?" he asked.

I snorted. "Hell, no. I wasn't as sober as I am now and made a poor choice."

"You looked pretty hot, regardless," Maddox answered.

"Thanks. I wanted to shock the hell out of Cody by dancing on stage. I chickened out at the last minute," I said.

"He would have shit his pants," Maddox said. "I would have loved to see that myself."

"Me too. At least I got him back by smashing the hell out of his car," I said, thinking back. "I heard that he'd lied to one of the strippers about being in the military and getting jilted by his fiancée. I saw red after that. All I wanted to do was kill him."

"I don't blame you," Tank said, frowning. "I would have used the bat on him."

The waitress returned at that moment with my wine, and we ordered our meals. Tank and Maddox requested breakfast food and I ended up ordering a cheeseburger and fries. After she left, Maddox excused himself and went to the bathroom.

Admiring his behind as he walked away, I asked Tank where they were from and about their club.

"We live in Jensen, Iowa," Tank said. "And are members of the Gold Vipers. Mad Dog just transferred over from Florida recently."

"Ah. And, you're the president?" I replied, staring at the patch on his vest.

Tank nodded.

"Why exactly did he transfer over?"

"Family reasons. I'll let him explain."

"No problem." I took a sip of wine. "So, what's it like being in a biker club? I imagine everyone is scared shitless of you?"

He laughed. "Some people are, but we have a pretty good reputation in our city. We don't fuck with anyone unless they fuck with us."

"Sounds like my dad's philosophy in life. Only, he seems to be doing a lot of the fucking around," I muttered.

"What does he do for a living, if you don't mind my asking?"

I told him what I knew.

"Investor, huh? What's his name?"

"Tony Armati. I doubt you've ever heard of him."

Tank's eyebrows shot up. "Armati?"

"Yeah. Why?"

He smiled grimly. "Well, now things are making more sense."

"Why?" I asked.

"He's mafia."

"No," I replied firmly. "He's always getting labeled as Mafioso, but that's because our Uncle Bill, God rest his soul, had connections. My father said he's in no way affiliated with them."

Tank gave me a curious look. "That's what you believe?"

"Honestly, after today I don't know what to believe anymore. He lied and paid someone off to stay away from me. Who knows what else he's involved with?"

"I'm going to be honest with you, darlin'. I know for a fact that your old man has his hands in some shady stuff. Rumor has it involves what I like to call the 'Three Gs'. Gambling, guns, and girls."

His words shocked me. "What? You're kidding? Why would he get his hands dirty like that when he's already making a killing with investment properties?"

"That's something you can ask him about. Just don't mention my name. I have enough enemies as it is," Tank said in a low voice.

My head felt like it was spinning. "You're sure about this?"

"Pretty much. I know some people who know some people who've done business with your old man."

I sat back in my chair. "I need to move my ass out of his house and get as far away from him as possible," I replied. It was shocking and saddening to learn such horrible things about my father. Part of me had always wondered, but I'd buried my concerns and ignored the signs.

"You're still living at home? How old are you?"

"Don't judge. I'm twenty-three."

"I'm not judging. If I had it my way, I'd keep my kids with me forever. I was just curious. What about your mother? Are your folks still married?"

I nodded. "But they don't live together."

"I don't blame her."

Maddox returned to the table. "So, what did I miss? Did she make any confessions about me while I was gone? Like how she can't stop thinking about me?"

I laughed. "Good one."

"No. We just talked about her family a little," Tank replied, an amused look in his eyes.

"Oh, yeah?" Maddox looked at me. "Let me guess, you're still living at home. Your father has always had his nose in your business. Your mother and he are divorced—"

"Separated, although neither admit to it," I replied. "I guess I know why my mother is afraid to make it official."

He gave me a curious look and I explained what Tank and I had talked about.

"No, shit? You had no idea?" Maddox replied afterward.

"I knew he was hanging out with some sketchy people. I just didn't know he was as equally rotten," I said. "I really need to get the hell out of Buffalo and as far from him as possible."

"You have a place to go?" Maddox asked.

"Not yet. I mean, I could stay with my mother, but I was thinking about going to a culinary arts school."

"You should," Tank replied. "I know someone who went to one in Davenport as is now running her own French restaurant. We eat there all the time."

"Funny, I never pictured you eating French cuisine," Maddox replied.

"It's good. I just have to order two or three meals to fill me up. The portions are tiny," he explained.

"See, that's what I'd love to do someday. I'd open up an Italian restaurant, though," I replied.

"What do you do now?" Maddox asked.

"I work in my Uncle Vinnie's restaurant as a hostess," I replied.

"Is he associated with the Mafioso?" Maddox asked.

"Honestly, I don't know. My dad is, so he might be, too," I said.

We talked some more about my uncle until the waitress brought our food. As we were eating, I asked Maddox about his personal life.

"How old is your daughter?"

He smiled. "She's five. Light of my life."

"What about her mother?" I asked, dipping my French fry into ketchup. "You're not together?" At least, I hoped not. Especially after the way he'd been flirting with me.

Maddox explained that he and his ex had been separated for four years.

"We tried to make it work, but argued all of the time. To this day she still hates the fact that I'm in a biker club. She doesn't understand the lifestyle or comradery, even though we met during a club party," Maddox explained.

"A lot of people don't," Tank replied.

"How do you get along now?" I asked.

"We're friends. Not close ones, but we have an amicable relationship," he replied. "Anyway, I moved to Jensen because the two of them moved out here to help take care of Aubrey's grandmother, who's terminally ill."

"Ah. Poor kid. I never knew my grandmothers, unfortunately," I replied. "Will they move back to Florida eventually, do you think?"

"Good question. I don't know," he said.

We talked more about Maddox and his relationship with Aubrey. It sounded like he spent a lot of his free time with her and was a fun dad.

"I wish my father would have been more like you," I replied after he told me about the things they did together, like visiting the zoo, going to the beach, and finger-painting. I knew my father loved me, there'd never been any doubt, but he hadn't been a hands-on dad. He paid for everything and had always been in the background, but there weren't any fond memories of park visits or bedtime stories.

"I try. I mean, I have a lot of faults she doesn't know about yet. I just hope that when she's older, she doesn't turn out hating me," he replied.

"I'm sure when she's a teenager, she'll hate you no matter what," I said, smiling. "That's just how they are."

"Not Aubrey. I won't let her," he said with a confident smile.

Tank, who'd finished his meal, pushed his food away. "You guys, I hate to say this, but I've got this splitting headache that just won't go away. If you don't mind, I'm going back to my room." He pulled out his wallet and threw a hundred dollar bill onto the table. "This should cover everything."

Maddox started to protest.

"Brother, it was my turn to pay so don't argue with me," he said sternly.

"Fine. You're the boss," Maddox replied.

"Damn right." Tank stood up. "It was nice talking to you, Charlie."

"You, too," I replied.

"I hope we meet again. You should come out to Jensen and pay us a visit. I know Mad Dog would like that," he said, winking at Maddox.

"Thank you. I have so much on my plate right now, though. I don't know where I'm heading, to be honest."

"I get it. Just, if you do ever visit, don't be a stranger," he replied.

"I won't," I replied, thinking he was a real sweetie for someone who looked like such a badass.

"How's your burger?" Maddox asked, when we were alone.

I'd eaten most of it. "Pretty good. It's wrecking my buzz, though," I said with a sad smile.

"That's not good."

"No. It's not." I pushed my plate away. "I think I'm finished."

He reached over and grabbed a couple of my French fries. "I'll walk you back to the hotel."

"Thanks.

EIGHT

MADDOX

AFTER PAYING FOR the food, we grabbed what was left of the wine and I purchased a six-pack of beer before walking back to the Holiday Inn. Instead of going our separate ways, we decided to head out to the pool area in back. The hotel had turned off the lights in the courtyard and we had the area all to ourselves.

"This is nice," Chuck said, after we sat across from the pool on two white lawn chairs.

"Yeah. Too bad the pool is closed," I replied, pulling out a bottle of beer and cracking it open. "A swim would be nice, right about now."

"I know, right? My father just spent a ton of dough on an underground pool. I mean, it's amazing and has everything, even a grotto." She frowned. "I'm sure he paid with it with his blood money."

"Probably." Of course, the Gold Vipers weren't angels, and we had our own special dealings going on behind closed doors. We kept our hands clean of drugs, prostitution, and murder, though.

As if reading my mind, she asked if I'd ever done anything illegally.

"Let's just put it this way—I go to bed every night with a clear conscience," I told her.

"So, you don't lie, cheat, or steal?"

"I try to keep it real, unless I'm being asked about Santa Claus or the Tooth Fairy."

She smiled.

"I don't cheat. As far as stealing, I did get caught taking gum from a grocery store when I was a kid. My old man spanked the hell out of me and I learned my lesson there."

She smiled. "Is he still around?"

"Yeah. He's living in Florida." I told her about Bastard and how he was the founding president of the Gold Vipers.

"Wow. That's impressive," she replied. "You must be very proud of your old man."

"Yeah."

Admittedly, he'd been hard on me growing up, as well as his other children, but not in a mean way. He'd always been stern and demanding, which I now respected. We'd butted heads a few times growing up, and even now, didn't always see eye-to-eye. But, I loved him and there was a mutual respect between us.

"So, what do you do when you're not hanging out with your club buddies?"

"I paint," I replied.

"Like, as in portraits?"

"Mostly cars. I do custom paint jobs."

"Like flames and stuff?"

"Yep."

"That's cool." She took a sip from the bottle of wine she was holding. "You start your new job on Monday?"

"Yeah."

"Well, good luck."

"Thanks."

"What else are you passionate about? Besides art and Aubrey?"

I had to bite my tongue to keep from saying "fucking" which was something I was real passionate about at the moment.

"My club," I said instead.

"And?"

I stared past the pool, at some fireflies making their way across the courtyard. "Riding motorcycles."

"That's it? Don't you have any other hobbies or into any sports?"

"I like watching football, hockey, and baseball."

"I'm talking about playing something? Do you?"

I thought back to my teenage years and early twenties. Most of my free time was spent surfing on Jacksonville Beach. "I used to surf a lot. There won't be much chance of that now that I'm living in Iowa, though."

She looked surprised. "Wow, I didn't expect that. You don't look like a surfer-boy. You look more like a wrestler."

I smirked. "I'd prefer water-warrior."

Chuck laughed. "Oh, my God. I just realized that you look a lot like that guy who played Aquaman—and he's a definitely a water-warrior."

"Jason Momoa?" I'd been told that more than once. We had similar facial features.

"Yeah. You'd look more like him if you grew your hair out," she replied.

I raised my eyebrow. I didn't know how to take that. "Are you saying that I should?"

Charlie laughed. "No. Not at all. I'm just saying that people would probably mistake you for him."

"Or maybe they'd mistake him for me," I said before taking a swig of beer.

"Yeah. You never know."

"What about you? What kind of things are you into?"

She listed off a bunch of things, including waterskiing, tennis, and rollerblading. "I try to stay active in the summer. It's been easy to do since I've been living with my father and have a lot of free time."

"That's cool."

We sat silently, staring ahead toward the pool. I could feel my eyelids getting heavier, but I didn't want to fall asleep. I was enjoying the moment too much.

"Have you ever tried snowboarding?" she asked after a while. "Since you like to surf."

"Yeah. It's fun, but not the same thing."

"I've never done either," she said, staring off toward the pool. "I also have never been on a motorcycle. I should add those to my bucket list."

"If I had my bike right now, I could help you with that," I replied, still ticked off about that.

"Where is it?"

I explained.

"That's too bad."

"No shit. Another reason I'm not impressed with your ex."

"Let's not talk about him. You'll ruin my good buzz," she replied with a lazy smile.

"You're right. Let's talk about this 'bucket' list. What else is on it? Maybe I can help you out with some things."

Charlie laughed. "There's nothing sexual on it."

"Did I mention anything about sex?" I teased. "Get your mind out of the gutter, girl."

She snorted.

"So, if nothing sexual is in your bucket list then I have to imagine that you've had a very adventurous sex life?"

"Probably nothing compared to yours."

I smiled. "Let's just say I'm pretty much up for trying most things, and haven't much left on my bucket list either."

"That crazy, huh?"

I smiled. It wasn't as crazy as some of the guys I knew, although I'd been with two girls before and had sex in some pretty precarious spots, like the zoo and an airport. Once I even had sex in an igloo while visiting Alaska. Well, it wasn't really an igloo, more like a huge, half-assed snow fort. I'd been sixteen at the time and the girl, seventeen. We'd stayed with her family because our fathers had been in the service together. She'd flirted with me the entire time and then one night, asked if I wanted to see the fort her younger brothers had made. The thing had been huge, too. They must have spent days building it. Although we couldn't stand in the fort, there'd been enough room to sit and do other things. And we most certainly did.

"Actually, I'm full of shit. I'm not as daring as I'm pretending to be."

"So, no club orgies or whips and chains action?"

"Afraid not. You?"

"Nope. None of those are on my bucket list either."

"What about girl-on-girl?" I asked with a devilish grin.

"Not interested. What about you?"

"Definitely," I replied. "Watching, that is."

"I'm sure most guys are."

"We're pigs. What can I say?"

She smiled. "Have you ever been skinny-dipping?"

"Yeah."

"Well… I haven't. And guess what? It's on the list." She took another swig of wine and then stood up. "I suppose now is as good a time as any."

My eyebrows shot up. "Here?"

"Sure. Why not?" She began unbuttoning her blouse.

I looked around. Although we were alone in the courtyard, anyone glancing out of their hotel window would definitely see what was happening.

"You coming?" she asked, removing her shirt. Underneath she wore a lacy, black bra that cupped two healthy mounds.

Fuck.

Instant boner.

My throat went dry as I watched her unbutton her shorts and slide them off.

"Hello?" She turned and then looked at me over her shoulder, smiling coyly. "Cat got your tongue?"

"Yeah. I think so."

She looked up toward the windows. "We'd better go in slowly. If anyone hears us splashing, it's all over."

"Good idea."

"Well, what are you waiting for?" she whispered, nodding toward my clothes as I stared at her luscious curves.

I stood up and began unbuttoning my pants while she slid into the water, still wearing the bra and thong panties. I knew if I got a piece of that ass tonight, every fucked up thing that had occurred earlier in the day, was well worth it. Hell, in the past twenty-nine years.

NINE

CHARLIE

T HE WATER WAS feeling pretty damn good, and so was I.

I swam slowly to the middle of the pool and turned around to watch Maddox undress. Seeing him remove his cut, T-shirt, and jeans was sexy enough, but watching him under the moonlight, wearing nothing but his boxers, took it to a whole new level.

"You know, it's not really skinny-dipping unless," he pushed his boxers down and stepped out of them, "you're completely naked."

Ohmygod.

I stared up at him. He was all gleaming skin and rippling muscle under the light of the moon. He was also hung like a damn horse. A delicious shudder passed through me at the thought of him inside of me.

"I guess we know who brought the bat this time," I said, swimming to the edge of the pool. I crossed my arms on the cement and smiled up at him. "You're pretty proud of yourself, aren't you?"

He smiled. "You mean of Happy Dog?"

"What?"

He looked down at his manhood. "I'm Mad Dog. He's Happy Dog."

I stared at both dogs with amusement. "You'd better get in here before someone calls the cops and puts us both in jail."

He chuckled. "Yeah. I'd never hear the end of it from Tank."

"I imagine not."

Still smiling, he dipped his foot into the water. "It's cooler than I expected."

"It feels good once you're in," I replied, unable to tear my gaze from his hips.

He slid into the water. "Brrr." He swam to the middle of the pool. "I'm surprised it's not heated."

"You wimp. It's not cold," I said, splashing him lightly.

"Wimp? Hey, you still have your bra and panties on. That's why you're not feeling it," he teased.

"Whatever, you goof," I replied.

"Come on. Your turn. I just put myself out there for you and all of the Peeping Toms staying at the Holiday Inn."

I looked up toward the windows above us, making sure nobody really *was* watching. Of course, it was hard to see anything in the darkness. For all I knew, someone could have been filming an entire movie.

"You're not a virgin, are you?" he teased.

Our eyes met. "Do I look like a virgin?"

"I don't know how to answer that without getting myself into trouble," he said, wading closer to me. "Your body is banging. If you haven't been having sex, then all of your old boyfriends must have suffered miserably."

I reached between my breasts and unclasped my bra. "Some of them probably did," I admitted. "I'm choosy with who I have sex with."

"You should be."

"Do you think I'm going to fuck you, Maddox?" I asked with a little smile.

He groaned. "We don't even have to touch if you just keep talking to me like that. I'm already about to come and I don't even know what color your nipples are."

"Dusky pink? That's what I've been told at least."

"Dusky pink? Is that even a real color?"

I laughed.

"Now I have to see them. So, I know what in the hell dusky pink actually looks like."

"Check your daughter's color crayons."

He groaned. "You're killing me again, Chuck."

I smiled and tossed my bra onto the cement, followed by my panties.

"I bet you're freezing your ass off now," he said. "Why don't you come over here and let me warm you up?"

"I said we'd swim. I never mentioned sex."

He moved closer to me. "Neither did I."

I pushed off of the wall and swam away from Maddox. Before I could get to the other side of the pool, he grabbed me around the waist and pulled me back against his chest.

"You're not getting away so easily this time," he whispered in my ear. His hands stroked my ribs and then cupped my breasts. He squeezed them gently at first and then his hands grew rougher. "Unless, it's what you want."

With his hands on my breasts and his hard cock pressed against my buttocks, I moaned my answer.

"Fuck, you feel so good," he groaned in my ear.

I closed my eyes as his lips trailed hot kisses along my neck. One of his hands slid down between my legs, making me gasp in pleasure. He rubbed my clit and worked his fingers into me, igniting my core. We hadn't even officially kissed and my senses were already shattered. My moans and whimpers soon turned into jagged gasps as his fingers sent me into shivers of ecstasy. On the brink of an orgasm, I reached behind and wrapped my hand around his thick, hard shaft, hungry for it. The tension inside of me grew and grew until I finally exploded. Coming, I threw my head back and he put his hand over my mouth, quieting my gasps of ecstasy.

TEN

MADDOX

I WAS ON FIRE and nearly came with her. I had one hand on her soft tits and the other on her pussy when she let go. My only regret was that I couldn't taste any of that sweet honey between her legs. There was nothing like watching a woman squirm and moan while your tongue drove her insane.

When I felt her relax, I turned her around and kissed her roughly on the mouth, my dick rock-hard and pulsating. I wanted to impale her and feel her wet tightness while I drove in and out of her. But, we didn't have any protection and I'd already learned my lesson there.

After exploring her mouth, I lowered my lips to her breasts, savagely licking at the tips, which were indeed a rosy color. Her nipples tightened as I sucked and teased the hard buds. She moaned and grabbed my cock.

"Fuck me," she begged, sliding her hand up and down the shaft.

Growling in the back of my throat, I tried to hold back from exploding as she worked my cock. "I don't have a condom."

"I'm on the pill. Are you… healthy?"

My cock grew harder at the news. "Do I *feel* healthy?"

"Very."

"What about you?"

"Clean bill."

That was all I needed to hear. I picked her up and she curled her legs around my waist.

CHARLIE

ACHING TO HAVE him inside of me, I positioned his cock against my opening and wiggled my pelvis against his head.

Maddox tightened his grip on my thighs and plunged into my hole.

I gasped.

His length and girth speared and stretched me as he buried himself deep into my center. He was impossibly huge, but the hurt was so, so good.

"Fuck," he growled in the back of his throat. "You're so tight."

Our lips met as he pulled out slightly and then entered again and then again. Body to body, mouth to mouth, we moved together. His strokes were slow, smooth, and possessive, eventually growing to hard thrusts. The water was soon splashing around us as he slammed into me, rough and gasping with every thrust. Heat streaked through me as he hit my G-spot, vibrating my entire core. The pressure began to build and within moments, another orgasm took me by surprise. I pulled at his hair as hot pleasure stormed through me.

Maddox stiffened up and then came with a shuddering cry himself. His lips closed over mine and I could feel his cock pulsate deep in my center as he released inside of me. Sated, he held me in his arms and nuzzled my neck as our bodies wound down.

"That was an epic ending to a shitty day," he whispered. "Thank you."

"For both of us."

"Now, the real question is, where do we go from here? Your room or mine?"

"Mine is the Honeymoon Suite."

He raised his eyebrow.

I smiled. "Don't worry. Neither of us are *that* drunk."

"I'm not drunk at all."

"I'm a little tipsy," I admitted.

"Shit. So it was the booze that made you want me," he joked.

"It was everything," I replied, kissing him on the lips. "And then some."

"Good." His fingers slid down between my legs again. "Just so you know, I have more 'then some' you haven't even experienced yet. But you will."

I smiled. "Oh, yeah? What's that?"

"Let's get out of here and I'll show you."

"Can I at least have a teaser?"

Maddox gave me a devilish smile and then went under the water. Before I could figure out what he was doing, I felt his hands on my thighs and his lips on my pussy. It only lasted for a few seconds and then he was back up for air.

"How's that for a teaser?" he asked, running his hands through his wet hair.

I smiled. "You're killing me, Maddox."

WE MADE IT to my suite without incident and jumped in the shower together to wash off the chlorine. We started fooling around again and spent the next hour making love. This time, he went down on me and drove me wild with his tongue until I was bucking and carrying on like a crazy woman. When we were both sated, he pulled me against him and we fell asleep. As I drifted off, I thought about him leaving for Iowa and was already missing him.

ELEVEN

CHARLIE

I WOKE UP in Maddox's arms, with him behind me, and smiled. As campy as it sounded in my head, it felt like I belonged there.

"You awake?"

"Kind of." I began stroking his forearm, wishing we could lie in bed all day together.

"This isn't where you kick me out of bed and make me do the Walk of Shame, is it?" he murmured in my ear.

I laughed. "No, this is where I kick you out so you'll get us something to eat."

"How about we both get out of bed and try the diner across the street again?"

My stomach growled as I thought about the huge plate of food he'd devoured. I was craving morning food. I could almost taste the hash browns Maddox had put down. "Sounds good. How was the breakfast?"

"Big and bountiful. Like these," he said, cupping my breasts. "I highly recommend."

"And the sausages?" I asked, feeling his erection against my back. "Will I be satisfied?"

"Allow me to serve you one so hearty, you'll never look at another the same way again."

I laughed. "You already accomplished that," I reminded him.

He kissed my neck. "You sure? Maybe I should give you another portion?"

"Sounds yummy," I replied.

His hand reached between my legs. "Feels like you're already drooling."

"You make me hungry," I replied, writhing against him as he began strumming my clit.

"Not as hungry as you make me," he growled in my ear.

Maddox entered me from behind, grunting as he worked himself inside of me and pulled back out. I met his hips eagerly, fueled by my own passion. The delicious friction penetrated every nerve and within no time, we were both reaching our plateaus and soaring over them.

"You able to walk?" he asked later, a smile in his voice.

"Hardly. Mind if I take a shower?"

"Only if I can join you."

"If you join me, something tells me you're going to get very dirty."

"The shower is the best place for that," he replied, squeezing my ass.

WHEN WE FINALLY made it out of the shower, it was almost ten a.m.

"Someone's phone is vibrating," he said, walking out of the bathroom with a towel around his waist.

I grabbed mine and frowned. It was my father.

"What's wrong?" Maddox asked. "Is it the douchebag calling for forgiveness?"

"No, and if it was, I'd tell him where to take it. It's my dad. It looks like he's called a couple of times."

"You going to answer it?"

"No. I'm not talking to him. If it's urgent, he can leave a message."

"I don't blame you. He's probably worried about you, though."

"It's more like he's going nuts because he's not in control of what's happening right now." I smirked. "I'm sure he'd blow a gasket if he knew I had sex with a guy I met at a strip joint."

"Or that I'm in biker club," he added.

I chuckled. "Oh, that would really set him off. I could hear him right now…" My voice trailed off as I saw the dark look on his face.

"Go ahead. Say it. He'd probably tell you that we're no good thugs, drunks, and addicts."

"Who cares what he says? I know you're not."

"I'm not a saint either."

"You don't have to explain anything to me. Especially considering how my father does business. And with whom."

Maddox walked over and pulled me into his arms. "Unlike him, I would also never go behind your back to fuck with you or those you care about. Even if I thought it was for your own good. You're an adult and can make your own decisions. I expect the same from you."

"For sure. I'd never play with your head. Well… "I smiled wickedly.

Grinning back, he pulled the towel off. "Play all you want, Chuck. In fact, I insist."

"You just won't let the whole 'Chuck' thing go, will you?"

"Nope."

"Fine, what should I call you then? Mad Dog just doesn't slide off the tongue very well. Little Dog doesn't really work for me either."

He groaned. "Slide off the tongue—now you're starting to get me hard again."

"Maybe I should just call you Mad-*dick*?" I replied, touching his cock. "With the mad skills?"

"Baby, you call me anything you want. Just keep calling me."

I groaned at his joke.

TWELVE

MADDOX

THE HOGS WERE supposed to be ready for us by one, which was fine. I wanted to have a leisurely breakfast with Chuck. She was funny, smart, and sexier than hell and if we lived in New York, I'd make her my woman in a heartbeat. But, I knew a long distance relationship wouldn't work. Especially since I'd be obsessing daily over who was trying to get into her pants. I wasn't usually a jealous guy, but she was insanely beautiful and I wasn't the only one who thought so. Even the bus-boy at the diner was eyeballing her when we walked in and he didn't look old enough to stay out past midnight.

"So, you two talk shoot the shit all night, or what?" Tank asked when he joined us. "You both look pretty damn tired."

"Yeah, we didn't sleep much," I replied, picking up the menu.

Tank smiled like the Cheshire Cat. "Funny, I would have thought you would have been exhausted after that late night swim."

"Busted." I chuckled.

Her eyes widened. "You saw us?"

"Not you, exactly, but I did catch a glimpse of Mad Dog prancing around buck-naked. I'd like to burn that memory from my brain," he replied, picking up the menu. "Kids. I tell you."

Chuck and I shared a smile.

"So, was your burger good?" Tank asked. "I'm thinking about getting one myself today."

Chuck and he discussed the menu and I decided on a steak sandwich and onion rings. After ordering our food, I asked Chuck how she was getting home.

"I'll call an Uber," she replied.

"Don't do that. We can drop you off at home," I said. "Before we pick up the bikes."

"Yeah," said Tank. "Don't waste your money."

"Okay. Thanks," she replied.

"How far away from here do you live?" Tank asked.

"About twenty miles. Too far?" she answered.

Tank shook his head. "No. Of course not."

She looked relieved. "Otherwise, I can ask Jackie, too. I have to call her back anyway. We've been texting each other."

"Did you tell her you were hanging out with us?" I asked.

"Some of us more than others," Tank said out of the side of his mouth.

Chuck nodded.

"What was her response?" I asked, sitting back as the waitress walked over and set down three water glasses.

"Not much," Chuck replied. "She likes you guys."

"Thanks, darlin'," Tank said to the waitress, Betty, who looked like she was somewhere in her sixties, rail-thin, with shaky hands. "Is it too late to order a strawberry shake?"

"No, of course not," Betty replied. "You might also want to get some pie afterward. The owner, Jerry, makes *the* best ones in the state. Especially our cream pies. People come from miles to try them all out."

"I doubt I'll still be hungry, but we can always get some to go," he said. "Thanks for the suggestion."

"You're welcome. I just didn't want you missing out. You guys aren't from around here, are you?" she asked.

"No, ma'am," I replied. "We're from Jensen, Iowa."

"Goodness. I know exactly where that is. What a small world. Are you here for some kind of biker convention?" she asked.

"No," I said.

Tank told her why we were in town and afterward, the older woman nodded. "I see you're with the Gold Vipers. Do you know someone named Slammer?"

Tank's eyes filled with emotion. "Yeah. He was my old man."

"*Was?*" Betty raised her hand to her chest. "Did he pass away?"

He nodded. "A few years ago."

"I'm so sorry for your loss," she said softly. "He was such a nice guy."

"How did you know him?" Tanks asked.

"I have a cousin who used to live in Jensen. She took me to some of the club parties. Those were fun times," Betty explained.

"Glad you enjoyed them," Tank replied.

"You know, I remember Slammer talking about his son. He was very proud of his boy."

Tank smiled sadly.

"I should go and check on your food. Oh, and by the way," Betty lowered her voice, "the pie is on me. For all three of you. In honor of Slammer, God rest his soul."

"Thank you, darlin'. That's awfully kind of you," Tank said.

We also thanked her before she headed away.

"If you don't mind my asking, how did your father die?" Chuck asked Tank softly.

"He was killed," he replied and then mumbled something about a club war.

Chuck's jaw dropped. "Wow, I had no idea. I'm sorry."

He nodded and looked at me. "Speaking of fathers, have you talked to Bastard lately?"

"Not recently. I should probably give him a call here pretty soon," I replied. "I'll do it on the way back to Iowa."

"I wish you guys didn't have to go back. You're still leaving today, right?" Chuck asked.

"Afraid so," I said.

"Well, I'm glad we met. You've changed my attitude about bikers and clubs. Yesterday, I would have been too afraid to talk to either of you."

"Yesterday, I *was* afraid to talk to you," I joked, remembering her with the bat. "You definitely know how to make a first impression."

She laughed. "That's not 'me'. The alcohol fueled that fire."

"So did numb-nuts." I looked at Tank. "Speaking of which, he'd better not try swindling us. I'll have to send Chuck and her bat on him."

She laughed. "It wasn't mine. It was one of the strippers'. When she heard about him lying, she lent it to me. It was actually her idea to use it."

"Well, you did a good job. It looked totaled," Tank said.

"He can afford to buy a new one," Chuck muttered.

The diner door opened up and a man wearing sunglasses and an expensive business suit walked inside. He looked around the restaurant, and then his eyes rested on our table.

"You've got to be kidding me," Chuck said, stiffening up. "How in the hell did he know I was here?"

"Who is he?" I asked, already knowing the answer.

She let out a frustrated sigh. "My dad."

THIRTEEN

CHARLIE

F UCK… JUST WHAT I needed.

I groaned inwardly as my father walked over to our table, a displeased look on his face. I had to admit, he wasn't big or bad-assed-looking like the two men at the table, but he put off an intimidating presence.

When he reached our booth, he removed his sunglasses and smiled coolly. "Charlotte, you haven't been returning my calls. Do you have any idea of how worried I've been?"

"How did you find me?" I asked crisply. "Did you have someone tailing me last night again?"

"*Tail* you? No, of course not. I just checked with the credit card company and they told me there was an authorization for the Holiday Inn, across the street."

I sighed. I really needed my own VISA. At the moment, I was just a co-signer. Of course, I was spoiled because he paid my balances off every month. Now that I knew he was mixed in with the mafia, the idea of where the money could be coming from left a bad taste in my mouth.

He went on. "After I arrived, they told me you checked out, so I figured I'd take my chances over here." He looked at Tank and Maddox. "You going to introduce me to your friends, Charlotte?"

"This is Mad Dog and Tank," I replied, enjoying the pained expression on his face as I said their names. "Guys, this is my dad."

"Nice to meet you," Tank said. "Would you like to join us for a bite to eat?"

I gave Tank a dirty look, but he didn't notice.

"Unfortunately, I have some business to attend to. Thank you, though," my father replied, studying him. I could tell by the look in his eyes that he was seething inside.

Good. He deserved it.

"No problem," Tank replied.

"Anyway," Dad looked at me again, "I wanted to make sure you weren't lying dead in the road somewhere. Fathers worry when they get 'ghosted' by their own children."

"Sorry," I replied. "You know, I *am* an adult. I shouldn't have to report where I am twenty-four-seven."

"No, you don't have to do that. But, when you don't come home at night and ignore my texts and phone messages, that's going to worry a person, Charlotte. Please, be more respectful next time."

I wanted to scream at him about respect and the shenanigans he'd pulled with Cody, but the diner was not the place for it. I was also embarrassed at the way he was treating me and wanted him gone, so I apologized instead.

"Apology accepted. Now, would you like a ride home? I'm heading there now," Dad said, looking at his watch.

"She just ordered her food. We can give her a ride after breakfast," Maddox piped in.

Dad looked at him. "On your motorcycle? Do you have an extra helmet?"

"No. I don't have my Hog with me either. We'll be using a cage to get her home. Don't worry," Maddox replied.

"Hopefully it won't give us any more fucking problems," Tank said, staring outside into the parking lot.

My father pursed his lips. Although he was known to through around the F-bomb, he was old fashioned and didn't approve of 'vulgar' language in public.

"A cage," he said to Maddox. "What do you mean you're giving her a ride home in a *cage?*"

"Sorry. That's slang for a car or truck," Maddox replied. "We call it that because it feels like you're caged in when you're driving."

"Interesting. I see you're with the Gold Vipers. How did you come to meet my daughter?" he asked, as if I wasn't even there.

"We met in a bar last night and had a threesome," I said dryly, before anyone else could speak up. "Would you like details?"

Dad's face turned red. "Charlotte," he snapped. "You don't need to be rude. I'm just making conversation."

"Really? I thought you had somewhere to be?" I replied.

"What in the world has gotten into you? I don't deserve to be treated like this," he replied.

I didn't reply. I was too angry and didn't trust myself. "Charlotte?"

"It looks like our food is on its way," I said, staring past my father. I was relieved to see the waitress was coming toward us with a tray.

"Great, I'm so hungry I could eat a horse," Maddox said, unwrapping his silverware.

"Yeah, me too," Tank added.

"I'll get out of the way. See you back at the house, Charlotte," Dad said tersely. Turning on his heel, he walked away from the table without another word.

Tank shook his head. "Damn. You weren't kidding. He needs to chill the fuck out. Does he actually have you followed sometimes?"

I nodded. "He always denies it, but I'm not stupid. I've even confronted some of them at the mall," I replied as the waitress set the tray down and began passing out our meals.

"I'm surprised you stuck around this long," Maddox said.

"It's hard walking away when you're lavished with gifts and money all the time. He's spoiled the hell out of me."

"Yeah, but there's obviously a price," he replied.

I nodded. "Yeah, well, I'm done paying it."

"Good for you," Tank said. "And good luck sorting everything out."

"Thanks," I replied.

FOURTEEN

Maddox

FTER WE ATE, Tank and I drove Chuck home in the Tahoe. Her house was located in a ritzy neighborhood, which I expected. I just had no idea of how loaded her old man actually was until we pulled up to the gated fence surrounding the property. Once we were allowed through, we drove down a long cobblestone driveway to a magnificent, brown and white Victorian mansion.

"No wonder why you never wanted to leave," I said, impressed.

Once we reached the front of the house, Chuck said goodbye to Tank and then I walked her to the door.

"Well, I guess this is it," I said, turning to face her. It was the first time ever that I wanted a one-night stand to turn into something else. Knowing we probably wouldn't see each other again was a little sad.

She nodded.

"If you ever make it out to Jensen, Iowa, call me." We'd exchanged phone numbers, but I knew that after a couple of weeks, the time we had together would just be a nice memory to look back on.

"Yeah. If you're ever in New York, let me know, too. We'll grab drinks and I'll show you around town."

"Sounds great." I pulled her into my arms and gave her a kiss. "I'm going to miss you," I said afterward.

"I'm going to miss you, too."

I kissed her again and *that* was when her father opened the front door. We stepped apart and I could see from the look on his face that he was trying to stay composed.

"Oh, good. You're home, Charlotte," he said, forcing a smile to his face.

"Yeah. Um, do you mind?" she muttered, obviously still very pissed off at him. "We're having a moment here."

"My apologies." He looked at me again and smiled slightly. "Thank you for getting her home safely."

"No problem," I replied, shoving my hands into my pockets. Although I didn't care for what I'd heard about him, I could understand his wanting to protect his daughter.

"I'll be in my office if you need me," he said to her.

She didn't reply.

Nodding to me, he went back into the house and closed the door.

"Sorry about that," Chuck said, looking embarrassed.

"Not a problem. You take care of yourself."

"Thanks. You, too."

We had one more kiss and then she went inside. I turned and headed back down the steps to the Tahoe.

"I guess this trip turned out better than expected, huh?" Tank said after I hopped back into the SUV.

"Yeah. She definitely made up for Cody's fuckup."

"You think her old man really paid him off?"

"Yeah."

Tank looked at the house and shook his head. "Cody's a jackass."

I agreed.

WHEN WE ARRIVED at Cody's shop, we checked on the Road Kings we'd ordered. Mine was a dark cherry color and Tank's was black. Comfortable and easy to drive, I couldn't wait to test them out.

"With those meaty 180s, you're going to get more grip in your turns. Not to mention, more tire life," Cody said as we looked them over.

Pleased with the bikes, we talked him into giving us an additional discount, because of our wait, and he reluctantly agreed.

"What happened with your car? Did you get it towed?" Tank asked.

Cody scowled. "Yeah. That fucking bitch. I know she did it, too."

"Was it true that her father paid you to stay away from her?" I asked.

He looked away. "She's obviously psycho. I don't need anyone to pay me to stay away from her."

"You going to try and go after her for damages?" Tank asked.

"The only witness around was her cunty friend, Jackie. I'm screwed. I'm just going to get it fixed and be done with it," he said with a disgusted look.

"Her old man is Tony Armati. It's probably better for your health if you let it go, anyway," Tank said.

"How do you know who he is?" Cody asked.

Tank looked at me and then back at him. "I know everything about everybody," he said with a cool smile. "Just like I know you're going to return the Tahoe to the rental company for us and pay for the extra day."

The two stared at each other for a few seconds and then Cody nodded. "Sure. Where'd you rent it?"

TWENTY MINUTES LATER, after calling our insurance companies, Tank and I were on the road and heading back to Iowa on our new rides. I had a smile on my face for two reasons—the Road King rode like a fucking dream, and I'd had an unforgettable night with a beautiful woman. One I knew I wasn't going to forget easily.

FIFTEEN

CHARLIE

OF COURSE, WHEN I finally confronted my father again about Cody, he remained firm on the notion that he didn't have anything to do with our breakup. I also asked him about the Mafioso.

"I'm not involved with that bunch," he replied sternly. "Why? Did you get another phone call?"

"No. I've just heard rumors that you've been doing business with them."

"Lies." His eyes narrowed. "Who's been feeding you this garbage?"

I'd promised Tank not to mention his name so I left him out of it. "It doesn't matter. Is it true?"

"I just told you it's not. I know many people, some aren't saints, but that doesn't mean I'm in league with them. In my line of work, I meet all kinds of characters, Charlotte. Unfortunately, being in the same room, or hell, restaurant with them, will bring about rumors. People are jealous of my success and will do anything to tear me down. I have to say that I'm disappointed that you would jump on their bandwagon so easily. I'm your father and I've given you everything you've ever wanted. And yet, you believe strangers over me? It breaks my heart."

I could see how much it was upsetting him and it was making me have doubts. I wanted to believe he was innocent, and there *was* a chance he was telling me the truth.

"I'm sorry," I replied, sighing. "You're right. I shouldn't be jumping to conclusions."

He smiled sadly. "I love you, Charlotte, and I only want the best for you. I also want you to be able to trust me. Haven't I always taken care of you?"

"Yes."

He walked over and gave me a hug. "And I will continue to, even when you're married and have your own children."

Although he meant well, I didn't want him monopolizing my entire life. He'd end up scaring every guy away I was interested in.

"If you love me, you'll give me some space," I murmured.

Sighing, he released me. "I will try. I realize now, after all of this, that I'm holding on too tight. You're an adult and I need to start treating you like one."

I relaxed. "Thank you."

"It's just you and me tonight. I was thinking about ordering some Chinese food for dinner. How does that sound?"

"Good."

I WENT UPSTAIRS, took a shower, and then called Jackie. I told her what had happened after she dropped me off.

She gasped in shock. "No, way. You and one of the bikers? What was that like?"

I smiled at the memories. "Amazing. Now, after being with him, I wouldn't take Cody back if he begged me. I have never had that kind of sex with anyone before. He's ruined me for other guys."

"Uh oh."

"I know. I'm in trouble. Oh, and get this…" I told her about Tony showing up at the diner.

"How did he know where to find you?"

"He checked the VISA records. Anyway, you should have seen the look on his face when he saw me sitting there with Maddox and Tank."

"I wish I would have been there. He must have been pissed."

"Yeah. Understatement. Anyway, I'm home now."

"I still can't believe Tony was checking up on you like that. You really need to put some space between you. Have you given college any more thought?"

"Yes. In fact, I have an idea," I said, thinking about Tank's mention of the culinary school in Iowa. I knew there were others, better and closer, but I wanted to get away. Plus, I wanted to see Maddox again. I couldn't stop thinking about him and watching their Tahoe pull away had left me a little depressed. Normally, I never did one-night-stands, so I didn't know if it was a normal reaction because the sex had been so damn good. Or if it was simply because I was on the rebound. Regardless, Maddox had driven away any lingering feelings I may have had for Cody. He'd also stirred up something inside of me and I needed to figure things out.

"Wait a second, Iowa? Is that where Maddox is from?"

"He's originally from Florida. But, yeah, he lives in Jensen right now."

She sighed. "You can't let what happened between you last night decide your future. You're setting yourself up to be disappointed. Either with the school or what may happen between you if you move closer to him."

"I'm not doing this because of Maddox," I said, the words sounding hollow even to myself. "Tank just mentioned that he knew someone who went to a culinary school in Davenport, and how much she enjoyed it. Maddox and I may never even see each other again."

"Wait, are Jensen and Davenport close to each other?"

"Yeah."

"And this isn't about Maddox?" she said dryly.

"Fine. Knowing he's going to be out there is also a plus. But, we just met. I don't expect anything from him nor am I looking for a relationship. I just want to get away from here."

"At least check out the other schools before you make any rash decisions."

I promised her I would.

"If you end up going to this school, and your dad finds out it's close to Maddox, he's going to blow his lid," she said, sounding amused.

"He'll get over it."

"Talk to Bianca. Get her on your side."

"Good idea."

No matter what I chose, I knew my mother would support me one-hundred percent. I decided to call her as soon as I was done chatting with Jackie.

We talked some more and then hung up. I quickly called Bianca, but she didn't answer, so I had to leave her a message. Then I began researching different culinary schools. Of course, I kept going back to the one in Davenport. As I was searching through the different programs and degrees being offered, I received a text from Maddox.

Maddox: *Stopped to eat something and am missing you already, Chuck.*

Me: *Funny, I miss you, too.*

Maddox: *I might have to take another road trip soon.*

Me: *Here?*

Maddox: *Yes, ma'am ;)*

Me: *I'd love that. BTW, I'm considering the culinary arts school Tank was talking about in Davenport.*

Maddox: *Seriously? That would rock.*

I smiled. I hadn't known how he'd react, so this was good.

Me: *Yeah. Just because he recommended it, of course.*

Maddox: *So, not because of me at all? I'm hurt.*

Me: *You'd be an added bonus. I just don't want you to think I'm stalking you or anything. We can just be friends.*

Maddox: *Fuck that.*

I laughed.

Maddox: *Gotta go. I'll call you when I get home. We'll discuss this some more.*

Me: *Sounds good. TTYS XX*

Maddox: *Definitely.* XX

I put my phone away, a smile still on my face. Going back to my laptop, I filled out the questionnaire on the school's website and requested more information. As much as I knew I should be taking Jackie's advice and looking at other schools, my mind was already made up.

MADDOX

HALFWAY THROUGH OUR trip, we stayed in Indiana at the Gold Vipers Chapter in Mooresville. I knew the president and a few of the other club members, as did Tank, so it was a good reunion. We stayed in their clubhouse, had a few beers, and were in bed by one a.m. After the last couple of days, I was out like a light by the time my head hit the pillow.

The next morning, we had breakfast with some of the guys, made some plans for a road trip before winter, and then headed out.

When we finally arrived in Jensen, it was around seven. I followed Tank to his place, where I was currently staying until I found a house of my own. As we were walking out of the garage, his phone rang.

"It's Raptor," he said, looking at the screen. He answered it. "What's up, brother? You itchin' to see our new rides?"

Raptor was the V.P. and the two were lifelong friends. He was a good guy and one who would always have your back.

Tank's smiled faltered. "Fuck, you think this is a real threat, or just someone talking out of their ass?" He listened to Raptor's response and then swore again. "She needs round-the-clock protection if this is legit." Tank looked at me. "I have an idea."

I listened to the rest of their conversation and knew it had to do with his stepmom, Frannie. She and Slammer had only been married a few years when he died.

After a few more words, the two hung up.

"So, what's up?" I asked.

"Raptor received some intel that Frannie's life is in danger."

"Yeah, I caught some of that. Who's threatening it?"

"The Devil's Rangers."

It didn't surprise me. There was a lot of bad blood between our two clubs. In fact, everyone was pretty certain that they were behind Slammer's assassination.

"Has she reported any threats or strange stuff happening?"

He shook his head. "No. It looks like they haven't made any moves yet. Raptor thinks it's a matter of time, though. I was wondering if you'd stay with her until this thing is taken care of?"

"For sure," I said. "I can be ready to go in ten minutes." The majority of my shit was in a storage garage up the road, so there wasn't much to pack.

"Thanks, brother," he said, looking relieved. "The thing is, though, I don't want her to freak out, which she will if she learns the truth. So, we're going to have to keep this low-key."

"In other words, you don't want her to know she's in danger?"

"Not unless we see anything suspicious. She's usually pretty good with staying alert herself. Being married to my old man taught her that. But, I don't want to cause any hysteria. She already worries enough."

"I understand. Does Raptor have someone watching her at the moment?"

He nodded. "Yeah, a couple of prospects are parked near her townhome in one of our vans. They'll take off when you get there."

"Okay. So, how are you going to set this up?"

"Easy. I'm going to call and ask if you can rent out her basement for a few weeks. She's been talking about leasing it out, anyway."

"Sounds perfect."

"Of course, I'll pay for everything."

"Fuck that. I was planning on giving you money to stay here, anyway. It would be my pleasure to pay her."

He tried arguing about it with me.

"Forget about it. I'm paying. You want to give her money, let her use it for a trip or something."

His eyes widened. "You are a fucking hero, man. Her birthday is coming up soon. I'll kill two birds with one stone by sending her on another cruise with her sister, Cheryl. Pops did that when Jessica's life was in danger awhile back."

Jessica was Frannie's daughter.

"Just book it last minute so the Devil's Rangers don't find out about it."

Tank grinned and put a hand on my shoulder. "Good idea, brother. Glad you're on board with us. You're already a life-saver."

"I'm glad I could help."

Tank took out his phone and made the call to Frannie. Fortunately, she was more than happy to rent out the space to me.

"He'll be over soon," Tank said to her and then winked at me. "You remember Mad Dog, right?"

She said something and he grinned. "Okay. I'll give him the directions."

They spoke some more and then he hung up.

"Okay. She's going to watch for you. Keep an eye on her and keep me posted."

"Will do."

"Thanks. I appreciate this," he said. "I'll talk to her about the cruise tomorrow. Don't say anything."

"No, of course not. So, she remembers me?" The last time I'd seen Frannie had been over a year ago when I'd driven up from Florida with my old man.

He chuckled. "Oh, yeah. She was practically fanning herself on the other end of the phone. I think she might have gotten all hot-and-bothered knowing you were the one coming over. She remembered something about you having a nice smile and big muscles."

I chuckled. "She said that, huh?"

Frannie was much older and wasn't the cougar type, so I knew that whatever she'd said to him was all in fun.

"Swear to God, I love you, brother, but she's off limits. I don't care if she visits you in the middle of the night, you don't touch her. Unless it's to protect her from stray bullets."

I could tell he was joking. "What if she decides to do the touching? I'm pretty irresistible, you've got to admit. She might not be able to help herself."

"You fucker," he said, chuckling and pushing me toward the house. "Get your ass moving before I change my mind and send Raina instead."

We both knew his wife would have been a good replacement, the little badass.

I greeted Raina when we got into the house and then hurried upstairs to pack my shit. When I came back down, she handed me two small brown paper bags.

"What's this?" I asked, smelling something sweet.

"We made some chocolate chip cookies today," she said. "Tank mentioned you two haven't eaten for a few hours, so I figured they might tide you over for now."

I groaned in appreciation. "You have no idea how much I love you right now." I pulled one out and ate it quickly. "Delicious. Thank you."

She smiled. "You're welcome. The other bag is for Frannie. Tell her I said 'Hi' and give her a hug for me."

I nodded toward Tank. "I'd love to, but he'd kick my ass."

She looked at him.

"Don't ask," he said with a twinkle in his eyes.

"I've learned it's better not to," Raina said with a smirk.

MADDOX

"**I** HOPE YOU like the place. Watch your step," Frannie said as we headed downstairs to the lower level of the townhouse. "Everyone seems to trip on that last one."

"Will do, thanks," I replied, looking around the basement in approval. I'd been half expecting little old lady furniture, cat nick-knacks, and doilies, but had been pleasantly surprised to find an actual man-cave. One that Slammer had obviously put together at one point.

"Did you have a hard time finding the place?"

"No, ma'am."

"Please, don't call me that," she said. "It makes me feel like a grandma. Although, I am. I just don't want to be reminded about my age."

"Sorry. Would it help if I told you that you didn't look anything at all like a grandma?" I said, taking a closer look at her. Tall and slender with bobbed dark-blonde hair and hazel eyes, she reminded me quite a bit of her daughter, Jessica. I'd have guessed Frannie to be in her late forties, but Tank had mentioned she was closing in on sixty-two.

"I'm not one to fish for compliments, but they certainly *do* help," she replied with a chuckle.

"Well, it's not just a compliment, it's the truth."

Her cheeks turned pink. "Well, thank you. Oh, not to change the subject, but Tank just called back before you got here and he's stopping over tomorrow night. He said he has some kind of a surprise for me and wants to make dinner. Do you know what that's all about?"

"Maybe. Maybe not," I replied with sly smile.

"You boys. I tell you," she mused. "Anyway, how was your trip to New York? I heard you two purchased a couple of new bikes. Is that the same one you rolled up on?"

"Yeah. It was good," I replied, my thoughts returning to Chuck again. I couldn't wait to see her and the idea that she might be going to school nearby kicked ass.

"Good. I love the color of your Hog, by the way. It's beautiful, that dark red. Slammer used to have one in that shade, too."

"Thanks. I remember seeing Slammer's up in Sturgis. It was one reason I decided to try this color." My last two Hogs had been black and I'd decided to change it up.

She sighed in memory. "Yeah, he loved to ride. I guess you all do, though, right?"

I smiled. "Yeah. That's one thing I'm going to miss about Florida—not being able to ride in the winter months."

"You'll just appreciate it that much more when you do, though. How's your daughter, Aubrey, by the way?"

"She's doing well, although, she has to have her tonsils out. Her mom says she keeps getting strep and just got over Tonsillitis again."

"Oh, no. Well, it's better to get them out now instead of later. The older you get, the harder the recovery."

We talked some more about Aubrey, who I was supposed to see the following weekend. With threats against Frannie's life, however, I didn't know if I wanted my daughter anywhere near this place.

The conversation turned back to Tank.

"He's bringing over the steaks, which is good considering he has a bottomless pit for a stomach. That man can eat an entire cow if he wanted to," she said, after showing me the spare bedroom.

I grinned. She hadn't seen me eat. I had a healthy appetite myself. Even after the cookies, my stomach was growling at the mention of steak.

"I almost forgot, I need to get to the grocery store" she said after the tour. "Why don't you get yourself settled in? If you want a snack right now, help yourself to whatever's here while I'm gone."

As much as I would have loved taking her up on the offer, I knew she couldn't go shopping without me. Especially since it was almost nine and would be dark soon. Anyone could follow her to the store and grab her.

"I'm good for now. Why don't I join you? I need a few things of my own," I replied, grateful there was a refrigerator in the basement she said I could use. It would give me an excuse to go shopping with her.

"I can probably get them for you if you'd like," she replied.

I could tell from her expression that she wanted to go alone, but it was out of the question. "I'm not exactly sure what I need, so if you don't mind, I'd like to tag along."

"No problem. Well, I should be ready in fifteen minutes," she answered. "Will that work?"

"For sure."

She went back upstairs and I took another quick glance around the basement, liking the fact that there was a pool table, dart board, and even an old jukebox. Definitely a place to relax and unwind. Unfortunately, knowing her life was in danger, I wasn't sure if there'd be much of that going on.

Before leaving, I opened up my duffel bag, strapped my ankle holster on, and took out the .357 Magnum. After loading it, I shoved it into the holster and waited for Frannie.

THIRTY MINUTES LATER, we were in the grocery store, talking about her family and Slammer. We didn't discuss his death, however, just some of the fond memories she had with him.

"He obviously loved you a lot," I said, after we laughed about an incident where he'd ordered flowers over the phone and the shop had screwed up. Instead of the note saying "I love you, Frannie", it had said "I love your Fanny." Apparently, he'd been drinking, too, so they figured it had been just as much Slammer's fault as it had been the shop's.

She nodded. "He was such a good man. Honestly," she smiled wanly. "I don't think he ever cheated on me either. I'd like to hope not, at least. I know it's not uncommon in the club life."

Frannie was right, especially with all of the parties and chicks willing to do anything for a guy in a Gold Viper's cut. Some of the things I'd seen go down at the parties were pretty crazy. Hell, on any given day of the week, you could walk into a back room of the clubhouse and find two or more people having sex, majority of them not married to each other.

"So, your daughter, Jessica, is from a previous marriage?" I asked, changing the subject.

"Yes. Her father died a few years ago in a car accident. He was a great man, too. Served in Vietnam."

"Wow. That's a shame. Sorry for your loss. It's been a rough few years, huh?"

"Yes and no. I've lost a lot but gained, too. Anyway, do you like spinach?" she asked, as we moved toward the vegetables. "I have a great recipe for creamed spinach. I was thinking about making that on the side."

"Yeah, sounds good," I replied before my attention was diverted toward the deli where two guys were standing. Both had Devil's Rangers cuts on and one of them kept looking our way.

Fuck.

Considering that they were a long way from home, and with the recent threats, this was no coincidence.

"I know Tank loved it when I made it last time. Of course, there's not much he doesn't love," she said, grabbing a few bags of fresh spinach. "Could you go over and get me a couple of those red onions?"

"Sure," I replied, meeting the biker's eyes who'd been watching us. He smirked and nudged the other guy, a dumpy-looking man who had to weigh three bills, none of it muscle. Dumpy turned and looked at me too.

"Do you like mushrooms?" Frannie asked, pushing the cart toward some. "I usually make the Portobello ones. Those are my favorite."

"Sounds good," I said, still staring toward the deli.

"Is everything okay?" she asked.

"Right now, yeah," I said, knowing we couldn't keep her in the dark any longer. It would make her too vulnerable.

Frannie followed my gaze and sucked in her breath. "Those are Devil's Rangers, aren't they?"

"Afraid so."

"What do we do?" she asked shakily.

"Ignore them." I turned toward her with a reassuring smile. "They're just shopping. Like us. So, what else do you want me to get?"

"The red onions?"

"Oh, sorry. You mentioned that already." I walked over and started bagging some, while still keeping my attention on the two men.

"I just need two," Frannie said, standing next to me again. "Not seven. Are you sure everything is okay? You seem tense."

"Yeah. Sorry. Here," I said, taking the extra onions out and handing her the bag. "What else do we need?"

WE FINISHED UP the rest of our shopping and fortunately, didn't run into the pricks again.

It was dark outside when we left the store and the parking lot was mostly clear. As we headed toward Frannie's SUV, I kept my eyes and ears peeled, but we made it to the vehicle without any issues. I'd been bracing for something to happen and was relieved when it didn't.

"Thanks for driving," she said, locking the passenger door. "I have poor night-vision and forgot my glasses. Not to mention that I'm a little shaky after seeing those two Devil's Rangers."

I started the engine. "No problem."

"Is there still a war going on between the two clubs?" Frannie asked.

"Honestly, I'm not exactly sure, but they can't be trusted. If you see any of these guys around again, let me or Tank know."

Her forehead scrunched up. "Should I be worried?"

"Not around me," I said, looking in the rearview mirror. There was a gray van parked in the back and looking very suspicious. I decided to send Tank a quick text before leaving the store. He quickly responded and asked if I needed backup. I replied stating I didn't see an immediate threat and told him I had my gun with me.

Tank: *Good. Let me know when you get back home safely. I'm sending a prospect to keep watch outside tonight, just in case.*

Me: *Ok*

"Are you telling Tank about the two men?" she asked, watching me type.

I nodded.

"I imagine he'll be worried." She swallowed. "I have to admit, this is giving me an ulcer. What are they doing in this area?"

"Nothing good," I admitted.

Frannie put her seatbelt on. "I'm really glad you tagged along tonight. I don't know if those two would have recognized me, but if they would have…"

I put my phone away. "Don't worry. I won't let anything happen to you. I promise."

"Thank you."

I pulled out of our parking spot, keeping an eye on the van. Fortunately, it didn't follow us.

"Did you see someone back there?" Frannie asked.

"I wasn't sure. It doesn't look like we're being tailed though. I think we're good."

"Maybe this is just a coincidence and they have family in the area," she said, looking out into the darkness.

"Maybe."
Deep down, I think we both knew better.

EIGHTEEN

BUSTER

Five minutes earlier

"THEY'RE COMING OUT," Joe said, sitting up straight in the passenger seat.

I looked up from my phone. I'd been texting our president, Rusty, about running into Slammer's old lady and one of the Gold Vipers. We'd traveled from Chicago and were waiting on orders to snatch the bitch. Seeing them in the store had actually been an accident. We'd gone there because Joe had been hungry for fried chicken.

"What should we do?"

I tapped my fingers on the steering wheel. "Nothing yet. We already know where she lives, and if we follow them, it's going to look suspicious."

"Why? They wouldn't know it's us."

"Bullshit," I said, watching as the Gold Viper scanned the parking lot and then looked directly toward our van. "He's already made us."

"Looks like it. You think he's banging Slammer's widow?"

"Who knows? She looks good for her age. I'd fuck her."

Hell, I thought, *maybe I will fuck her when I get my hands on the bitch.*

"Me, too," replied Joe.

"You believe that asshole? He was staring at us in there almost as if he was daring us to make a move."

Still thinking about it pissed me off. He was big, though. Well over six foot and pretty fucking ripped. My theory was that he had no life and spent all of his free time trying to compensate for a little pecker. Not to mention he was probably on steroids and that shit was known to shrink your junk.

"I say we should blow this fucker away and take the bitch right now."

I sighed, reminding myself that Joe was only twenty-two and patience wasn't his strongpoint. He'd just recently been patched, and although he'd spent the last year as a prospect, the kid had a lot to learn. Especially about the Gold Vipers. They were sly motherfuckers who needed to be handled carefully. My cousin, Mud, had obviously failed in that department. Now there wasn't even a Devil's Rangers charter in Iowa, but that was going to end. If things worked out the way I wanted, the Gold Vipers of Jensen would be annihilated before the end of the year. Not just disassembled, but totally fucking gone. Nobody screwed with my family, or club, without paying the price.

"You text the prez?"

I nodded.

"What he say?"

"He hasn't gotten back to me yet."

I was the V.P., and although I'd been a Devil's Ranger for almost two decades, it had taken me far too long to talk Rusty into backing me on this plan. Fortunately, he was finally on board and now all we had to do was get our hands on Frannie and go from there. We'd been holding up in a motel for the last week and I was starting to get a little anxious myself, though.

"What now?" Joe asked, opening up the box of chicken. He pulled out a drumstick and began stuffing his face.

"We wait for Rusty to get back to us. Hey, don't you dare get fucking crumbs in here," I growled.

Joe was a slob and I, admittedly, was a little obsessive about keeping things neat and orderly. It was more for precaution, however. The less DNA we had floating around the van, the least likely we'd get in trouble if shit went south and we had to ditch it.

"I'll just wait until we get back to the motel," he muttered, throwing the leg back into the box.

"Yeah. Save some for me, too," I said, starting the engine.

"I thought you didn't want any."

Hearing the whine in the slob's voice irritated me. "We ordered sixteen pieces. You weren't planning on eating it all yourself, were you?"

"They're small pieces."

"If you keep shoveling it in like this you're never going to make it to thirty," I warned, looking toward his stomach. He'd gotten winded walking out of the store and spent most of his time playing video games and jerking off in the bathroom.

Joe didn't say anything.

My phone rang and I quickly answered it.

"Of all the fucking places you had to get food, why a grocery store near Slammer's old lady's house?" Rusty snapped.

"Joe had a craving for chicken," I replied, giving him a dirty look. I knew we'd get reamed out for this.

"And there wasn't a KFC anywhere close?"

"No," I lied, staring at one across the street. I hated the chicken there and had wanted to stretch my legs, too.

"Fuck. Well, now that one of them has seen you bozos, they'll be expecting you to make a move," Rusty said. "I want you to hold off for a few more days."

I sighed. I was already anxious and tired of waiting. Not to mention that I was getting sick of being with Joe twenty-four-seven.

"How about we wait for two days and then grab the bitch?" I suggested.

"Absolutely not. Do that and you'll get caught. You need to lay low for a while. I'm sure Tank is ordering protection for Frannie as we speak. You'd just better hope it's not the Judge, or I'm going to have to find myself a new V.P. if that's the case."

Although we'd never seen him, "The Judge" was supposed to be a hired assassin used by the Gold Vipers to do their dirty work. Including blowing up Mud's clubhouse. At least, that was what we'd heard through our intel.

"I'm not afraid of that fucker," I said, my stomach tightening in anger at the mention of the guy. "Hell, I'd like to meet him face-to-face and pay him back for my cousin's death."

"You'd never see *his* face or anything else again if he's after you. Stay low and wait for my instructions."

I sighed. "Fine."

"I know you're pissed, but you did this to yourselves."

He was right and if we had to wait, we would. I wanted vengeance, but new it wouldn't come easy. We couldn't afford to fuck up again either.

"Good. I'll call you in a couple of days. I finally have someone on the inside who'll let us know when it's safe to move."

That brightened up my spirits. "Who is it?"

He told me and it shocked the hell out of me.

"Keep your phone close and your enemies far away until I tell you when to move."

"Will do," I replied.

NINETEEN

CHARLIE

I HADN'T HEARD from Maddox all day and kept checking my phone for messages. I knew I was in trouble when my phone buzzed and I jumped to get it, hoping it was him. Instead, it was Jackie calling, which shouldn't have disappointed me, and yet it did.

"So, have you applied at any of the culinary schools?" she asked with a smile in her voice. "Or, just Jensen?"

I told her I'd already made up my mind and was waiting to see if I would be accepted.

She groaned.

"What?" I asked, feeling defensive.

"I know you think I'm being a nag. I just can't stop thinking about this and what could happen. You're my best friend and I don't want you to get hurt."

"I love you, too, Jackie. Look, worst case scenario is that I go out there and nothing happens between the two of us. I still get my degree and an exciting career. Not to mention," I lowered my voice, "I'm out from under my dad's thumb."

"No, the *worst* case scenario is that you get your heart broken and it won't happen if you just forget about Maddox and go to a different school."

She really didn't like this guy. "I'll be fine. May I remind you that my heart didn't get broken with Cody and we were engaged?"

"You didn't love actually love him, Charlie. You know that. By the way, I read about this great culinary school in Maui. Now, doesn't that sound like a lot more fun?"

I sighed. "Yeah, but I'm looking for a school. Not a vacation."

"You're not going to even give any other colleges a chance, are you?"

"I like the Davenport one. I really do. They have an excellent program."

"You're so damn stubborn."

"But, you still love me," I said with a smile.

"Of course."

We spoke for a few more minutes and then I hung up. Afterward, I checked my messages again and saw that there was still nothing from Maddox. Disappointed, I thought about Jackie's warnings and agreed that as much as I liked him, I needed to be careful. Especially now that he was under my skin and I couldn't stop thinking about him.

TWENTY

JACKIE

"WHAT DID SHE say?" he asked.

I put the phone down and turned to Tony Armati, a man I despised with every fiber of my being. Unfortunately, I was indebted to him and a despicable traitor to my best friend. Even though I hadn't been able to talk Charlie out of going to Iowa, I'd tried. Not because I thought it would be better for her. But, her father had forced me into it.

And I owed the bastard.

He'd paid for my mother's hospital bills after she'd been in a car accident. Unfortunately, she hadn't had insurance and the bills had been staggering, especially for the physical therapy she needed afterward.

This was before she'd met my stepdad, Tom. It had just been the two of us. I'd been nineteen at the time and desperate to find a solution. Meanwhile, Tony had heard about our struggles through Charlie, and had paid me an unexpected visit one evening. After pretending to be concerned, he made me an offer which would I should have never agreed to. He promised to help pay off all of her hospital bills and credit card debt. For a price.

Me.

At first, I'd told him where to shove it, but then things went from bad to worse for Mom. She lost her job and couldn't pay the mortgage. Because she was upside down on the loan, she couldn't even sell the place for a profit. When I offered to quit school and get a fulltime job, she refused to allow it. I couldn't stand to watch her suffer, so I made a deal with the devil.

Worth it?

For my mother's health and sanity—yes.

137

But, I hated myself for deceiving my best friend and whoring my body out to a man as sinister and evil as Tony. She had no idea of the secret relationship I had with her father, or the kind of pig he really was, and I hoped to God she never would.

"Charlie still plans on going to Davenport," I told him.

He began swearing in Italian.

"Hey. I tried."

"My daughter is a stubborn fool. Who put this idea of college into her head anyway?" he asked. "Her mother? You?"

"I have no idea," I lied.

I loved Charlie and knew she had to get away from her father and everything he stood for, so I'd definitely encouraged it.

"It must have been that biker. Maddox," he growled, getting out of the bed. He pulled his pants on and zipped them up. "I'm not going to let him ruin her life."

"What are you going to do?" I asked, knowing that he was capable of anything. I knew Tony was involved in the mafia and had a lot of bad people working for him. He wasn't someone who said or did things lightly.

"I'm going to take care of it," he said. "Like I always do."

"When is this going to end?"

"What do you mean?"

"This thing between us? Brian has been talking about marriage and having kids."

"The poor schmuck. Little does he know his girlfriend sucks my dick more than his," he said with dark smile.

I gave him a dirty look. "Not by choice."

138

Unaffected by my jabs, Tony reached over with his finger and lifted my chin. "Fine, you want it to end. Pay me back what you owe."

"How much is that?"

He did a mental calculation and then shrugged. "Seventy-six thousand dollars."

"What? I know for a fact it wasn't that much," I argued, thinking back to the bills.

"Ah, but you forget about interest. Nobody borrows out that kind of money for free."

I stared at him, speechless.

He picked up his shirt and pulled it over his shoulders. "You've been very lucky. I haven't demanded payment from you and I very well should have. You're friends with Charlie, though. That's why I haven't come down on you."

I fought the urge to slap him in the face. "I've given you payment for the last four years. With interest."

"What? *This?*" he scoffed, nodding toward the bed. "You think that this is part of the deal?"

I glared at him. "Excuse me?"

Did he actually think that I'd been fucking him for pleasure?

Obviously, he knew I didn't like him touching me. There'd never been any foreplay on his part and I needed lube just to get him inside of me. Fortunately, he didn't last long so our visits were usually short.

"I mean, sure… what we've been doing bought you more time on the loan."

"You seriously expected me to fuck you *and* pay you back?" I said, incredulously.

"Jackie, we don't have to have sex if you don't want to," he said, smirking again. "We can end it right now if you wish."

I stared at him suspiciously.

Tony went on. "Of course, you'll need to write me a check and pay off your loan before I walk out the door."

"This is bullshit. You never once mentioned I'd have to pay you back *financially*. You made it clear what you wanted from me from the very beginning," I snapped.

"Show me a contract in which I agreed to have sex with you as payment."

"This was all done verbally and you know it."

"Was it?" he said with a smirk. "You should have gotten it in writing. As of right now, you owe me the entire amount. I'll knock of any further interest if you keep opening those legs of yours."

I stared at him, shocked that my sweet friend had a father so evil.

He went on. "Don't worry. I'm not going to force you to pay the balance anytime soon. Just keep giving me what I want."

"And what exactly is that, Tony?" I asked, trying not to cry. "I mean, why do you even keep coming over here? I know I'm not the only one you're having sex with. It's obvious even to you that I don't enjoy it."

"That's okay because this is about me and… we both know how much I enjoy fucking you, Jackie," he said with an ugly smile. "In every sense of the word."

He was such a bastard. If only I could turn the tables on him. There was only one weakness I had access to, however. "What if I told Charlie everything?"

Tony looked ready to kill me. "Threaten me and you'll end up in the back of someone's trunk. Maybe even your mother's." He chuckled at the idea. "Her fingerprints on the weapon used to shoot her you. I wonder how she'd do behind bars?"

I stared at him in horror.

Amused at himself, Tony finished dressing and then left.

TWENTY-ONE

MADDOX

AFTER RETURNING TO Frannie's, we put the groceries away and I made myself a frozen pizza. As it was cooking in the oven, she got ready for bed and I kept checking outside for any unwanted guests. Fortunately, Tank was good with his word and sent a prospect over to keep an eye outside. A guy we called Fabio, who was soon to be patched. His real name was Jake, but he was a pretty boy and had modeled a couple of years ago, appearing on a few book covers, so we liked to give him shit. I noticed he'd parked his SUV across the street so I texted him.

Me: *You see anything message me right away.*

Fabio: *Will do.*

Me: *You want coffee?*

Fabio: *Brought some. Thanks, though.*

Me: *TTYL*

Fabio: *Okay*

Tank sent a text around eleven and I verified that everything was good. Afterward, I sent a message to Charlie, apologizing for not calling her back.

Me: *Can I call you now or are you getting ready for bed?*

Charlie: *Call me*

I dialed her number and we talked for an hour. It was good hearing her voice and all I could think about was our night together. As we were winding down the conversation, I promised to try and give her a jingle the following day.

"I'm going to be tied up during the day because of the new job. I also have some club stuff to take care of afterward, but I'll try calling you earlier than I did tonight."

"You know, I'll understand if you'd like to move on," she said, surprising me.

"What do you mean by 'move on'?"

"I just don't want to force myself into your life. We can just be friends, too, you know. I'm sure you have a busy life with your job, your daughter, and all of the club activities."

"Darlin', there is no 'forcing' going on. I definitely want you in my life," I admitted. In one way or another. "I miss the fuck out of you already."

"I miss you, too," she said, a smile in her voice.

"I *will* give you a call tomorrow," I promised. "But, I'll text you first to make sure it's not too late."

"Sounds good."

I yawned. "Night, beautiful."

"Goodnight, Maddy."

I raised my eyebrow. "Maddy?"

"If you're going to keep calling me Chuck, I'm calling you Maddy."

"Yeah, but it sounds too much like a girl's name." The moment the words came out of my mouth, I chuckled. "Okay. Touché."

She laughed. "Night, Maddy."

"Night, Chuck."

MY ALARM WENT off at five a.m. I checked on Frannie and saw that she was still sleeping peacefully. I looked outside and noticed that Fabio's SUV was gone, but one of the other prospects was now parked in his place. Satisfied, I took a shower and got dressed. Afterward, I made myself a couple of sandwiches from the food I'd purchased at the grocery store and grabbed a bottle of water. I was putting my boots on by the front door when Frannie called out my name. I turned around.

"Did you get breakfast?" she asked, standing in the living in her robe with a cup of coffee.

"No, but I'm good," I said. "Thank you, though."

"I suppose you're hurrying to work. Feel free to use the stove whenever you want. And the coffeemaker."

I thanked her.

"Where are you working?"

"An auto body shop close to the clubhouse. Tank helped me get a job there."

"Are you a mechanic?"

"Custom painter," I said.

"Oh, you paint cars?"

"Yep. Cars, trucks, bikes, boats, you name it."

"Sounds fascinating."

"I enjoy it."

I'd started out just as a regular paint technician and eventually took some graphic design classes. I now specialized in airbrushing and 3-D paint affects.

"Well, good. You have yourself a nice day," she said before sitting down in the recliner.

"Thank you. Are you working today?"

I knew she was an office manager at some nursing home.

"Yeah. I don't start until nine, though. Lucky me."

I smiled. "Have a nice day."

"You, too."

"Thanks."

ON THE WAY to work, I stopped at McDonalds and grabbed some coffee and a couple of breakfast sandwiches. After scarfing them down, I drove to the shop and met with the owner, who gave me a personal tour and introduced me to the other people working there. Afterward, I met with a client in the parking lot. He was an older guy in his fifties. His name was Stan and he wanted a custom flame job on a classic truck he owned.

"I want orange and yellow flames across the front and side," he said, showing me his black 1954 GMC pickup, which had been recently overhauled and painted.

"Sweet ride," I said, looking it over. "You said it was a 496 big block?"

"Yep." He lifted the hood and proudly showed me what was underneath. We talked engines for a while and then went back into the shop, where we discussed the art he wanted. I showed him my portfolio and then created a design for his truck using a new virtual program I'd recently installed on my laptop.

"That's going to look real nice. I'm excited," he said, rubbing his chin and smiling. "Okay. So, what kind of figures are we talking?"

We went over pricing, which he agreed upon, and then scheduled the service to begin the following day.

"You do nice work," he said, shaking my hand. "I'm excited to see my truck when you're done with it."

"I'm looking forward to working on it."

After he left, I kept myself busy by helping out around the shop until lunchtime.

"So, you're with the Gold Vipers, huh?" Morris, one of the welders, asked me while we were in the breakroom. He was in his thirties and walked with a limp. A quiet guy, a loner in fact, but everyone had great things to say about him.

"Yup." I unwrapped my second turkey sandwich and took a bite.

"Tank still president?"

I finished chewing and nodded. "Yeah, you know him?"

"We went to high school together. Great guy."

"Yeah, he is."

"Tell him I said hello, will you? Morris Johnson."

"Will do, Morris."

He was quiet for a while and then asked if we had a lot of parties.

"I just transferred a short time ago from Florida, so I'm not exactly sure myself. I know they throw them, I just don't know how often."

"Gotcha."

"The next time we have a bash, I'll let you know," I said. Normally, I didn't invite many citizens, but Morris seemed like a stand-up guy.

"Thanks."

"No problem."

"Of course, my girlfriend might have a fit. She'll probably want to come with."

"You can bring her. Just don't let her out of your sight when she's there."

He laughed. "She's about six months pregnant."

I grinned. "Some guys find that sexy. You still better watch out for her."

"You have any kids?"

I nodded and told him about Aubrey. "Which reminds me…" I took out my phone. "I need to check in and see how my daughter's doing."

He stood up and tossed his lunch bag into the garbage can. "I'm going outside to have a smoke. Catch you later."

I nodded.

He left and I called Kathy. She answered on the third ring and sounded out of breath.

"What's up?" she asked.

"Just calling to see how Aubrey's doing. Everything okay? You sound winded."

"I was just outside filling the pool for her."

"You didn't leave her out there alone, did you?"

"No, of course not," she said in an annoyed voice. "Mom's out there with her."

"How are they?"

"Aubrey's finally feeling better, although her pediatrician still recommends that she get her tonsils out. Mom's doing okay, I guess" she said wearily.

"Maybe we should get another opinion. Just in case."

Kathy groaned. "This one knows what she's talking about. It would be a waste of time. Not to mention, I'd have to pay for another office visit."

"Okay. If you trust her, I guess that's good enough for me."

"I do. Completely. So, you're still taking Aubrey this weekend, right?"

"That's what I wanted to talk to you about. There are some things going on… I don't know if it would be a good idea."

She swore. "I shouldn't be surprised. There's always something going on. Is it a 'club' thing?"

That was bullshit and she knew it. I didn't want to argue with her, though. Instead, I kept my cool.

"Kind of."

"What's going on?"

I wasn't about to tell her about Frannie's life being threatened. She hated the club life and the dangers involved. It was one of the reasons we'd split up in the first place.

"Hello? What am I supposed to tell Aubrey?" she snapped. "She's been looking forward to seeing her daddy."

I felt like shit. I'd been missing her, too. "Can I stop by after work today and see her?"

"Yeah, I guess. Will you be staying for dinner?"

"Probably not. I have some things I need to take care of. I won't be able to stay for long."

She sighed. "Fine. At least you're coming over to see her."

"I moved all the way out here to see her," I reminded Kathy. "You know how much I love Aubrey."

"If you really loved her, you'd quit the Gold Vipers. Mom was telling me about how much trouble they've been getting into over here. They're worse than the group you left behind in Florida."

"They haven't been getting into trouble," I said. "That was a long time ago."

149

Slammer's death, along with the murders related to our club war, had happened about five years prior. Since then, the Iowa Chapter had stayed out of the news. Of course, the Minnesota Chapter, hadn't. They'd been dealing with another rival club—the Blood Angels. That situation had been resolved the year before, however.

"So, why can't you have Aubrey over then?"

"I might be working overtime this weekend. At the new auto shop I'm at," I lied.

"Did it ever occur to you that I might have had plans this weekend, Maddox?" she replied angrily. "And, my mother is too weak to watch Aubrey. So, where does that put me?"

I wanted to ask her who'd be watching Aubrey if I hadn't followed her out to Iowa. I'd left an entire life behind just so that I could be near my daughter. Kathy didn't seem to appreciate any of the sacrifices I'd made. Not to mention, I *never* stood up Aubrey. This was different and for her protection.

"I'm sorry. I'll make it up to you," I replied.

"Whatever. I've heard it before."

"You keep saying that. When have I ever canceled on Aubrey?"

She was silent for a few seconds. "You've been late a few times."

"Yeah, bringing her home," I said sarcastically. "That's because she wanted to spend more time with me."

"Fine. Whatever. Just, don't disappoint Aubrey. She's already going to be upset about this weekend."

"I know. I'll talk to her tonight when I see her."

She hung up.

I sent Tank a text and explained the situation. He told me not to worry about it and to take my time with Aubrey. Apparently, he had another prospect watching the house until he showed up for dinner.

THE REST OF the day flew by smoothly and when my shift was over, I stopped at a store and picked Aubrey up a stuffed kitten, along with a pint of her favorite ice cream. Fifteen minutes later, I was at Kathy's mom's place.

"Daddy!" squealed Aubrey, racing into my arms.

Hugging her back, my heart swelled with love for the tiny little imp.

"I didn't tell her you were coming over," Kathy said as I swept Aubrey up and placed her on my shoulders.

"I'm the tallest person in the world!" Aubrey cried out as I walked her into the living room where her grandmother, Lana, was. She was seated in her robe and looked very weak. Her head was shaved and she wore a beanie.

"That's because you're my princess and should be above everyone," I teased and then looked at Lana. "Hi."

She gave me a weary smile. "Hi, Maddox."

I put Aubrey down on the sofa and sat next to her.

"Why are you here, Daddy?" she asked, looking up at me with her big brown eyes.

"I've missed you so much I just had to come over and see you."

"I missed you, too. What's in there?" she asked, looking at the plastic bag I was holding.

I pulled out the white, stuffed kitten. "I just picked this up for myself. Isn't she cute?"

Her little jaw dropped down and then she smiled. "You didn't really buy it for you, did you?"

I held it to my cheek and grinned. "Of course I did. I'm thinking of naming her Sparkles, because of her collar. What do you think? Will she like that name?"

"Da…ddy," she said with a knowing grin. "That's for me."

I teased her a little more and then gave up the toy.

"Thank you. She's so cute," she said, hugging me again.

"Not as cute as you and you're welcome, monkey. Oh, I also bought you some of this." I pulled out the ice cream. "But, you have to wait until after dinner and *only* if your mom says that it's okay."

Aubrey looked at her mother, who'd been watching us quietly. "Can I? Please."

Kathy didn't look happy about it, but she agreed.

"Daddy, I want to show you my new room. Come and see," Aubrey said, pulling my hand toward the hallway.

"Okay." I handed Kathy the ice cream. "Sorry, is this okay?"

"The ice cream? Yeah, it's fine. Just please ask me next time. Or at least bring enough for the three of us," Kathy said.

"I thought you and your mom were lactose intolerant?" I replied.

"They have ice cream for us, too, you know."

I apologized. "I'll remember next time."

"It's fine. I'm on a diet anyway and Mom hasn't been very hungry," she admitted.

I looked over at Lana, who had fallen asleep.

"Daddy, come on," Aubrey said, pulling me away.

I let her lead me to the bedroom and for the next hour, we hung out, talked, and she colored me a couple of pictures.

"Those are really good," I said when she was finished. Like me, Aubrey had always been into art since she was old enough to hold a crayon. Although she was only five, her pictures were very detailed for someone so young.

"You should go to art school," I said.

Aubrey smiled. "Yeah."

"You should just teach her yourself," Kathy said, standing in the doorway with her arms crossed.

"I wish I had more time to do that. I'll teach you what I can though, kiddo," I said to Aubrey before Kathy could respond.

"Do I still get to be with you this weekend, Daddy?" Aubrey asked, staring up at me innocently.

Fuck.

"I might have to work," I said softly. I wanted to see her as well, but it was too risky. "But, I'll see what I can do."

She began to pout.

"If I can't have you over this weekend, for sure the following," I said, making a promise to myself as well. No matter what happened, I would find a way to be with her. Even if we stayed at a hotel. "And, we'll do something later in the week, too. Maybe Friday evening?"

"We have plans," Kathy said.

I sighed.

"What about tomorrow?" Aubrey asked. "Maybe you could bring me swimming?"

"I have to work during the day," I replied. "How about Wednesday night? I'll take you out to eat?"

Aubrey looked disappointed but she nodded. "Okay."

"Is that all right?" I asked Kathy.

"I guess it's going to have to be," she said before turning around and walking away.

153

TWENTY-TWO

CHARLIE

I WENT INTO my father's office and broke the news to him about culinary school in the early evening. He took it very well. In fact, he actually encouraged it, which surprised me.

"There are a couple of very reputable schools in New York that are worth taking a look at," he said. "You should talk to Uncle Vinnie's executive chef and find out where he went. I believe it's some place in SoHo, if I'm not mistaken."

"Actually, I've already found a school that I'm interested in and have applied."

"Is that right? You've done all of your research and have found an exceptional college offering everything you need to succeed?" he said wryly. "In, what, one day?"

"No. I've been thinking about it for more than a *day* and yes, I did the research. Anyway, I'm waiting to hear back from them," I said, knowing this was still going to be a tough sale. Especially when he found out I was going out of the state.

He leaned back in his chair. "Where is this school?"

I told him and as suspected, he wasn't impressed.

"Why on God's earth would you want to go to some hick town in Iowa just to take cooking classes?" he asked, looking at me like I'd lost my mind.

"Davenport isn't a *hick* town. There are over one hundred thousand people living there. And… and it's a nice, quiet place near the Mississippi River."

He grunted.

I went on. "There are interesting museums and beautiful, botanical parks." I'd been doing my research, knowing he would insult the city in any way he could.

He pursed his lips together. "Look, I know why you want to go to Iowa. It's obvious. You're fixated on that biker you were kissing the other day."

"He doesn't live in Davenport and I'm not going there because of him."

"We'll talk to Uncle Vinnie's chef and find out where he went. If you want to become successful, you should go to a reputable school. One that has more to offer than just a view of the Mississippi River and a couple of nice flower gardens," he said, looking back at his computer screen. "Is there anything else, sweetheart? I have a meeting in an hour and need to print out some tax forms for my accountant."

"I'm going where I want to go," I said firmly. "And it's Davenport."

He looked up at me with disapproval. "Charlotte—"

"No. I don't want to hear it," I said firmly. "I'm a grown woman and can make my own decisions."

"You're acting on an impulse. You're not thinking clearly," he said. "Don't jump into this without taking some time to really think about it."

"I've already make up my mind," I said to him. I turned around and headed toward the doorway. "And don't try to talk me out of it. You'll be wasting your breath."

He didn't say anything, but I knew he wasn't going to let it go. Neither was I.

TWENTY-THREE

MADDOX

I MADE IT back to Frannie's around six. Tank showed up a half an hour later with Raptor and his brother-in-law Cole, who was also a club member.

"Where are Raina and the kids?" Frannie asked, looking disappointed. "I thought you said they'd be coming over as well?"

Tank, who was holding a bag of groceries, sighed and scratched his forehead. "Sorry, I forgot to mention that Gracie Lee and Billy are both sick. Raina stayed home with them, obviously."

Her eyebrows knitted together. "Sick? What's wrong with them?"

"Some kind of stomach flu," he said, heading toward the kitchen. "Hope you don't mind that I invited Raptor and Cole in their place?"

"Of course not," she said, smiling at them as he disappeared into the next room. "Obviously, I'd like to see my grandkids… but you two are a sight for sore eyes. How've you been?"

"Been good. Kids are running me ragged, though," Raptor said, settling down on the recliner. He kicked the footrest back and looked up at her with a lopsided grin. "It's hell, I tell you. I can't seem to get anything done anymore."

"Running *you* ragged, huh? Good thing you have Adriana around to pickup the slack," she said, looking amused.

"Yeah, she helps when she can," he replied.

Frannie laughed. "You're so full of it."

Raptor chuckled. "Honestly, I've been so busy I haven't seen much of the kids this week. That storm last week brought us a bunch of new business."

I knew Raptor had a son and twin toddler girls. He also owned and managed a small roofing company.

"What's Adriana doing tonight?" Frannie asked. "You could have invited her and the kids over."

"They're over at Grandma's house," he replied. "She got a new puppy and the kids have been begging to see it."

"What kind?" Frannie asked.

"A Miniature Schnauzer she named Babs," Raptor replied.

"Oh, how fun. How's Vanda doing?" Frannie asked.

"Good, as far as I know."

"I'll have to give her a call soon." She looked at Cole. "What about you? How've you been?"

"Me? I'm doing great," he replied from the sofa.

"Anything new in your world?" Frannie asked.

"Terin and I just got back from Vegas last week."

"Oh, really? Did you gamble?" she asked.

Cole crossed his ankle over his knee and gave a sly smile. "Sure did. Drove by a chapel and didn't get sucked in. I guess that was a win."

Frannie clucked her tongue. "Oh, *you*. When are you two going to tie the knot?"

"I don't know. To be honest, she's the one dragging her feet on this. Hell, I'd get married tonight if she was ready," he said, brushing off a piece of lint from his jeans. "It's her call."

"Why do you think that is?" Frannie asked.

He shrugged. "She blames it on work. Now that she's transferred to the *Crime Scene Investigation Unit*, the hours she's been putting in are nuts. But, she loves her job and to be honest, I'm proud of her dedication. She's a damn good detective."

Frannie nodded. "I'm sure she is. Tank mentioned that she's involved in that case near the college campus."

He nodded.

My ears perked up. "Which college?"

"Jensen Community College. Some poor freshman was raped and murdered the other night," Frannie replied sadly.

"Damn. Hopefully they'll catch the bastard who did it," I replied, thinking about Chuck. I knew the school she was thinking of attending wasn't anywhere near that campus, but it still made me anxious.

"Do they have a suspect yet?" she asked Cole.

"No, unfortunately they don't. It's driving her mad," he replied.

Tank walked out of the kitchen. "You talking about the freshman? Gina something?"

"Yes. What a shame," Frannie said. "Hopefully he'll be caught before another girl is hurt. No leads, though, huh?"

Cole shook his head. "Terin couldn't tell me much, but she mentioned that the killer must have taken a lot of precautions. There wasn't much for DNA, so whoever did it knew what he was doing. She said it probably wasn't his first victim and won't be his last if he doesn't get caught."

"Maybe we should ask the Judge to look into it?" Tank said to Raptor.

"Are you kidding me? He won't. He's adamant about being retired," Raptor replied.

"I doubt he'll find anything new, anyway," Cole replied.

"Oh, I don't know about that. He's pretty savvy when it comes to investigating things," Tank replied.

"Retired, or not, you should still see if he might be willing to help," Frannie said. "At least ask. It can't hurt."

"I will," Tank said. "Knowing him, he'll bitch about it and then pull through with some intel. It's how he is."

Raptor nodded.

"You two talk a lot?" I asked.

Tank shrugged. "Not really.

I'd heard that the guy was pretty reclusive, but from the way it sounded, Tank had him on speed-dial.

"I still don't know how he can help when there's no evidence," Cole replied.

"You have to look beyond the physical evidence, or lack of it, and that's what he does," Raptor replied.

"I'd love to meet him. He sounds so… mysterious," Frannie said.

"Not as much as you might think," Tank said, his lips twitching.

"No shit." Raptor smiled and scratched his head.

"*I'll* be the 'judge' of that," Frannie quipped.

Tank snorted.

"So, you brought us some steaks?" Frannie said, walking toward the kitchen.

"Yeah. They're on the counter," Tank said. "You need any help?"

"No. Just get the grill ready. There's some beer in the garage, too. Help yourselves."

"Thanks, Ma," Tank replied and looked over at us. "Let's go grab us some brewskies and get it fired up."

We walked out to the garage, grabbed some cold ones, and headed to the patio.

"Okay, now that we're alone, tell me again about the incident at grocery store," Tank said, raising the grill cover.

I went over exactly what had happened. When I was finished, the other three looked at each other.

"Too much of a coincidence," Raptor said, frowning. "We need to find out what the hell they're up to."

"I don't get it. Why are the Devil's Rangers starting shit again after all of this time?" Cole asked.

"Because of what happened in Minnesota, I'm sure," Tank said, scraping black crud off of the grill grates with a wire brush.

The Devil's Rangers had been implicated in the deaths of Cane and Jet, the president and V.P. of the Blood Angels. The truth was, my old man had set it up to look like they were responsible, to keep both clubs off our backs and focused on each other. Unfortunately, it didn't appear to be working.

"You think they knew we were involved?" Cole asked.

"All was quiet before then. I'm sure they got wind of the shit going on between us and the Blood Angels and made some connection." Tank scowled. "Going after Frannie, though… my old man's widow? That's fucked up."

"What are we going to do about it?" Raptor asked.

"First off, I'm sending Frannie on a cruise," he said. "Then we'll go from there."

"You'd better talk to Jordan and let him know what's going on," Raptor said. "Jessica could be in trouble, too. Knowing him, he'll watch her like a damn hawk. As far as Frannie goes, I agree. We need to get her out of here. I'd even send a couple of members on the cruise to keep an eye on her."

"Good idea," Tank said and looked at Cole. "Too bad Terin is busy with that college case. You two would have been perfect."

"Yeah. She won't take any more time away from work," he replied. "Especially now that she's investigating the murder."

"I understand. I'm sure we can find someone willing to go on a free cruise," Tank said.

"I'd go myself if I wasn't busy with this new job," I said.

Tank looked at me. "Maybe I could talk to the owner and see if he'll give you some time off."

"Nah. It's too soon and you've done enough to help me as it is. Just send a couple of the prospects. I'm sure most of them will jump at the chance," I said.

"Hell yeah they will," he replied.

A sudden scream from inside of the house made us all jump.

TWENTY-FOUR

BUSTER

"RUSTY JUST SENT me a text," I said, staring down at my phone. We'd been sitting in the motel room for most of the day, biding time and waiting for further instructions.

"What he say?" Joe asked.

I typed a response and he answered back. "He wants us to try and grab the broad Friday night. He thinks we're being paranoid about Frannie having twenty-four hour protection."

"What do you think?" Joe took a bite of the meat-lovers pizza we'd ordered. It was a deep-dish and he'd already polished most of it off himself.

"That he might be right. Unless someone else is after her and it's not just us."

"Maybe the Blood Angels are."

"I don't know."

They blamed us for the deaths of two of their own. It was bullshit, but they were convinced our club was behind the assassinations.

"So, when? Late at night?"

"Earlier. Apparently, the Gold Vipers have church at eight, so they'll be preoccupied. She should hopefully be home by herself."

"Friday can't come soon enough. This town is as boring as all hell."

"Tell me about it."

"So, afterward we can head back to Chicago right away?" he asked through a mouthful of food.

"Yup. He wants her alive though."

"What kind of condition?"

I smiled. "He didn't specify. Why? You still thinking of taking her for a spin?"

"Knowing how much it will piss off Tank and the rest of those Gold Viper fucktards, you'd better believe it. I'd think you'd want to have a go at her too, considering everything that's happened."

I thought about the pretty young thing I'd had the week we arrived in Jensen. After dropping Joe off at the motel, I went out for cigarettes and to get away from his annoying ass for a while. That was when I'd seen her. It had been just after nine p.m. and she'd been jogging alone by one of the college campuses. It had been a dangerous move, but I couldn't help myself. I forced her into the van after following her for a while. Things got a little rough and I ended up killing the bitch. I bagged and dumped her body into a dumpster on the other side of town. Of course, they'd found her already, but I wasn't worried. I'd been pretty careful to not leave any evidence.

"I don't rape women," I lied. As much as the thought excited me, I didn't want my DNA on Frannie. Just in case.

"You'll change your mind," Joe said. He burped loudly and wiped his greasy hands on his jeans. "Let's get out of here for a while and see a movie or something. I'm going nuts staring at these four walls."

"Sounds good."

Joe disappeared into the bathroom.

I stood up and reached into my duffel bag for a clean T-shirt. As I took it out, the tennis bracelet I snatched from the jogger also slipped out of the bag. I picked it up and examined it. It was gold and had small diamonds around it. It definitely looked expensive. I was going to give it to my Old Lady, Rita, as a peace offering. Before leaving Chicago,

166

we went to a party and both of us got pretty wasted. When we made it back home, I lost my temper when she accused me of fucking one of the club whores. Shit happened and I ended up smacking her around a couple of times. We had sex afterward, but she wouldn't talk to me for several hours. I apologized and promised to make things right. Rita, being the good woman that she was, eventually forgave me, but things were different. There was a wall between us now, which, truthfully, I didn't exactly mind. I just wasn't into her as much anymore. Not sexually, at least. She was a damn good cook and involved with the club heavily. Everyone loved her and in my own way, I probably did too. She just didn't thrill me anymore. Nobody did, unless they put up a struggle. I knew it was wrong, but it wasn't enough to stop me. The jogger had been my fourth victim, the other three had occurred in Chicago. I'd been very careful with each of them, although admittedly, taking the college student had been a risk I probably shouldn't have taken.

"Where'd you get that?" Joe asked, zipping up his fly as he stepped out of the bathroom.

I put the bracelet away. "It's a gift for Rita."

"Ah. Is her birthday coming up?"

"No. Sometimes you gotta surprise 'em with gifts, you know? Make 'em feel special."

He chuckled. "I've got a gift that makes them all feel special," he said, grabbing at his balls. "And it doesn't cost me a dime."

I knew very well that Joe barely got laid and it probably cost him five *thousand* dimes to get a woman into bed. He was a sloppy, fat fuck who often smelled like ammonia and dog shit, especially when he took off his boots. Driving around with him in the van had been challenging, and at one point, I'd ordered Joe to take a shower. Unfortunately even that hadn't helped much. It was another reason why I'd been chain-smoking. It blocked out his rancid smell.

"Good for you. If you want to see a movie, you'd better shower because you smell like shit again," I said in a serious tone.

Joe's smile fell. "I just took one yesterday."

"Take another one. This time, use soap," I replied.

"You're a real asshole, you know that?"

"Yeah, well at least I don't smell like one."

He flipped me off.

I smirked.

TWENTY-FIVE

MADDOX

"WHAT'S WRONG?" TANK asked, after all four of us raced into the house. We found Frannie in the kitchen, standing on a chair and looking angry. "I saw a damn mouse," she said, pointing down toward a small hole in the wall. "It ran in there."

We all relaxed and turned to look.

"Do you have any mousetraps?" Tank asked, walking over to the wall. He crouched down and began inspecting the hole.

"No. I've never had mice in the house before," she said, wringing her hands. "Be careful, it might jump out and bite you. It could have rabies."

"There's another one," Cole said, pointing toward the other side of the kitchen where there was a tall potted plant. "It just ran behind the pot."

Tank swore. "I hope you're not infested."

Frannie's eyes widened and her face turned pale. "Me, too. We have to do something. *Now.*"

Tank pulled his keys out. "Relax, Ma. I'll take care of it. Think of it this way: at least they're not rats or shrews."

"I'm sorry, but that doesn't make me feel any better," she replied, staring down at the floor. "Do you see any more? Is there one near me?"

I crouched down and looked. "I don't see anything. They're probably on the run again."

She groaned.

Tank headed toward the hallway. "I'll go to the hardware store and pick up some mousetraps. You guys stay

170

here and protect her from Mickey Mouse," he added, looking back at us with a smirk.

"You should get a cat," Raptor said, as we all started looking around the kitchen for more rodents. "They keep the mice away."

"I'm allergic to them," she replied. "But, I think I'd rather deal with allergy medication than those little bastards."

"Wow, I don't think I've ever heard you swear before," Raptor said, chuckling.

"Me neither," said Cole with a twinkle in his eyes. "This must be serious."

"Could one of you get the broom?" she replied, ignoring them. "It's in the pantry."

I grabbed the broom and handed it to her. She stepped off of the chair and searched the floor for more intruders.

"I'm sorry," Frannie said with a faint smile. She let out a weary sigh. "I'm sure you're all starving and I'm fretting over a stupid mouse."

"It's fine," Raptor said, putting his arm around her shoulders. "And, you're going to be fine, too. When Tank gets back, we'll set the traps and take care of them. Why don't you mix yourself a drink, go outside, and relax at the picnic table?" He looked at me. "Mad Dog will join you while Cole and I start getting the food ready."

"For sure," I said.

"I think that actually sounds like a good idea." Frannie looked at me and smiled. "You can get my mind off of what's going on by talking about Florida and what you did for fun."

"I don't know if you'll look at me the same way again if we open up that can of worms," I joked, winking at her.

"It can't be that bad," she said.

"His road name is Mad Dog, remember?" Raptor said with a chuckle. "Not to mention he's single and loves to party. Try to tone your stories down to an 'R' rating. Tank will have your head if you give her a heart attack."

"Hell, we don't have much to talk about then," I joked.

"Oh, *you*," she said, swatting my shoulder playfully.

THE REST OF the evening went by pretty well. Tank returned with the mousetraps and set them up while I helped Frannie get the steaks on the grill. As we were eating dinner on the patio, Tank asked her about her sister Cheryl.

"She's doing well," she replied. "Still single, but busy with all of her volunteer work."

"You and her are like two peas in a pod," he replied. "Always working and never relaxing. You could both use some 'me' time."

She laughed. "I have plenty of 'me' time. In fact, sometimes I feel like I have too much."

"Nonsense. You can never have too much," he replied.

Raptor's phone vibrated. He pulled it out of his pocket, checked the screen, and then nodded to Tank.

"What's going on?" Frannie asked, noticing the exchange.

Tank wiped his hands with a napkin and stood up. "Someone's here. I'll be right back."

She looked confused. "What do you mean, someone's *here*? Who?"

"A prospect is at the front door. I'll be back in a minute," he said and disappeared into the kitchen.

"I should have told him to invite the guy for dinner," Frannie said. "There's another steak that nobody has touched."

"Tank bought himself two," Raptor said. "Believe me, it won't go to waste."

A minute later, Tank returned to the patio with a large manila envelope. He sat back down at the table and handed it to Frannie.

"What's this?" she asked.

"Open it," he replied, picking up his knife and fork.

She did what he asked and pulled out a handful of brochures from a popular cruise line. "I don't understand. What's going on?"

"Happy Birthday. You and Cheryl are going on a cruise together, beginning Saturday," he said.

Her jaw dropped. "What? It's not my birthday and… as much as I'd love to go on a trip somewhere, I can't get away from work."

"Think of it as an early present and I've already talked with your boss at the nursing home. He's giving you the time off next week, so you can go and have some fun."

"Talked with or *convinced* him?" she said with a frown.

"We talked and he's fine with it. You don't seem too happy," Tank replied. "I thought you'd be thrilled."

"I am thrilled, don't get me wrong. And, I'm very grateful that you want to give me such a wonderful present. It's just… happening so quickly. I don't know if Cheryl can get the time off."

"I talked to her and she's found a way, too," he replied. "You're both good to go. The tickets for the airline and cruise will be arriving before the end of the week. The travel agent promised."

She was silent for several seconds and then pursed her lips. "Is my life in danger? Is that why you're sending me away? Does it have something to do with those Devil's Rangers?"

Tank sighed.

"Tank. Talk to me," she said sternly.

"Fine. I have intel that you might be a target."

She gasped. "Why on earth didn't you tell me?"

"I didn't want you to panic," he replied. "I'm sorry."

"What about Jessica? Is she safe?" Frannie asked, looking very upset.

"There haven't been any threats made against her or the other wives. Jordan's taking her and the family out of town, too. Just in case," Raptor said.

"Is this why you're here?" she asked, looking at me. "To protect me?"

I nodded.

"He needed a place to stay, too," Tank added. "There's more room here."

"I still can't believe nobody said anything. If there is a threat against my life, I need to know," she said angrily. "Keeping something like this a secret is putting me in more danger. You should know that by now."

"I'm sorry," he repeated. "If it makes you feel better, we should have this problem cleared up by Friday night."

"Why is that?" she asked.

His lip twitched and he smiled. "Let's just say that the Devil's Rangers aren't as crafty as they give themselves credit for."

TWENTY-SIX

CHARLIE

THE REST OF the week, I avoided my father and put in some extra hours at the restaurant. Of course, my Uncle Vinnie must have heard the news about me wanting to attend culinary school, because he pressured me into talking to one of his head chefs, Paul. Fortunately, Paul didn't give me the kind of advice my father had been hoping for.

"As long as it offers a diverse program with career assistance, you should be good to go," he said, looking rushed.

"It's supposed to have state-of-the-art training kitchens and even opportunities to study abroad."

"I'm sure the programs there are just fine," he said. "Can I ask why you're thinking of going all the way to Iowa, though?"

My answer was honest. "I want to go somewhere else and start fresh without being under my family's thumb."

He gave me a knowing look. "Yeah, I get it."

"I'm sure my father and Vinnie wouldn't be too pleased with our conversation. I'll tell them that you recommended your school, so you don't get into trouble. Where did you go?"

"I went to ICE. The Institute of Culinary Education. In New York City."

I'd read that ICE was an award-winning school and it didn't surprise me. If things had been different, and my father wasn't such a manipulator, I might have even considered it.

"Thanks, Paul."

"Good luck," he replied.

THE FOLLOWING EVENING, Jackie and I met for drinks.

"So, are you and Maddox still talking?" she asked, after we both ordered Cosmopolitans.

I smiled. "Yeah. Every night."

We'd made plans to get together in three weeks while I visited Davenport. I hadn't yet heard from the school, but I had a good feeling about getting into the program. They had a high acceptance rate.

"Any news about the school in Davenport?" she asked.

"Not yet."

"What about your dad? How is he handling it?"

"I've been avoiding him. Thankfully, he's been busy. There's nothing he can say to make me change my mind, though." I sighed. "He's not going to give up, either. I know it. I swear to God, I should have moved out a long time ago."

"Well, at least you have some money saved, right?" she said, opening up the menu.

I had over ten thousand dollars. I planned on trying to find a job in Davenport, too. "Yeah. Some."

She gave me a sad smile. "I hope it all works out for you."

Relieved that she wasn't trying to talk me out of it again, I thanked her.

"How's Brian?" I asked.

She looked down at her napkin. "Okay, I guess. We got into an argument last night. I don't know if it's going to last."

"Oh, no," I said, reaching over and touching her hand. "I'm sorry."

She shrugged and looked at me. "It's okay. He… he just wants more than what I'm ready to give."

"Like marriage?"

"Yeah. He also wants to find a house together."

"I thought you loved him."

"I do," she said softly. "It just won't work."

I didn't understand. I tried asking her why, but she changed the subject.

"How's your mom?" she asked. "Is she excited about you going to culinary school?"

"We haven't been able to talk much, but she seems happy for me. She mentioned that she was going to try and fly in to New York before the fall."

"Did you tell her you were going to Davenport?"

I smiled, remembering our conversation. "Yeah. She keeps trying to talk me into Le Cordon Bleu, in Paris."

"Paris? How awesome would that be?"

"I'm sure it would be great, but I've still got my heart set on Davenport."

"Yeah. Well, whatever you decide, I'm happy for you. Just, don't forget about me when you move away."

"I would never," I replied.

She smiled.

"How's *your* mom doing?" I asked.

"Okay. Same as always."

"Does she ever have any more problems with her back?"

"If she does, she hasn't complained about it."

"Tell her I said 'hi'."

"I will."

Our waitress brought our Cosmos and then we spent the next couple of hours chatting, eating, and drinking. Because I was driving, however, I played it safe and only had two cocktails.

"Let's try and get together this weekend," I said to Jackie when we were walking out of the restaurant.

"Sounds good."

We hugged each other and then I headed home and called Maddox.

"I can't wait to see you," he said. "Have you heard from the school yet?"

"No."

"I'm sure you'll get in. Have you been looking at any of the apartments in Davenport?"

"Not really. I want to make sure I get in first."

"I hear you. If you need help finding a job out there, Tank said he knows quite a few people in the restaurant business and could put in a good word for you," Maddox murmured.

"That's nice of him. I might take him up on the offer."

We talked some more and then I asked about his daughter.

"She's doing well. We went out for pizza tonight."

"Oh, how fun. I can't wait to meet her." I wondered if he'd told her about me, but didn't ask. We had a big family and I'd always loved being around my nieces and nephews. I truly was excited to meet Aubrey. I just hoped that she approved of me. I knew some children weren't exactly keen on their dad's girlfriends, especially if they wanted their parents together. From the way it sounded, however, Maddox and Kathy had broken up when she was very

179

young and there wasn't a chance in hell the two would rekindle anything.

"I can't wait for you to meet her, too. By the way, not to change the subject, but I might not be able to call you until late tomorrow," he said. "We have some things going on with the club and I'll be tied up."

"It's okay." I wondered if he was going to a party. I'd heard biker clubs were notorious for holding crazy ones, which made me nervous. As hot as Maddox was, I knew women would be hitting on him. We weren't in a committed relationship and just getting to know each other. It didn't stop me from feeling a stab of jealousy at the thought of other women coming on to him.

"If it's too late, I can call you Saturday if it works better."

"Just call me when you're free," I said, wishing I was already out in Jensen with him. The more I thought about him partying, the more anxious it made me. "I don't care if it's one a.m."

"What about four a.m.?" he said with a smile in his voice.

"I don't care. Unless, you have company and can't talk," I said.

He chuckled. "Don't worry, Chuck. I'm not planning on *any* company at that time of the morning, unless it's you."

I relaxed.

"I've told you this every night—I can't stop thinking about you. Hell, you've probably ruined other women for me."

"The feeling is mutual."

"So, you're not seeing anyone else?"

"Nope."

"I was hoping you'd say that. The thought of any guys touching you drives me insane."

"You *not* touching me is driving me insane," I said softly.

"I'm countin' down the days until we can fix that."

TWENTY-SEVEN

MADDOX

"**M**E TOO. I wish I could come out there earlier. I feel like it's such a long time away," she said into my ear, as if reading my thoughts.

I closed my eyes. "Baby, I wish you could too."

As much as I wanted to see her, however, we were still on high-alert with the Devil's Rangers. Of course, we had plans for them, which was why Chuck needed to stay put until I was convinced it was safe. Things were tense. I almost felt like I was being followed now, and the hell if I was going to risk putting her life in danger. With sneaky bastards like them, you couldn't be too careful.

She yawned. "As much as I'd love to talk to you all night, I'm going to sleep. Call me tomorrow night. Like I said before, I don't care what time it is."

"I will," I said softly. "Goodnight, Chuck."

"Goodnight, Maddy."

AFTER HANGING UP with her, I walked upstairs and peeked outside. Nobody seemed to be lurking outside and we'd stopped sending prospects over to guard the house at night. Frannie was staying over at Jessica and Jordan's until her flight on Saturday. Regardless of what happened, she and Cheryl were taking their cruise and would be out of harm's way. Tank had also arranged to have Slater, one of the other club members, and a prospect named Fish, on the same cruise. Slater was getting up there in age and needed a vacation, anyway. Fish was in his mid-twenties and had a good head on his shoulders. He'd also served in the military and took his responsibilities seriously. I was already pushing for him to become a fully patched member because I had so

183

much respect for the guy. Tank was planning on trying to get him voted in after things settled down.

My cell phone went off, startling me.

It was Kathy.

"Hey, what's up? Is everything okay?" I answered, sitting up. She never called me in the middle of the night.

"You never gave me the money for the tonsillectomy," she said in a thick voice.

"I'll pay for it once you're billed," I said. "You sure the insurance company isn't paying for any of it?"

"Nope. It's not covered."

"I'll call them tomorrow."

"Who? The doctor?"

"No, the insurance company."

"They're not going to give you any information. It's my policy and you're not on it."

I sighed. "Fine. Whatever. Just schedule the procedure and give me the date so that I can be there for the surgery."

"They want payment first."

"What?" I snapped. "That doesn't make any sense. These places don't work that way."

"It's thirty-five hundred dollars. Please, just give me the money and I'll take care of everything."

Something was definitely off. "What's going on, Kathy?"

"Nothing."

"Are you gambling again?"

She paused. "No."

Her 'no' didn't sound too convincing. "Dammit, you are, aren't you? Do you owe this money?"

I heard her begin to cry on the other end of the phone.

"Talk to me," I said, trying not to lose my cool. I knew she used to have a problem, back when she was in her late teens. She'd gotten into some problems gambling and had even worked as a stripper to pay off some people.

"Hold on." I heard her blow her nose and then she got back onto the phone. "I'm in trouble, Maddox. I didn't want to tell you. I'm so ashamed."

I closed my eyes.

Fuck.

"How much do you owe? Thirty-five hundred?"

"I owe four grand. I have five-hundred. But, if I don't pay them by Monday, I'm afraid they're going to kill me." She started crying.

"Why in the fuck did you start gambling again?"

"I was stressed out with my mom being sick. I did it to keep my mind off of things. I actually started winning big for a while."

"And then lost bigger."

"Yeah."

I started lecturing her again.

"Enough. I know I fucked up, okay? I can't go back in time and fix it. If I don't pay them, I'm a dead woman."

"Who are these guys you owe?"

She told me that they were bookies living in Florida.

"They found me here, though. They know where I'm at and they said I have until noon on Monday to wire them the money or send it through PayPal."

"And these guys threatened to kill you if you didn't pay?"

"Basically. Yeah. They're not a bank."

I swore again. I was backed into a corner. I had to give her the money. I couldn't allow my daughter to grow up without her mother.

"I don't know what I'm going to do. Mom doesn't have the money. She already has two mortgages on the house. I couldn't ask her, anyway. I'm such a fucking fool."

"Yeah, well, if you're looking for sympathy, you're not going to get it from me."

"I'm not, trying to get any," she snapped.

"You not only put your life in danger, but Aubrey's, too. You need help. Join Gambler's Anonymous or something, for Christ's sake."

"I stopped already."

"Because you have no fucking money," I snapped.

She started crying again.

"Listen, calm the fuck down, okay?"

"I don't know what I'm going to do."

"I'll pay for it."

"You will?" she squeaked.

"Yeah, but if this ever happens again, I'm filing for full custody of Aubrey and you'll never see her again. Plus, I want you to join a support group *and* I want proof of it."

"I will. I promise. Thank you. Thank you so much."

I sighed. "What's your PayPal address? I'll send you the money tonight."

She told me.

"You pay them as soon as possible. Don't wait. Tell me when it's done too, so I can relax."

"I will. I'll send it as soon I get it from you."

"Okay."

"Thank you."

"This is it, Kathy. No more bullshit."

186

"I swear to God, I won't ever do this again. I've learned my lesson."

I wanted to believe she did, but I wasn't so sure.

After I hung up, I transferred her the money. Five minutes later, she sent me a screenshot of her sending a payment of four-thousand dollars to a man named Lou Farris. I recognized the asshole—he was a bookie from Tampa Bay with a bad reputation. If she wouldn't have paid, there was no doubt in my mind that her time of death would have been Monday, at 12:01, on the nose.

I texted her one final warning about her gambling and then set my phone down on the nightstand. Fortunately, I'd had some funds saved and was getting paid pretty well at the auto body shop. But, it still ticked me off. I'd worked damn hard and now all of that money was gone with the press of a button. Closing my eyes, I made a promise to myself that from now on, I wouldn't let anyone else take advantage of my good side. Including Kathy. If she fell into a hole like this again, she was going to have to claw her way out of it herself. Without me *and* without Aubrey.

TWENTY-EIGHT

CHARLIE

FRIDAY STARTED OUT as usual. I slept in, had a shake for breakfast, played tennis with Abby, and arrived back home around two. As I was heading to my bedroom, I passed by my father, who seemed to be in very good spirits.

"How's your day going?" he asked.

"Fine. You're looking particularly chipper today."

"It's Friday and I'm taking the weekend off."

"Oh. Good for you." I almost made a comment about the mafia never taking a day off, but stopped myself. I still had my doubts, but knew it was pointless to keep stressing about it.

"Abby and I were thinking about having dinner at Chop's Steakhouse tomorrow night. Would you like to join us?"

Chop's was my favorite restaurant. "Yeah, that sounds nice. Thank you. I don't work tomorrow, either."

"I know. That's why I thought I'd ask."

"Just let me know what time we're heading out there."

"I'm going to make the reservation for seven."

"Sounds good. Thanks."

"Of course. There's some mail for you on the credenza by the front door."

"Okay."

After taking a shower, I went downstairs and grabbed the mail. Noticing there was a letter from the culinary school in Davenport, my heart began to race. I tore it open, read their decision, and immediately wished I hadn't.

They'd denied me.

The letter stated that the school only allowed a certain amount of students every year and I should consider applying the next term.

I swore.

"What's wrong?" my father asked, coming down the spiral staircase.

I looked up from the letter. I knew if I told him, he'd be pleased. Not to mention, I felt like a loser.

How could I not be accepted when they supposedly had such a high rate of approval?

I'd sent them my transcripts and they'd been decent. My SAT scores hadn't been off the charts, but they weren't horrible either. Better than average, actually.

"Charlotte? Are you okay?" he asked, approaching me.

"I'm fine."

He looked at the envelope I was holding. "What do you have there?"

"It's nothing." I turned around headed up the stairs.

"Are you sure you're okay?" he called out.

"Yeah," I replied, trying not to cry.

I went to my room and closed the door behind me. I knew it was crazy to be so upset, but I'd been making so many plans and now everything was going to hell.

I crumpled the letter, threw it into the garbage can, and called Jackie.

"I didn't get in," I said when she answered.

"The culinary school?"

"Yes. They fucking denied me. Can you believe that shit?"

"I'm sorry."

"I just don't get it. It's Davenport, Iowa. I can't imagine many people are applying *there*," I replied walking over to my bedroom window. "It just pisses me off so much."

"I know."

"I guess I'll just have to look for another school in Iowa. There were others. That one was just the closest," I said, staring off.

"The closest to Maddox?"

I didn't say anything.

"See, it is all about him. Don't choose a school just because of a guy. You'll get burned in the long run."

"You don't know that for sure," I replied. "Anyway, Maddox and I have been talking every day. I'm going to be flying out to see him in three weeks, too."

"Just… careful, okay?"

"I will."

"And, don't forget Paris. Or, your mother."

I laughed. "That's so far, though. Are you trying to get rid of me, Jackie?"

"No. I just want what's right for you. Not to mention that the farther away you are from Tony, the less control he has."

"I agree, but I don't think I need to fly all the way to Paris."

"I'm not so sure," she said in a strange voice.

"Are you okay?"

She cleared her throat. "Yeah. I'm fine."

"Listen, I'm going to research some other colleges. I'll call you later, okay?"

"Sounds good."

After hanging up, I immediately got back onto my laptop and began researching other culinary schools. After applying to another one, farther away from Jensen but still impressive, I sent Maddox a text about not getting in to Davenport. He immediately replied and told me to keep my chin up and not to take it personally.

Maddox: *You'll find another one. A better one.*

Me: *Thanks. I just applied to a couple others.*

Maddox: *Good. Just don't give up.*

Me: *I won't.*

Maddox: *TTYL beautiful.*

Me*: Okay. XOXO*

Maddox: *XOXO*

A FEW HOURS later, Dad, Abby, and I were sitting in a booth at Chop's and my spirits felt lifted again. I'd decided to not let the denial get me down because it just wasn't meant to be.

During our appetizers, my father told Abby about my interest in culinary school and she smiled at me.

"Really? That's fabulous. Where have you applied?" Abby asked.

I told her.

Her eyebrows raised. "Oh, really? You're not thinking of going anywhere in New York? I hear the schools around here are excellent."

"Maybe, but I'm thinking of going somewhere out of the state so that I can try something new, you know?" I replied. "Expand my horizons."

She spread some caviar onto a cracker and smiled at me. "I understand. Still, you could always travel after you earn your degree. I'm sure if you attend one of the schools here in New York, it'll look better on your resumé, too."

I glanced at my father and knew the two of them had already discussed this. More than likely, he'd asked her to try and talk me out of leaving. I didn't want to make any accusations, nor did I feel like arguing, so I simply played dumb.

"I doubt I'd get into one of those swankier schools anyway." I looked at my father. "By the way, you'll be happy to hear Davenport said 'no'."

"What? They denied you? See, they're idiots at that school. There is no reason you should have been turned away," he replied with a look of distaste. "Did they say why?"

"Yeah. They could only allow so many students per term and that I should try again later. Anyway, I've applied at some other schools. I'm sure I'll get in somewhere," I said.

"What other ones?" he asked.

I listed the other three I'd submitted applications for.

"I've never heard of them," he answered.

I snorted. "I don't know why you would unless you've been doing your own research."

"Actually, yes. I have," he replied. "You're my daughter and I want what's best for you."

I knew he loved me, but the fact was, he wanted what was best for him so he could continue to keep an eye on me.

Dad went on. "And Abby is right. New York has some of the best culinary schools in the United States. It would be a pity for you to not even consider them just because you want to 'explore your horizons'."

I sighed. "Can we just talk about this later? I'm really not in the mood."

He shrugged. "Fine. But, just promise me you'll think about broadening your choices?"

"Fine. I will."

He relaxed. "Thank you. Also, if you need anything from me, let me know."

"Thanks. I'm fine, though."

He looked at Abby and smiled wanly. "She's becoming so independent. It's hard for a father to see his baby girl grow up."

"Dad, I'm twenty-three. I've been 'grown up' for quite a while now," I said dryly.

"You will always be my little girl," he said, reaching over and touching my hand. "Someday when you have children, you'll understand."

I understood there was a difference between being there for your children and trying to run their lives. Unfortunately, he didn't. I held back from saying it out loud, knowing it would be like beating a dead horse.

"I'm sure I will, too," I replied and then changed the subject. "How's the caviar?"

TWENTY-NINE

MADDOX

"IF ONLY THAT chick from New York could see you now," Tank said in the doorway.

"Fuck off. You should be the one doing this," I replied, staring at myself in the bathroom mirror. I had on a curly blonde wig similar to Frannie's hairstyle, and a house robe that stopped above my knees.

"Maybe, but then I'd have to shave," he replied.

I looked over at his five o-clock shadow and grunted. "So, if I wouldn't have shaved this morning, we could have rolled the dice on this one?"

He leaned against the doorframe. "No. I would have still made you do it. Let's face it, you make a better looking chick than I do."

"I'm not sure how I should take that."

He grinned. "By the way, she keeps her lipstick in the medicine cabinet. You should put some on."

I opened it up and took out a silver tube. I removed the cover and was about to apply some to my lips when I stopped. "What the fuck am I doing? They're not going to see my face," I muttered, recapping it. "And if they did, they'd run like hell."

He laughed. "Damn, I was hoping you'd fall for it. What's it called?" He grabbed the tube and read the name. "Hot Stuff."

I flipped him off and then grabbed the lipstick. I put some on and rubbed my lips together. "There, satisfied?"

He roared with laughter.

I shook my head and smiled.

"Oh, man… I've never laughed this hard sober or straight," he said, wiping at his tears. "Raptor! You've got to see this!"

Raptor appeared in the doorway and whistled when he saw me. "Damn, girl. Where've you been all my life?"

I put my hand on my hip and raised my voice. "In your dreams, tough guy, and you can't handle me there either."

The two laughed.

Tank took out his cell phone. "I've gotta get a picture. Hold still."

"You take a fucking picture and I'll kick your ass," I said firmly. "Seriously, man, don't."

"Touchy, touchy." Looking disappointed, he lowered his phone.

Tail, another club brother, appeared also. He took one look at me and laughed. "That is some scary shit. You should wear this on Halloween. The guys would laugh their asses off."

"Don't hold your breath," I replied, looking in the mirror again. I leaned forward and wiped some lipstick from the front of my tooth. "You're free to steal the idea, though."

"It wouldn't be the same, considering I would make a much hotter chick than you," Tail said.

I looked at him and agreed. Pretty-boy was right.

"What time is it?" I asked.

"Almost eight," Raptor replied.

Tank sighed. "Okay. I have a feeling that this is going to happen sooner than later. I'll check in with Fabio and make sure he's ready."

"Sounds good," I replied.

As of that moment, the rest of the Gold Vipers were at the clubhouse in a meeting, where we were also supposed to be. In the meantime, there were six of us holed up in here. We were setting up a trap for the Devil's Rangers who thought Frannie was home alone and an easy target. Little did they know that we'd found out about their 'insider' who was feeding them information. She was a woman who'd been dating one of the other club members. He'd been suspicious and had managed to grab her cell phone a few nights back. After learning what she was up to, he told Tank. Now, we were using her to take care of business. Everything seemed to be falling into place, and now all we had to do was wait for them to show up.

"We're going to have to move fast on this," Raptor said. "We don't want the neighbors getting involved."

"Don't worry. This will be over quickly. Once we nab them, we'll take the fuckers to the warehouse and do what we need to do," Tank answered.

Ten minutes later, I was sitting in the dark and watching *The Golden Girls*, my back to the doorway. I felt like a fool, but it was worth saving a woman's life. Especially one who'd been married to a guy we all admired and respected. Not to mention, she was a pretty terrific lady.

THIRTY

BUSTER

BY THE TIME Friday hit, I was ready to murder more than just a Gold Viper or family member. I wanted to put a bullet between Joe's eyes. The guy was driving me fucking crazy. Fortunately, I'd managed to slip out on Thursday night and find myself another honey. She'd been a manager at a sandwich place we'd visited earlier in the week and had given me the cold shoulder when I'd tried flirting with her. Now, the stuck-up broad was just another headline in the news. After having my way with her, I'd dumped her body in Lake Halper. I doubted her death could be linked to me, unless they found the necklace I'd taken from the snooty bitch. An emerald pendant dangled from the rope and I knew it was worth a lot more than the bracelet. Rita was going to love Christmas this year.

"How are we going to do this?" Joe asked, bringing me back to reality. We were on our way to kidnap Slammer's Old Lady and had just gotten done eating at Denny's. Of course, I'd had to watch Joe put down enough food to feed an army, which had ruined my own appetite. So, now the van smelled like my greasy leftovers instead of Joe's body odor, which actually worked out in my favor.

"I'm going to have you drop me off a block from Frannie's. You stay away until I give you the 'all clear'."

"Then what?"

"You'll pick us up."

"Okay. What if she's not alone?"

"That's why I'm going ahead. To make sure she is," I said, leaving off "Knucklehead." It amazed me that Joe was a functioning adult with his own apartment. The past few days I'd gotten to know him more and couldn't believe what an absolute putz he was. I couldn't fucking wait to get back to Chicago.

FIFTEEN MINUTES LATER, Joe dropped me off a block away from Frannie's.

"I'll let you know when it's safe," I told him. "Don't come until I text you."

He nodded. "You want the rest of your burger?"

"Yeah."

Joe looked disappointed.

"Fine. Eat it. Just pay attention to your phone and don't get ketchup on the steering wheel."

He perked up. "Okay."

I shook my head. Somehow, I had a feeling he might still fuck this entire operation up.

Trying to stay positive, I left the van and headed to the townhouse. As I approached the place, I could see that there were low lights flashing in the living room. Someone was watching television.

Staying in the shadows, I slipped behind her house to the sliding glass door. After jimmying the lock, I slid the door open and then sighed in relief. She had a security system up, but the dumb broad had forgotten to set it.

I quietly closed the door behind me and headed toward the sound of the television, my gun ready. When I reached the living room, from the hallway, I saw a woman sitting on the sofa, her back to me. Noticing that her shoulders were too large for such a small woman, I froze in fear.

Fuck.

That was no lady.

Backing away, I turned around and headed toward the kitchen, my heart racing. As I was opening up the slider, I felt something hard press against the back of my head. It was followed by the sound of a gun cocking.

"Freeze, motherfucker," a man whispered.

Fuck.

"Drop your gun or I'll blow your head off," he ordered.

I did what he asked and it was kicked away from my feet. He then grabbed me by the back of the neck and shoved me into the middle of the kitchen. I quickly turned around and found myself face-to-face with the president of the Gold Vipers. Tank.

"Where's the other guy?" Tank asked, glaring at me.

"I don't know who you're talking about," I said, staring him in the eyes. Unfortunately, he was a whole lot bigger than me, but it was well known he wasn't a cold-blooded killer. So, I had an advantage.

"Don't fuck with me," he said angrily, aiming the gun at my forehead this time. "Where's your sidekick?"

"I'm here alone," I replied. "Otherwise, you'd hear shots by now. Right?"

Two more Gold Vipers showed up. One of them was Raptor. The other one looked familiar, but I couldn't remember his name.

"Grab his phone," Tank said to Raptor.

Raptor pulled it out of my pocket.

"What are you doing here?" Tank asked.

"Not sure. I guess I'm lost," I said, smiling coolly.

"You're lost, all right. You're so far from home, something tells me you won't be able to find your way back," he answered.

I didn't reply.

Tank looked at my cut. "V.P. huh? Which chapter?"

"None of your fucking business," I said.

"Fucker, it is my business. See, you're in our territory and everything you say and do here *is* my business," he growled back angrily.

I flipped him the bird.

"Tail," Tank said. "Grab the pliers from the garage. I'll hold him down while you cut off his fingers. Start with his middle one."

He nodded and headed out of the kitchen.

"Wait." I told him that I was from Chicago.

"What's your name?" Tank asked.

"Buster," I said.

"You still want me to grab the pliers?" asked Tail.

"Yeah. We might still need 'em," Tank answered.

He disappeared.

"Find anything?" Tank asked Raptor, who still had my phone.

"His phone is locked," he replied.

"What's your passcode?" Tank asked.

"That's not my phone. I found it," I lied.

"I'm really not in the mood for games," he said. "What's the fucking passcode?"

I shrugged.

Before I could react, he grabbed me by the throat and slammed the butt of the gun against my forehead.

THIRTY-ONE

MADDOX

AFTER HEARING THE commotion from the living room, I raced into the kitchen where Tank was grilling one of the Devil's Rangers I'd seen at the grocery store.

"I'm really not in the mood for games," Tank said, holding up what I presumed was the thug's phone. "What's the passcode?"

He shrugged.

Tank grabbed him by the throat and slammed the butt of his gun against Buster's forehead a couple of times and released him. The guy crumpled to the floor, blood dripping from where he'd been hit, groaning in pain.

Noticing me, Tank asked if Buster was the same guy from the grocery store.

"Yeah. That's one of them," I replied.

"And there were two?" he said.

I nodded.

Tail returned with the pliers. He handed them to Tank.

"You have two choices: Tell me your passcode, or I use these." Tank said to Buster, his jaw ticking in annoyance.

He glared at him.

"Brothers, hold him down. Looks like he doesn't believe me," Tank said.

"Five-four-three-one," Buster growled.

"Got in," Raptor said, smiling down at the phone in triumph.

"Good," said Tank.

"Looks like his partner, someone named Joe, just texted him. Apparently, there's a cop in the area and it's making him nervous," Raptor said.

"Text him to come to the house," Tank said. He looked down at Buster and smiled coldly. "We'll have ourselves a party."

"Will do," Raptor replied, typing into the phone.

A few seconds later, there was a reply.

"He's on his way," Raptor said.

"Let's go and wait for him outside. We'll hide until he pulls up." Tank looked at me. "Watch Buster."

"Okay." I took my gun out and aimed it at him while the other three slipped into the backyard. Looking down at Buster, I noticed he was older. Probably in his forties.

"Come here often?" Buster rasped after spitting out some blood.

"Shut up."

"I almost didn't recognize you," he replied, chuckling as he looked me up and down. "With that get-up and lipstick, you look like one bad fucking dream."

"Right now, I'm *your* fucking nightmare."

"I bet you've been waiting all your life to say that to someone."

I rolled my eyes.

"You know, I wasn't aware that Gold Vipers allowed cross-dressers into their club."

"And I didn't know Devil's Rangers were stupid enough to try and fuck with us again and *again* and still not learn their lesson," I replied sarcastically.

"Whatcha going to do, shoot me?"

"If you don't shut your pie-hole, I will. Just in the leg, though," I said, aiming toward his calf. "Or the thigh. I know Tank is going to want to personally take care of business, considering you're fucking with his family."

Buster's face turned red with anger. "You want to talk about family? Your fucking club killed my cousin! Don't get all high-and-mighty on me, boy. You guys aren't saints."

"Who was your cousin?"

"Mud," he snarled.

I remembered how he'd kidnapped Raptor's wife. She'd almost been raped and killed under his command. "He deserved everything he got."

"You're going to deserve everything you get, too, when my club is finished with you," Buster replied with a gleam in his eyes.

"Maybe your club should pull their heads out of their asses and stop making stupid, idiotic choices. Like getting killed for trying to avenge rapist assholes who deserved what was handed to them."

"Fuck you."

"You know it's true. Unfortunately, you'd rather keep this war going instead of looking at the big picture."

"And what is that supposed to be?"

"Innocent people are going to continue to get hurt in the crossfire and it could all be avoided if you just leave well enough alone."

"*You* started this."

"No, your club started this with murdering Krystal. Not to mention, kidnapping Adriana and killing Slammer."

"Who the fuck is Krystal?"

"Tank's old girlfriend."

"I don't know anything about that. Her death was probably pinned on us, just like Slammer's. We didn't kill the bastard, although he deserved the bullet."

I glared at him. "I'm sure he'd say the same thing about you. I know Tank definitely will."

Buster glanced over toward the sliding glass door. I could tell by the look in his eyes that he was thinking of making a run for it.

"Don't even try it."

"Can I at least get up and sit at the table?"

I sighed. "Fine. You try anything stupid, I'll shoot your ass another hole."

Buster slowly got up and moved to the table. As he was sitting down, Raptor and Tail returned.

"Where's Tank?" I asked.

Raptor looked at Buster and smirked. "He's with 'Joe'."

Buster let out an aggravated sigh.

"Tank's taking him for a little ride. He should be back in about an hour, I reckon," Raptor replied. "In the meantime, we'll need to tie Buster up. Did you see any duct tape in the garage, Tail?"

"Yeah. I'll go and grab some," he replied and disappeared.

AFTER MAKING SURE Buster wasn't going anywhere, we questioned him, but didn't learn much. Not until Tail took out the pliers again. Fortunately, Buster's fear of pain outweighed his allegiance to the Devil's Rangers, because he began to talk. He admitted to being out there to kidnap Frannie and that his president had given the order.

"Why?" Raptor asked. "For what purpose? Why do you keep beating a dead horse? Can't you fuckers just move on?"

He didn't reply.

Raptor looked at me. "It's like talking to a brick wall. These guys have nothing better to do than fuck with us and our families. It's pitiful."

Buster got angry and brought up his cousin Mud again.

"Are you fucking kidding me? You're defending him? Mud was a scumbag who went after my wife," Raptor snapped back. "He was a murderer, a rapist, and a degenerate. So were his club brothers. The world is a better place without scum like him."

Buster glared at him.

"When is this supposed to end?" Tail asked. "Because the way things are going right now, your club keeps shrinking every time they fuck with ours. And why? To avenge the deaths of people who had it comin'?"

"Says the guys who all have blood on their hands," he replied, looking around the room.

"He's as bad as the rest. They just don't get it and they never will," Raptor said to Tail.

Buster rolled his eyes.

WE WAITED FOR Tank to return. Meanwhile, bored, Raptor turned on the television and started flipping through the channels, stopping on a news report about another death in Jensen.

"The body of twenty-three-year-old Tessa Jacobs was found earlier this evening by fishermen on Lake Halper," the reporter said. "Sources report that she'd been brutally stabbed and possibly raped, like Gina Peltier, who was abducted near the college just days earlier."

"Looks like we have a fucking serial killer on the loose," Raptor mumbled.

The reporter went on to mention that officials were evaluating some video footage taken from behind the sandwich place where she worked.

"Hopefully, they'll have a suspect in custody before this lunatic strikes again," the reporter said grimly. "Back to you, Steve."

I glanced over at Buster and noticed that he was staring at the television with a funny look on his face.

"Sounds like the work of a Devil's Ranger," I said, the wheels in my head spinning. "How long have you guys been in town?"

Buster looked at me. "We're not involved in this shit," he said firmly and looked away. "It was probably one of your guys."

"None of our brothers are into raping and murdering women," Raptor said leaning down and getting into his face. "That's definitely your club's M.O."

Buster shook his head and mumbled something.

Raptor's cell phone began to vibrate. He backed away from Buster and pulled out his phone. "Tank should be back in thirty minutes. Until then, I say we find out if there's anything else this prick is holding out on."

Tail and I agreed.

THIRTY-TWO

CHARLIE

I WORKED AT my uncle's restaurant until nine, and we were swamped. By the time I walked out of the place, my feet hurt from the heels I'd worn all day and I had a slight headache. On the way home, I picked up a bottle of wine and called Jackie to see if she wanted to drop by and go swimming in the new pool.

"Is your dad home?"

"I don't know," I replied. "I'm just getting off of work." I smiled. "You really don't like him, do you?"

"No, that's not it," she said quickly. "I was just wondering if he was going to be there with his goony friends."

"You mean his 'Mafioso'?" I said dryly.

"Do you really think he's mixed in with them?"

"I don't know, nor do I care anymore. I'm outta here soon."

"Did you get a response from any of the other schools yet?" she asked.

"No, but one of them has to accept me, right?" I said.

"I'm sure. Just don't give up."

"I won't, even if it kills me. So, do you want to stop by? I could even pick you up on the way if you want."

"No. I'll just meet you there in about an hour."

"Sounds good."

We hung up and I continued heading home. As I was driving, my thoughts turned to Maddox and I wondered what he was doing.

Party?

I thought of the skanks who might be hitting on him and reminded myself that we were crazy about each other. I needed to trust him.

My phone began to ring, startling me. I looked at the caller ID. Oddly enough, it was another anonymous number.

"Hello?" I said, answering it.

"Your old man is interfering with your college applications," a man said in a muffled voice.

"Excuse me?"

He hung up.

Who in the hell was this?

My stomach tightened. All I knew was that it was the same caller and I was being warned about my father once again.

Did he have something to do with the Davenport denial?

I couldn't imagine that it was even possible.

But then again…

Pressing harder on the gas, I headed home as fast as I could, determined to figure out what in the hell was really going on.

WHEN I ARRIVED home, nobody was there. I sent my father a text, asking what time he'd be returning.

Dad: *Why? Is everything okay?*

Me: *Yeah. Jackie is coming over. We're going swimming.*

Dad: *Fun. I will be home around midnight.*

Me: *Okay.*

Dad: *Say hello to Jackie for me.*

Me: *Sure.*

KNOWING I HAD the house to myself, at least for a couple of hours, I slipped into my father's office and sat down at his desk. I opened up his laptop and tried logging in, but found he'd protected it with a password. Fortunately, he was predictable, and after a couple of tries, I was able to log in using my name and birthdate. As secretive as my father was about his business affairs, I had to almost laugh at how easy it was for me to get into his computer.

After logging in, I went to his email and started looking around. Unfortunately, there really wasn't anything that looked suspicious. It wasn't until I went into his *sent* folder that things took a turn. I found an email, dated two days ago, he sent to the culinary school in Davenport.

I pulled it up and began reading. When I was finished, I was both confused and shocked. In the letter, there was an acknowledgment about a 'large school donation' being sent to an admissions officer. A man named Stewart Harding.

Another bribe?

Of course, there was no mention of me on the email, but my father was smart. He would have called Stewart and talked to him personally.

Mother... Fucker...

I couldn't imagine any other reason for my dad to offer a monetary donation other than it was related to my application. And, of course, I hadn't been accepted.

Angry and pissed off as all hell, I sent Maddox a text. I wanted to leave New York and get as far away from my father as I could—and from the look of things, he was my fastest way out.

THIRTY-THREE

MADDOX

W E'D JUST LOADED an unconscious Buster into the van when my phone began to buzz. I looked at it and found a text from Chuck asking me to call her.

It was an emergency.

I swore.

"What's up?" Tank asked.

"Chuck wants me to call her," I said.

"Chuck?"

"Charlie."

"Oh. Go ahead and do what you gotta do. By the way, you can probably take the wig and shit off," he replied.

"I'll be right back," I said, removing the hairpiece.

I turned and headed back toward the house, grateful it was dark and Frannie's neighbors couldn't see me. I quickly dialed Chuck and she answered on the first ring.

"What's wrong? Are you okay?"

She told me about what she'd found in her father's computer. She believed that he'd paid someone off so they wouldn't accept her into the school.

"Considering he also probably paid off Cody, that doesn't surprise me," I replied.

"I don't know what to do," she said, sounding almost in tears. "I'm so angry. I want to confront him, but part of me is afraid. I just don't know what he's capable of."

"Is your old man home?"

"No, that's why I snooped into his computer."

"Do you know who it was that called you?" I asked.

"I have no idea. I wish I did. I'd thank him."

"How would this person find out about the email and the donation? Not to mention Cody. It has to be someone close to him."

"I don't know. Maybe someone has hacked his computer and wants to get him into trouble?" she replied. "I just can't believe this is happening. I want to scream at him."

"Don't confront him alone, whatever you do," I said, stepping into the townhouse from the back slider. I shut the door behind me. "He'll just try and manipulate you into believing more of his bullshit."

"You're right. I need to get out of here."

"Go to Jackie's," I suggested.

"She's on her way here. Crap, I need to call her."

"You should. When you're done with that, call me back and I'll see if we can book you a ticket out here. I'll also try and get you a hotel room to stay in until we can figure this shit out."

She gasped. "You'd do that for me?"

"Of course. I don't like how your old man is playing you. He might love you, but he's acting like a selfish prick. He can't keep getting away with it."

"I agree."

"When you call back, if I don't answer… just leave me a message," I said, walking into the bedroom to change. "I'll call you back as soon as I'm available."

"What are you doing?"

I looked at myself in the mirror. If she only knew. "I'm just getting ready to deliver some shit to the clubhouse with Tank."

"Oh. Okay. I'll talk to you soon then."

"Sounds good. Stay safe."

"You, too," she replied and blew me a kiss.

I blew her one back.

After getting off of the phone, I changed into my street clothes, put my cut back on, and removed the makeup.

"You coming?" hollered Tank from the front door.

"Yeah."

We locked up the house and got into the van. Tail and Raptor followed us on their bikes.

"So, now what?" I asked.

"We reunite Buster and their informant and then wait for Bastard to get back to us."

"You already talked to him?"

Tank nodded. "On the way back from dropping off Joe."

"How *is* Joe?"

"Grateful that this shit is over with," he replied. "He's heading to Canada to stay with his sister."

"He's a good guy," I said.

Joe was our informant and had been feeding us information about the Devil's Rangers for the last year. I had to give him credit, he'd really stepped up to the plate and kept his composure, especially when he'd been a prospect. He hated the Devil's Rangers and I imagined had endured a lot of shit.

"Yeah, he is. Joe almost wouldn't take the money I gave him. He needs to stay away for the next few months though, so I made him take it. They need to believe he's actually dead."

I nodded.

"What was up with your girl?"

I told him.

219

"That's fucked up. You sure you want to get involved with someone whose father is part of the mafia?"

"I'm just trying to help her out. We're not serious or anything."

He looked at me and smirked. "Right. You keep telling yourself that. Just like I did with Raina."

I smiled. "You gotta admit, she's hot. Whether we get involved or not, I'm not turning down a few more nights with that chick for anything. Not even her father."

"Spoken like a guy who's already whipped."

"I'm not. I just like her. A lot."

He was silent for several seconds and then sighed. "You'd better be careful. Something tells me you're going to be next on her father's list of 'items that must go'."

"Let him try. It won't get him very far. Maybe a shallow grave."

Tank laughed. "You're already willing to kill for her. And her *father* to boot. You may not be whipped, but she means more to you than you realize."

Deep down, I knew he was right. I just hoped that it wouldn't come down to proving just how much. Something told me that as much as Chuck wanted her father out of her life, it wasn't permanent.

THIRTY-FOUR

JACKIE

I WAS ON my way over to Charlie's house when she called me.

"Change of plans," she said.

"What do you mean?"

She told me about an email she'd found on her father's laptop. Knowing he also sent me ones from time-to-time, my heart began to race.

"That's horrible," I said, trying to remain calm. "Was there anything else?"

"Not that I saw, although I didn't look at anything else after reading that bullshit." She laughed harshly. "I'm afraid to find out about whatever else he might be hiding."

"I would be, too. What you don't know can't hurt you, right?" I joked.

"In this case, it did. And in Cody's case. I should look and see if I can find an email between the two of them."

"I'd just let that one go. We both know it happened. Besides, the more you dig the more it's going to drive you crazy."

She let out a weary sigh. "True. I just can't believe he did this to me. He knew how much this meant, too."

"I know. I'm sorry," I replied sadly.

"Me, too."

"So, what are you going to do?" I asked, pulling over to the side of the road.

She took a drink of something. "Maddox is going to buy me a ticket to Jensen."

"An airline ticket? When?"

"Hopefully, tonight. Can I stay with you until then? I need to get out of this house. Just being here makes me sick to my stomach…"

She rambled on, expressing how angry she was, and I couldn't blame her. If she only knew how deranged her father really was, she'd want to do more than fly to Iowa. She'd want him locked up behind bars. But, I couldn't tell her anything. Not only would she hate me, but Tony would do exactly what he'd threatened to do—kill me and pin my mother for it.

"Of course we can hang out until you hear from Maddox," I replied. "You should make something up for your dad, though, so he doesn't think anything is wrong."

Not to mention that I didn't want him showing up at my apartment drunk and horny. I didn't want to take any chances.

"Good idea."

"Make sure you cover your tracks well. If he realizes you were in his computer, he'll freak out."

"I will. Where are you?"

"I was on my way to your place."

"Okay. I'm going to start packing. Thanks, Jackie. I don't know what I'd do without you. Probably go crazy."

"I don't know what I'd do without you, either," I said, my eyes filling with tears. She was my only friend and I was losing her because of Tony. He'd once been a godsend, but now was the ultimate evil. I hated the fact that I was so indebted to him and couldn't do anything about it.

"See you soon," she said.

"Okay."

THIRTY-FIVE

CHARLIE

AFTER SIGNING OUT of my dad's laptop, I quickly packed a suitcase and waited for Jackie to arrive. As I watched for her, I thought about calling my mother, but suspected that she might try talking me out of leaving. As angry as she'd be with my father, I knew she'd be against me running off to be with a man I barely knew.

Although, hadn't she flown to another country to stay away from a man she knew *too* well?

Five minutes later, Jackie showed up.

"Thanks for doing this," I said.

"Of course. If you can't rely on your friends, who can you rely on?" she said with a brittle smile.

"True."

She popped the trunk of her car open and I put my suitcase inside.

"You call your dad?" she asked when we were in the car together.

"I sent him a text," I told her.

I'd explained that we'd had a change of plans and informed him that I was staying at Jackie's instead. Of course, he couldn't just accept the excuse and had to ask if everything was fine. .

"And he was okay with it?"

"Yeah. Of course." I sighed and stared out the window. "I can't believe how underhanded he is. I wonder what else he's done in the past that may have influenced something important to me."

"I'm sure there's been many," she said, pursing her lips together. "Anyway, are you sure about going to Iowa? You could stay with me until you figure things out."

"I appreciate the offer, but I'm still within arm's reach of my dad and he'd be over in a heartbeat if he knew I was pissed at him. Lying and making up all kinds of excuses."

"True."

I pulled my phone out of my purse. "Maddox hasn't gotten back to me yet. He was going to check for flights out there."

"Okay. Did you want to stop somewhere and grab some coffee?"

"Actually, that sounds like a good idea. I have a feeling I'm going to need it."

We pulled into a Starbucks drive-through, and both ordered lattes. From there, we went back to her apartment and sat on the couch to talk. About an hour later, Maddox called me.

"There are no flights out there until tomorrow morning," he said. "At around six a.m."

"I guess that will have to work."

"Where are you?"

"At Jackie's." I looked over at her and relayed what he'd said.

"That's fine. I'll drive you to the airport in the morning," she replied.

I thanked her.

"Okay. I'll reserve the flight for you," Maddox said. "Call me when you get to the airport so I know you arrived there safely. I'll meet you in Davenport when your flight arrives. Oh, and text me your full name and birthdate for the reservation."

"I will. And thank you. I'm sorry for dropping all of this on you." I got up off of the sofa and walked over to the window. "In fact, I've been thinking about all of this and I want you to know that I can stay at a hotel. I just want to get out of Buffalo and figure things out. I have money—"

"Don't worry about it. I was the one who convinced you to fly out here. I want you with me. I miss you."

I smiled. "I miss you, too."

We talked for a few more minutes and then he said he had to go.

"Okay. I'll call you when I'm at the airport."

"Sounds good."

AFTER WE HUNG up, I turned around and saw Jackie smiling at me.

"What?" I said with a smile.

"Girl, you're in love, aren't you?"

"Love? We barely know each other."

"I know, but you have that look in your eyes. Anyway, for God sakes, you're flying halfway across the country to stay with him when you could just as easily stay with me."

I sat down on the sofa and pulled my knees to my chest. "Okay," I said, grinning even wider. "I don't know if it's love, but I can't stop thinking about him. I feel like he could really be the one and… it scares me to death."

"Just remember that as sweet as he is on the phone, he's *still* a biker and mixes with a very bad crowd. You know he does."

"Yeah, but… he's been telling me about his brothers and they don't sound so bad."

"His brothers? How many does he have?"

I explained that it was in reference to his club buddies.

227

"Ah. Well." She smiled wryly. "If he's really as awesome as you say he is, let me know if there are any others like him. I'll follow you to Jensen."

I laughed.

She gave me a serious look. "Just, be careful, okay?"

"I will."

Jackie moved closer to me and gave me a hug. "I'm going to miss you."

"I'll miss you, too," I whispered, feeling overwhelmed emotionally. I felt deceived and hurt by my father. Sad about leaving Jackie. Anxious about rushing out to Maddox. Although we'd talked on the phone for hours, we'd only had one night together, and guys like him didn't fall in love at the drop of a hat. I hadn't thought that I could either, but here I was. Not only was I leaving everything to be with him, but thoughts of a future together were already running through my mind. Deep down, I knew it was silly and naïve to think like that, but it didn't stop me from wanting it.

"You know, your father will ask me what happened to you," she said softly.

"Don't worry. As soon as I get out to Iowa, I'll send him a message."

"Are you going to tell him what you found in his emails?"

I sighed. "Yeah. If he's going to go snooping into my life then there's no reason why I should feel guilty about snooping into his."

Not to mention that he'd taken it even further. His interference and deception had not only changed my future, but it had driven us apart. For good.

"He'll fly out and try to bring you back."

"I'm sure. He'll be wasting his breath, though. Not only am I sick of his games, but I have a new boyfriend. One who doesn't get intimidated easily. Or take bribes."

"Let's hope not. Like you said—you don't know him *that* well. Your dad could offer him a shitload of money to help get you back here. Sometimes money *does* talk when it's the right amount."

"Maddox isn't like that," I said.

At least, I hoped to hell not.

"You'd be surprised what people will do when they're financially strapped," she said, staring off. "Just be careful, okay?"

I grabbed her hand. "I will. Are you okay?"

She smiled. "Yeah. Of course. Just worried about you."

"I'll be fine," I said.

I had to be.

THIRTY-SIX

MADDOX

AFTER BRINGING BUSTER back to the clubhouse, we sat him down next to Cherry, one of the club whores. She was also the chick they'd sent to spy on us. I'd learned from Tank that she'd slept with a few of the members, but, fortunately, hadn't gotten much intel. The club had figured out what she was doing after three of the guys talked about banging her. They noticed how she'd been drilling them about the club and asking the same questions, especially in regards to Frannie. Suspicious, they told Tank about it, who confronted Cherry. At first she tried denying everything, but then broke down and admitted she'd been helping the enemy. Her reasoning was that Rusty, who'd fathered her seven-month-old son, was keeping him from her. He refused to give the child back until she provided them with some intel on us. We also learned that he was a sadist who enjoyed beating women, which was why she was so scared of the maniac. She even showed us some pictures she'd been secretly storing on her phone as evidence. From puffy black-and-blue bruises, to cigarette burns, to teeth marks. Having a daughter of my own, it made me furious to think that a guy like him was torturing women like that as a pasttime.

"He's going to kill me when he finds out I've told you all of this," she'd cried afterward. "And I'll never see my son again."

Tank had asked her why she hadn't gone to the police, especially if she had pictures as evidence.

"Like they would do anything," she'd scoffed. "You, of all people, know that the clubs have their own laws and half the police force takes bribes from them."

We all knew it was true and in the end, Tank promised to help her if she helped us.

"How are you going to help me?"

"We'll get your kid back. I also know of someone who can get you a new identity, so you can start fresh somewhere."

Although Cherry didn't seem too convinced, she had to go along with it. She'd had no other choice now that we knew everything.

Buster, on the other hand, would still think she was on their side for her own safety.

After handcuffing him to a chair next to Cherry, who was also in restraints, Raptor, Tank, and I walked over to the bar and out of earshot.

"You talk to Bastard yet?" Raptor asked quietly.

"Yeah. He's leaving this up to me to handle it accordingly," Tank said.

I wasn't too surprised. My old man knew Tank had a good head on his shoulders.

"So, what are we going to do?" Raptor replied.

"In the past, Buster wouldn't be breathing by now," Tank said, scratching his chin. "But, I made a promise to myself that if we had to deal with this kind of shit again, I'd try another route. Now that I have kids, I don't want to take any chances."

"You have any ideas yet?" I asked.

"Oh, yeah. I'm already working on it," he said with a sly smile.

TEN MINUTES LATER, after interrogating Buster more about the Devil's Rangers, we un-cuffed him.

"So, what now? You going to kill me?" he asked, rubbing his elbows.

"No. We're going to let you go so you can deliver a message to Rusty," Tank said, glaring at him.

Buster touched his face, which had taken quite beating, and winced. "Oh, yeah, what's that?"

"To stay the fuck away from us, what the fuck else?" Tank glanced at Cherry, then to Buster. "Look, we're letting you go as a gesture of our desire to let bygones-be-bygones. Both of you."

Buster stared at him in disbelief.

"When my old man was killed, I wanted to come after you with guns blazing, too," he said to Buster. "But, I knew it would just lead to more bloodshed, and I don't want that for our families. Enough is enough. You feel me?"

Buster nodded.

"Now, I understand you're upset about Mud. We have something in common. We both lost a lot, but nothing we do is going to bring them back," he replied.

"Is it me, or do you feel like we're in a Lifetime movie?" Raptor murmured to me under his breath.

I smirked.

Tank went on. "We need to bury this shit. For the good of both of our clubs." He set down two shot glasses and filled them with whiskey. He pushed one toward Buster. "Have a drink. It'll help take the edge off. I'm sure your face is hurting right now."

"Yeah. You could say that," he replied, picking up the shot glass.

Tank and Buster drank the whiskey down.

233

"You want another one?" Tank asked.

"Fuck it. Why not? One more," he replied.

Tank poured them each another shot and again, they tossed them back.

"Wanna go for three?" Tank asked.

"Nah," he replied. "I'm good."

"Okay." Tank turned his shot glass over. "You two are free to leave."

Buster looked around, as if he was waiting for the punchline.

Tank handed him the keys to the van.

"What happened to Joe?" Buster asked.

"I let him go. He's just a new member, right? Only following orders." Tank looked at his phone. "I dropped him off at Denny's, on 80th Street, and told him to wait for you to pick him up."

"He's still breathing?" Buster replied, looking shocked.

"And eating, probably. Like I said, we're done with this war between us. It won't stop until one of us waves an olive branch. If it has to be us, it has to be us," he replied.

Buster just stared at him open-mouthed.

"You can leave anytime," Tank said.

Buster stood up. "Come on, Cherry."

Cherry swallowed and stood up. "Um, thank you," she said, looking scared.

Tank nodded.

The two walked out of the clubhouse.

"Think he fell for it?" Raptor asked quietly.

"It doesn't matter one way or the other. He's going to get what's coming to him," Tank replied.

THIRTY-SEVEN

BUSTER

C HERRY AND I got into the van. As we waited for the Gold Vipers to open up the gate and let us out of the parking lot, I looked at her.

"Can you believe this shit? Either they've turned into a bunch of pussies or this is some kind of a setup."

"Why would they let us go if it was a setup?" she asked.

"I don't know. Nothing is making sense." I pulled my phone out and sent Joe a text asking if he was okay. A minute later, he replied that he was having breakfast and doing fine.

I snorted and put my phone away. "Strange shit. But, still a win for us, I guess."

"I guess," she repeated in a hollow voice.

"Seriously, though, I don't care what Tank said about letting things go, though. Fuck that." I touched my face, which still ached from getting pummeled with the gun earlier. "My cousin is still dead and he never gave him an option to 'let things go'."

Cherry sighed and stared out the passenger window. "Do you think Rusty is going to be pissed at us?"

"What do you think? You must have fucking squealed which is why they busted us to begin with," I snapped. "How did they find out you were even spying on them?"

She looked at me. "I don't know. I never told them anything until they cuffed me and started threatening me with a knife."

I glared at her. "Maybe I should finish what they started. They're not known for killing women, bimbo. It's one thing everyone knows about the Gold Vipers. You should have known that."

"Well, *I* didn't," she said, her eyes filling with tears.

236

Cherry was one of Rusty's favorite club whores, and a hot one at that. I'd wanted a piece of her, but everyone knew she was off-limits. Of course, now she owed me.

"You return to Chicago, without any marks on that pretty face of yours, nobody is going to believe that you tried hard enough," I said.

She frowned.

"You should have at least been smacked around a few times," I replied, my fist itching to do the deed myself.

"Let me guess, you're volunteering for it?" she replied dryly.

I smirked. "If it saves your life, you should be begging me to slap you around a little."

The gate opened. As we drove by Mad Dog, I couldn't help myself. I flipped him off and grinned. He shook his head and closed the fence.

"Asshole," I muttered.

I took a right and started driving toward the freeway. "I still can't believe we're getting out of here so easily. And they call themselves a one-percenter club." I snorted. "Fuck that."

"I thought it was cool that they let us go," Cherry said softly. "And smart."

"You would think that," I said, glancing at her again. "Let's stop off at a motel before we pickup Joe. You play nice with me and I'll make sure Rusty knows you did your best when we get back home."

Her eyes widened in alarm.

"You've been fucking the Gold Vipers for the last few weeks, right? The filthy scum. You should be relieved that you're going to have a real man inside of you." I looked into my rearview mirror and saw a cop behind me with his lights flashing. "What the fuck is this now?"

Cherry looked back. "Shit."

I pulled over to the side of the road. Fortunately, the Gold Vipers still had my gun.

"Why is he pulling us over?" she asked.

"I don't fucking know. Hand me the insurance information. It should be in the glovebox."

"Okay." Cherry opened it up and pulled out what I need.

When the cop approached, I rolled down my window and handed him my license and insurance card.

"What's up, Officer?" I asked, forcing a smile to my face. The man had whitish-blond hair and blue eyes. He reminded me a little of Kiefer Sutherland.

"Did you know that you have a taillight out?" he asked.

Fuck. It must have just gone out. "No, I wasn't aware of it. Sorry, man."

"Have you been drinking?"

I realized that my breath probably still smelled from the shots of whiskey. "I just had one small drink."

"What happened to your face? Looks like you might have gotten into a brawl tonight," he said, studying it.

"Just a little one." I smirked. "You should see the other guy."

The cop smiled grimly and looked over at Cherry. Then back to me. "Can you step out of the vehicle for a minute?"

I glanced at Cherry. She looked as frightened as all hell. It figured that the dumb bitch didn't know how to play things cool.

The cop repeated himself.

I knew better than to argue with him and I wasn't worried about getting a DUI. My tolerance was pretty high.

"Yeah. Sure." I opened the door and got out of the van just as another squad pulled up.

"Now, put your hands behind your head," the cop ordered firmly. "And turn toward the vehicle."

"I thought you were just going to give me one of those tests," I replied angrily, looking at his tag. "Officer Peters."

"Hands behind your head, *now*," he snapped.

"Are you profiling me? Because of my club affiliation?" I asked as he cuffed me.

"Your behavior is suspicious enough to warrant a search."

"That's bullshit. I've been on my best behavior. I've been compliant and haven't hassled anyone. What the fuck, man?"

Two other officers appeared and one of them had a police dog.

"Check the van," Officer Peters said.

"Why?" I growled, annoyed. "This is ridiculous."

The other officers ordered Cherry out of the van and the dog searched the back.

"What's the duct tape for?" called out one of the other officers, a female.

"To fix things," I said wryly.

Officer Peters began patting me down, and it was then that I remembered the bracelet and ring. I'd stuck them inside of my pocket before leaving Joe in the van. I'd been paranoid about him going through my shit.

Remain calm…

Of course, Officer Peters found both of them.

"Whose is this?" he asked, holding up the jewelry.

"My girlfriend's. Cherry. It's supposed to be a surprise gift. Please, don't say anything to her," I replied, my heart racing.

"You have any receipts for this stuff?" he asked.

"I bought them at a pawn shop," I replied. "Tossed the receipts."

Suddenly, the dog began to bark, and deep down I knew I was totally fucked. And not just because of the jewelry I'd stolen from the dead girls.

"Looks like Bentley found something." Officer Peters pulled me behind the van and both of us stared in surprise at the large, white package the dog had sniffed out.

"Well, lookie here," the female officer said. "Looks like a kilo of coke. Good job, Bentley!"

My eyes bugged out of my head. "That's not mine! That was planted there by someone else!"

The officers gave me a knowing look.

"Yeah," Officer Peters said. "That's what they all say."

I was so angry I could barely breathe. The Gold Vipers had screwed me big time. I knew the cops would eventually link me to the jewelry, too.

I was so completely fucked.

And they were probably sitting around their table and laughing their assess off about it.

They'd been bullshitting about letting things go.

Motherfuckers...

THIRTY-EIGHT

CHARLIE

I ARRIVED IN Davenport at eleven a.m., and just as promised, Maddox met me at the airport. The moment I saw him smile in my direction, joy overwhelmed me. I wanted to throw myself into his arms, but was too shy to do anything about it. Now that we were facing each other, I could barely even speak.

"Hi," I said, staring up at him.

"Damn, girl, you're a sight for sore eyes," he said, his eyes twinkling.

"You're not so bad yourself," I replied, drinking him in. He had on low-riding blue jeans and a black form-fitting T-shirt under his cut. Everything he wore emphasized hard masculinity and muscles. I'd forgotten how sexy he was.

He pulled me into his arms, and covered my lips with his. His kiss was hard, exploding with pent-up lust, and I matched it with my own. When we finally parted, we were both breathless and all I could think about was getting him alone and naked.

"Jesus," he murmured, the corners of his mouth turning up as he stared into my eyes. "Talk about a memorable reunion."

I smiled back. "It's just getting started."

"Down, boy," he murmured, nonchalantly adjusting himself as he looked around.

I chuckled. "Let's get out of here."

"Good plan."

I noticed he had dark shadows under his eyes. "You look tired. Rough night?"

He nodded.

"You guys must party pretty hard," I replied as we walked toward the luggage claim area.

"We weren't partying. We had some business to take care of," he said quietly.

"What kind?"

"A dispute with another club. It's been handled, though."

My eyebrow rose. "That doesn't happen often, does it? Club disputes?"

He gave me a reassuring smile. "Not at all. You have nothing to worry about."

"Good."

"Have you talked to your old man yet?" he asked.

"Hell no." My stomach burned at the thought of my father. "I'm so angry at him right now, I don't want to even hear his voice."

"You'd better let him know you're okay, though. Knowing him, he'll call in the FBI and send out a search party."

"Good. Maybe it will somehow backfire and they'll dig into all of his dark secrets," I replied dryly.

"They probably already know about it," Maddox replied.

I sighed. "Maybe. Don't worry, I'll get in touch with him later. I certainly don't want him hassling Jackie. He usually plays golf on Saturday mornings, anyway."

"Okay."

We grabbed my suitcase and headed toward the parking lot, a comfortable silence settling between us. I knew he was tired and I hadn't slept much either, so I had a feeling it was going to be a lazy day. One that was hopefully spent naked and in bed together.

"We're in the black SUV," he said, pressing the key fob to unlock it. "I'd have brought my Hog, but I didn't know how much luggage you had. I have to say, I'm impressed there's just the one suitcase. Does this mean we'll be spending most of our time naked?"

I laughed. "Maybe. Where are we going, anyway?"

"I've been staying at Tank's stepmom's place," he replied, putting my suitcase into the back of the vehicle. "She's going to be gone for the next week, so we can hang out there until we figure things out."

"Okay."

We got into the Acadia and he started it.

"I still can't believe you're actually here," Maddox said, looking over at me with a smile.

I smiled.

"You hungry?"

"Actually, yeah. I am."

"Good, because I'm starving. I'm still new to the area, but the guys keep talking about this diner that's supposed to have great burgers and sandwiches."

"Sounds good."

He leaned over and kissed me. "The problem is, I don't know if I can make it to the diner with this hard-on," he murmured, reaching for my breast. "Fuck, I was ready to bend you over right there in the airport. We need to find us someplace private so I can give you a proper homecoming."

I rubbed my hand over his zipper, making him groan. "Let's do it," I whispered. "Wherever you want. I'm game."

Smiling, he started the engine and we practically tore out of the parking lot.

"Slow down," I said, laughing. "You'll get a ticket."

244

"Some things are worth a ticket," he replied, leaning over and reaching under my skirt. He touched my panties and sucked in his breath. "You're wet already. Fuck me."

"I plan on it," I replied, closing my eyes as he slid his finger under the fabric and began fingering me. Moaning, I squirmed and whimpered under his touch until he pulled away.

"Sorry," he said, turning down a gravel road. "I'll get back to that in a minute. I have an idea."

"Okay."

We drove down the rocky road for about a mile and then came to a farm field. Then next thing I knew, he turned the wheel sharply and we entered the cornstalk.

"Hang on," he said.

"Oh, my God," I gasped and laughed. "What are you doing?"

He grinned. "Sowing some oats. Or, at least hoping to."

It was a rickety ride and we were thrown around as the SUV continued forward. After a few more seconds, he slowed it down and then we came to a complete stop. He turned off the engine and smiled at me.

"Here?" I said. "What if the farmer comes?"

"He sees your body, he probably will."

I just stared at him in disbelief.

"Come on," he said, opening up the door. Turning to me he gave me sexy smile. "We don't have much time."

We spent the next several minutes fucking like rabbits. He bent me over the hood, raised my skirt, and was inside of me before I could catch my breath. Although there wasn't a lot of foreplay, his cock felt so good and hit all the right angles. It didn't take long before he had me screaming out an orgasm, which was quickly followed by his own gasps of pleasure.

"Fuck, do you hear that?" he asked.

"It sounds like some sort of tractor."

"Yeah, and it's moving closer."

We quickly pulled ourselves together, hopped into the Acadia, and tore out of the cornfield.

"You did a number back there," I said, looking back at the flattened stalks.

"It was a fast number, though. Sorry about that."

"I was talking about the flattened stalks."

"Don't worry. I'll send the farmer an anonymous pile of cash to pay for the damage."

I stared at him in surprise. "Seriously?"

"Yeah. We take care of each other in Jensen. Even the citizens."

"Citizens?"

"Non-clubbers."

"Well, I guess that would refer to me as well. A citizen."

He smiled. "For now."

THIRTY-NINE

CHARLIE

A FTER OUR LITTLE rendezvous in the cornfield, Maddox took me to the diner his friends had recommended. Both of us were ravenous, so we ordered both appetizers and meals. As we waited, he talked about his new job at the auto shop and how much he was enjoying it.

"I'm going to need to find a job," I said, stirring the strawberry banana malt I'd ordered. "I have some money, but it's not going to last."

"They're hiring for a receptionist at my place," he said. "I don't know what the pay is, but it's worth looking into."

"You sure you'd *want* me working with you? It won't be too much?"

"You kidding me? I'd love seeing you every second of the day."

My heart melted.

"The truth is, however, I don't spend a lot of time in the front of the building, so we'd probably hardly ever see each other."

"I don't know what to do, honestly. I've applied at a couple other schools, although…" I frowned. "My father might try interfering with those as well." I knew the schools wouldn't be too difficult to find. Especially, if he knew I wanted to move close to Maddox.

"Not everyone takes bribes, you know. Not to mention, it's illegal. If that guy, what's his name?"

"Stewart Harding."

"If he gets busted, he'll be in deep shit." Maddox smirked. "Hell, maybe I should pay him a visit."

My eyes widened. "You'd do that?"

"If you really want to get into that school, damn right I would."

I reached over and touched his hand. "As sweet as that sounds, I wouldn't want you getting arrested for threatening the guy."

"It would never happen. Guys in monkey suits are no threat to us, darlin'. They know if they mess with one of us, they're in trouble with all of us. Besides, he wouldn't want to cause a scandal. Especially since he took that money."

"Too bad my father isn't too worried about scandals."

"I'm sure he is. The difference is your old man has a lot of money and reach. He could cover up things a lot easier than most."

I couldn't disagree there. "He's going to be pissed when he finds out I'm out here and we're together." I could only hope he didn't try pulling something again.

"Too damn bad," he replied. "Let him try getting between us. It won't happen on my watch."

"Finally, a man not easily manipulated by him," I replied. "It's about time."

"I'm not easily manipulated by anyone. Only you," he said with a twinkle in his eyes. "And I have to say… I like it."

I took my foot out of my shoe, put it between his legs, and rubbed his zipper with my toe. "Good, because I'm not through manipulating you," I whispered before the waitress returned with our appetizers.

"Hope you're hungry," the woman said, setting a large order of wings and artichoke dip on the table.

"Yeah," Maddox said, caressing my foot. "We worked up an appetite."

"Well, good," she replied. "Let me know if you need anything else."

"Got everything I need right here," he said, winking at me.

The waitress noticed and smiled. "You two are so damn cute. You remind me of when my husband and I first met. Anyway, enjoy your food."

"Thanks," we said in unison.

She left and I grabbed a wing. "I think I could get used to this place. I always did like small towns and friendly people."

"Quite a change from New York, huh?"

I nodded.

"I'm liking it out here myself. Don't get me wrong, I love Florida and miss being near the ocean, but I don't feel as anxious out here as I did back home."

"So, you're happy you moved?"

"It's brought me luck so far. Among other things," he replied, squeezing my foot before letting go. "I'll be back. I need to use the bathroom."

"Okay."

I watched him walk away. I was also feeling less anxiety and it had everything to do with being in Jensen with Maddox. I didn't exactly know what my future held, but I hoped it was with him.

MADDOX

AFTER WE FINISHED eating, I took her back to Frannie's place and we spent the next couple of hours making love and plans. In the end, she decided to look at getting her own apartment and a job in town.

"I was thinking that I should even apply for that receptionist job you were telling me about," she replied, giving me a sideways glance. "Unless, you're having second thoughts about it."

"Hell, no. I'm the one who brought it up."

She looked relieved. As beautiful as Chuck was, her confidence level was shit. I figured it was because of all the B.S. her old man was putting her through. Then there was Cody, who'd given her up for cash. Piece of shit. She deserved better anyway.

"What about school?" I asked, cracking open a beer. I handed it to her and opened another one for myself. We were in the kitchen and had just gotten done taking a shower together. Something told me Frannie's water bill was going to be high that week. I made a mental note to give her some extra money.

"I don't know. I need to think about it some more," she replied. "Originally, I just wanted to go to get away, you know? But, now that I'm out of the house, I feel like I should slow down and re-evaluate what I really want."

"Don't forget about Tank's friend. The one with the French restaurant. Maybe he could talk to her and get you a job in the kitchen?"

She looked interested.

I went on. "That way you could decide if it's really something you want to even pursue."

Chuck smiled. "That's not a bad idea. I'm still interested in the receptionist job, too. Maybe I could work both?"

"Whatever you want to do," I replied. The truth was, I just wanted her to be happy. I also wanted her to stay in Iowa so that I could be within arm's reach. She'd gotten under my skin and was already making me feel things I wasn't used to. Not since Kathy. Scratch that. I'd never felt the same way about Aubrey's mother as I was already feeling about Chuck. Hell, just listening to her talk about getting her own apartment was making me want her to find a place with me. I knew it was too soon, though. Not to mention, her attitude toward my club was fine right now. But, who knew? She could pull a Kathy later down the line and I wasn't giving up my brothers. Not even for Chuck.

After we finished our beer, I took her for a ride on my Hog and she loved it.

"How hard is it to learn how to drive one of these things?" she asked when we stopped to get gas.

"It depends on how quickly you pick up on things. Some people learn in a day. Others it takes a while to get used to. Why? You want to learn?" I asked.

"Oh, hell yeah. I'd love to."

That pleased me. "We have some older bikes at the clubhouse. We could probably set you up with one and you practice in the parking lot."

She looked thrilled. "Yeah, I'd love that."

"That way, you can also meet some of the guys."

"Okay."

Her phone suddenly went off. She pulled it out of the jacket I'd given her to wear. "Oh, shit. My father. I forgot to call him."

"You'd better get it over with," I said, hanging up the gas dispenser. "Talk to him."

She sighed.

FORTY-ONE

CHARLIE

M ADDOX WAS RIGHT. I couldn't avoid him
forever.
"Hello."

"Hey, sweetheart. You've been gone all day. I was just
wondering if you were going to be home for dinner," he
asked, a smile in his voice.

"Ah, about that."

I told him that I was in Iowa and would be moving out
there for good. When I was finished, there was a long pause
and then he started in on me about making rash, bad
decisions.

"Actually," I said crisply, "I had all intentions of making
great decisions, but you pretty much fucked that up for me."

"Excuse me?" he replied, shocked.

I told him that I'd received another anonymous call
about him and checked his laptop.

"I found an email you sent to the school in Davenport.
Apparently, you paid them off so they wouldn't accept me."

"First of all, you have no right going through my
computer. Second of all, you should have come directly to
me. If you would have, I'd have told you that my donation
had nothing to do with your application," he replied just as
angrily.

Right.

Did he really think I was that naïve?

"Oh, really? What was it for?"

"I donated money toward the remodeling of their
kitchens. So that if you *did* go there, you'd have the best
appliances to learn from."

The college's website had boasted of having brand new state-of-the-art gourmet kitchens to learn from. That was before his 'donation'. He was so full of shit.

"That's just really sad. When do the lies stop?"

"I'm not lying."

"Just like you didn't lie to me about Cody accepting a bribe from you. That was bullshit, too."

"I did no such thing. Why? Did he tell you I paid him off?" he asked angrily.

"It doesn't matter. I know the truth about everything, and that's why I'm moving out here." I looked at Maddox and smiled. "With *Mad Dog*," I replied, emphasizing his road name. I knew it would rankle my father even more.

"You're not thinking clearly. A guy calling himself 'Mad Dog' has to be a degenerate with a dangerous and uncontrollable temper. Not to mention, it's pretty obvious that those two apes you were with in the diner are obviously on steroids."

I rolled my eyes. He assumed everyone with muscles used steroids and had rage issues.

"Listen to me, sweetheart. Animals like that will hurt you or even get you killed. You can't be serious about staying with either of those criminals."

"I'm *very* serious about this."

"You're making a mistake."

"So, what? Maybe I am. Maybe I'm not. But, it's my life. Whatever mistakes I make will be caused by *me*. Not by you."

My father began to ramble on about gang violence and drugs.

"Hold on, are we still talking about biker clubs or the Mafiosa?" I replied. "Because, from where I'm standing, the only one doing devious things right now is you."

"Please, Charlotte," he begged, ignoring the dig. "Don't do this. You're not thinking clearly."

"No, Dad. It's just the opposite."

"You're making a mistake," he repeated.

"The only one making them is you by trying to run my life, not to mention doing it *illegally*."

He kept protesting.

"I don't want to hear any more. Goodbye." I hung up on him.

Maddox frowned. "Let me guess, he went off on a tangent about me?"

I grinned. "Yep. He was especially pissed when I told him your road name. He thinks you're on 'roids and have rage issues. He doesn't know you like I do, though. If I was afraid of you, I wouldn't be here."

Maddox didn't reply.

"Are you angry?" I asked, my smile falling.

He shrugged. "No. I'm cool. I just don't like being talked shit about."

"My father talks shit about everyone," I replied. "Don't take it personally."

He studied my face. "You seemed to be really enjoying yourself by pissing him off."

"Can you blame me? He deserves getting his feathers ruffled."

Maddox didn't reply.

"What is it?" I asked, sliding my hands around his neck. "Are you mad at *me*?"

He smiled. "No. I don't know what I am. Just still tired, I guess. Maybe a little ornery. Don't take it personally."

I leaned up and kissed his lips. We then got back on the motorcycle and returned to Frannie's place. As we walked into the house, I could tell that Maddox was still a little cranky; he was quiet and even a little distant.

"You sure you're okay?" I asked him.

He smiled. "Yeah. Like I said, just tired. Nothing a little sleep can't cure."

"Okay," I replied, hoping it was the case and nothing more.

MADDOX

I KNEW I was probably being childish, but Chuck's conversation with her father had irritated me. Not to mention the satisfied smile on her face while he went ape-shit on his side of the phone.

About me.

What frustrated me was that not once had I heard her come to my defense. Not that there was much to defend, but she could have at least told him that I was a standup guy. I had a job. I had money. I was the one taking care of her for the moment.

Fuck it.

I was tired and over-thinking things I decided.

I closed my eyes and told myself to quit being a fucking crybaby. We had a good thing going and that was all that mattered. Her father could kiss my ass.

I SLEPT IN the next morning and woke with a much better attitude. It didn't hurt that I could smell bacon frying in the house.

"Damn, girl. You didn't have to do this," I said when she brought a tray of food into the bedroom before I could even get out of bed.

Chuck, who had on one of my T-shirts and a pair of boxers, smiled. "You might be repeating those words in a few seconds. I'm not much of a cook. It took me three attempts at getting those eggs to not look like yellow cottage cheese."

I looked down at the breakfast. There was a cup of coffee, two eggs over easy, toast, and a pile of bacon. It looked damn good to me. "I'm sure it's delicious. Where's yours?"

"I ate what I screwed up. I didn't want to waste the food," she replied, sitting next to me on the bed with her own cup of coffee.

Hungry, I dug into the food right away. Everything was good, although the eggs were so salty, I had to force them down.

"I found the website for the auto shop and filled out an application online. I used you as a reference. I hope that's okay?" she said, watching me eat.

"Of course."

"Um, also one more thing—my friend Jackie sent me a text early this morning. She's coming out here to visit."

"Already?" I replied. "You've only been here a day yourself.

"I know. She thought it would be better to do it now because I'm not working yet. She's supposed to fly in tomorrow evening."

"I don't mean to sound like a prick, but she'll need a hotel room. She obviously can't stay here," I replied. "I'm just housesitting myself."

"It's fine. I'm sure she'd feel more comfortable at one, anyway."

"How long is she staying?"

"I don't know. A couple of days?"

"You don't think your dad sent her out here to talk you out of everything, do you?"

"Hell, no. Jackie was just as shocked as I was about what he did. Honestly, I don't think she even likes him so there's no *way* she'd take his side."

Considering the antics her father had pulled, I wasn't so sure. Especially, if there was money involved. I only hoped that Chuck was right about her friend and I was being paranoid.

"So, you still want to learn how to ride a motorcycle?" I asked, after I was finished my bacon.

Her eyes lit up. "Yes!"

"Cool. I'll take you to the clubhouse and we'll see what you can do."

"I can't *wait*." She got out of bed and raced over to her suitcase. "I'm going to take a shower."

"Okay. You sure you don't want to wait for me?" I asked, wiggling my eyebrows.

She smiled at me over her shoulder. "How about I start and you come in when you're ready?"

I moved the tray away from my lap and pulled the sheet down. "Darlin', I'm always ready."

"Apparently," she replied, smiling at my erection.

WE ARRIVED AT the clubhouse around eleven. Not many of the guys where there, but I was able to introduce her to Dodger, Tail, Dover, and Old Man Hoss, who practically lived there. They were watching baseball in the rec room when we arrived. As we stepped inside, I noticed the usual banter going on between them. Mostly between Hoss and Dodger, who were always giving each other shit. All in good fun, of course.

"Damn, where in the world did he find you?" Hoss asked, staring at Chuck in appreciation. "And, even more importantly, do you have any sisters?"

I had to admit, she looked foxy as usual. Today she had on tight jeans and a white halter top under the leather jacket I'd loaned her for riding.

"New York," she said, blushing. "And no. I don't."

"Sisters? You mean *grandmothers*," Dodger said with a smirk. "You're getting a little too dusty to be flirting with girls who didn't arrive with you on the Mayflower."

Hoss flipped him off. "The only thing dusty around here is gonna be your face after I wipe the floor with it."

"Just don't forget your walker 'cause the floor is going to be slippery," he replied.

"I'm actually twenty-one," Hoss said to Chuck. "Dodger's aged me ever since he showed up. I used to be pretty, like Mad Dog and Tail. Now I look like Herschel from the Walking Dead."

Chuck gasped and put her hand over her mouth. "Oh, my God, you kind of really do," she said, laughing.

"I still have all of my limbs, though. I trip over the one in the middle sometimes," he said with a dirty grin. "I even use it for a kickstand sometimes."

She laughed again.

I rolled my eyes and shook my head. "Jesus. And you wonder why you're still single."

"I'm single because I'm still waiting for a girl like Chuck. You and Mad Dog break up, you give me a call, darlin'," he said to her. "What I lack in stamina, I make up for in technique and experience. By the way, I had my tongue pierced a couple years back." He showed her. "Strictly for pleasure. Because, that's the kind of gentleman I am."

Chuck looked at me. "Wow."

I frowned. "Sorry. Don't worry, though. He's all talk."

"No, I'm all tongue," Hoss replied.

"Don't tell me that's your pickup line?" Tail said.

"No. I was just testing it out," he said, picking up his beer. "I guess it's too much?"

"Depends on who the gal is," Tail replied. "Darla Mayers would probably welcome it. She's been eyeballing you for the last couple months."

"Darla Mayers weighs more than the both of us put together. I'd either get lost down there or she'd smother me. Not that I'm against death by pussy. Actually," he chuckled and scratched his whiskers, "I think I might call and see if she's free later."

I pulled Chuck against me and whispered in her ear. "I'm sorry. I should have warned you about our dirty old geezer. He's losing his marbles."

She grinned. "It's fine. He's obviously harmless."

"You're really going to call Darla?" Tail asked Hoss.

"Yeah. Not everyone looks like you, pretty boy." He looked at Chuck. "Did you know that they call him Tail because he's had more bush than half the country?"

"That was in the past," Tail replied, looking embarrassed. "I'm strictly a one-woman man now."

"She's a good one, too," Hoss said to him. "You all have good ones. Except me and Dover."

"True," said Dover, raising his beer to his lips.

"Dry spell for you, too, huh? Well, you can join me and Darla later. There's more than enough sushi to go around," Hoss said to him.

Dover spit out his beer.

"Enough with the sex talk," I said. "You're going to scare Chuck away."

She waved her hand. "No, I'm fine. I can handle it. Don't stop on my account."

Hoss smiled. "Chuck, you're a mighty fine girl. I think you'll get along fine with our little clan."

"Thank you," she said.

"Did Mad Dog tell you about Swap-Sunday?" he asked with an innocent look.

"No. What's that?" she replied.

I groaned inwardly.

He grinned and nodded toward the clock on the wall. "Everyone swaps their chicks at noon on Sunday. Of course, you're the only one here right now."

Tail rolled his eyes.

"Since I have seniority, I get first dibs. The rest of you bastards have to wait for… Swappy Seconds," he said before roaring with laughter.

"Someone cut him off," I said, going for his beer.

"Get away," he said, slicing his hand in the air. "I'm just having some fun."

"Let's go, Chuck," I said, grabbing her elbow. "He'll go on forever if we let him."

She laughed. "It was nice meeting all of you."

"You, too," they each replied.

I TOOK CHUCK to the warehouse where we stored the extra bikes, and for the next hour instructed her on the basics of riding. The parking lot was clear, so there was plenty of room for her to practice. She caught on pretty well, and by the end of the day, she even impressed me.

"So, what do you think?" I asked, after she took off the helmet I'd loaned her.

"Incredible. I love it. I want one," she said, her eyes glittering.

I chuckled. "You'll need to get your license before you're street legal, but I thought you did great."

"Thanks."

"We can even look into doing it this week if you'd like. I'm sure Tank will loan us the bike. Otherwise, I don't know… maybe we can find you a used one that's not too expensive."

She grabbed my arm. "Wait. My own motorcycle?"

I nodded.

Chuck squealed and gave me a kiss. "This is so great. We could go on road trips together, right?"

"For sure," I replied, amused at her excitement.

Chuck started talking about Sturgis and bike rallies.

"Jesus. If only my father could see me now," she said, revving the bike engine. "He'd flip his lid." Her eyes lit up.

"I should have you take a picture and send it to him. It would serve the asshole right."

I sighed.

"What else could I do to piss him off?" she said, talking more to herself. "Tell him that I'm now a patched member of the club?"

"It doesn't work that way, Chuck. You just can't join and become a member at the drop of a hat. There's a lot more to it than that." Not to mention, she was a woman and the Gold Vipers had restrictions.

"I understand that, but… he wouldn't have to know. Maybe I could just send him a photo of me taking shots with you, Hoss, and the others?" she mused.

"Don't you think you're taking this a little too far?"

"I'm just trying to set him straight. He needs to know that I'm in control of my own life."

"Fine, but do it truthfully. You don't have to pretend to be someone you're not."

"So, you're saying that I'm not part of your world?" she replied, taking off the helmet.

"No, I'm not saying that at all. It's just… you're trying to rub everything in his face and using me to do it."

Her face fell. "Oh, hell. I'm sorry. I didn't mean to."

"You sure about that?"

Chuck sighed. "I guess I just wasn't looking at it from your perspective. I'm sorry. You're totally right. I shouldn't even involve you in this. It's between me and my father."

"I want to be involved. Just not that way."

She nodded.

I tilted her chin up and kissed her on the lips. "You hungry?"

"Yes."

"Me, too. Let's get out of here and grab a bite to eat."
"Sounds good."

FORTY-TWO

CHARLIE

W E ENDED UP stopping at the grocery store and grabbing the items needed to make spaghetti. This time it was Maddox who cooked. We also had garlic toast and Caesar salad. Admittedly, he was better at cooking than me. Maybe I should rethink culinary school. I kinda suck at cooking.

"If I keep eating like this, I'm going to need to go on a diet," I said afterward when we were on the sofa.

"No. We just have to keep burning calories by having more sex," he replied, staring up at me from my lap with a twinkle in his eyes. We were in the living room, watching television.

"Yeah. It's kind of like a never-ending circle. You eat after having sex, because you've worked up an appetite. You then have sex to burn off the calories."

"It's the circle of life."

"Only, without kids. Speaking of which, when do I get to meet Aubrey?"

"Hopefully this week sometime. I'll check with Kathy and see if we can take her out for pizza or something."

"Don't you have weekends together?"

"I was supposed to see her yesterday and today," he replied with a frown.

"Oh, God… I'm sorry. Did I mess that up?" I replied, feeling horrible.

"No. It was the club business. She couldn't be here."

I asked him why.

"It's a long story."

"It had to do with your rivals, right?"

He nodded.

"Should I be worried?"

"No. It's all taken care of."

That was a relief. Although I'd enjoyed meeting his club brothers, there was an edge to all of them. I found it both fascinating and intimidating at the same time.

"What's up?" he asked, looking up at me.

I smiled. "I was just thinking about how nice this is. Us, being together."

He reached up and stroked my cheek with his thumb. "It is nice. I'm glad you're here."

"Me, too."

Maddox's phone rang. He sat up and answered it. "Oh, hey, Rob. What's up?"

I couldn't tell what the man on the other end was saying, but Maddox looked at me and smiled.

"Yeah, I know Charlotte. She applied for the receptionist position, huh?"

I smiled.

Maddox answered some questions about me and then hung up soon afterward.

"That was the office manager at the shop. I think he's going to call you for an interview," he said, sitting back down on the sofa. He put his feet up and grabbed the remote control. "You'd better keep your phone handy."

Sure enough, Rob called me a short time later and we set up an interview for the following day, in the early afternoon.

"How am I going to get there?" I asked Maddox, afterward.

270

"I'll see if I can find a prospect to give you a ride," he replied.

"What's a prospect?"

"Someone trying to earn their way into the club."

"Like a new recruit?"

He grinned. "Yeah, something like that."

"I can just take an Uber, too."

"Nah. I'll find you a ride."

"What about tomorrow night? Can you give me a ride to meet Jackie at the airport?"

"Fuck no. You two are on your own there."

My jaw dropped.

He laughed. "Of course I'll find you a ride."

"Don't you have another vehicle besides your motorcycle?"

"Not right now. I'm going to buy a cage before winter. Maybe sooner, now that you're here." He flipped through the channels and stopped when we both saw a familiar face pop up on the television screen.

Cody.

We watched in shock as a reporter spoke of how Cody's body had been discovered in his garage around two p.m. Apparently, he'd died of carbon monoxide poisoning.

"Authorities say there was a suicide note, but family members and friends aren't buying it," the reporter continued.

"Oh, my God," I said breathlessly.

They showed a clip of Cody's father, Bruce, being interviewed.

"My son was murdered, plain and simple. Someone is trying to cover it up and I know who," he said angrily.

271

The reporter looked shocked. "You're suggesting that someone killed your son and you know who it is?"

"Yes, and I'm going to make sure this family pays for what they've done Cody if it's the last thing I do," Bruce said, breaking down.

"Who do you think is responsible for Cody's death, Mr. Renner?" the woman asked.

"I'm not allowed to say, but these people know who they are. So do I. I'm not giving up until every last one of them is behind bars," Bruce replied.

Maddox and I looked at each other.

"You don't think he's blaming…" I couldn't even say it.

"Your old man?" he replied.

I nodded.

"Could be. Do you think he might have had Cody killed?"

The very idea made my stomach churn. I didn't want to believe it. As angry as I was with my father, I didn't want to even go there.

"I don't know," I replied, my eyes filling with tears. I got up from the sofa.

"Babe," Maddox said, trying to grab my arm. "Sit down."

"No. I've got to call my father. I need to know."

"You think he'd actually tell you if he had Cody killed?" Maddox said softly. "You of all people know he'd deny it just like he did with the bribes."

"He asked me yesterday if Cody had admitted to getting paid off. I don't remember what I said," I replied, pacing the living room. "What if *I'm* responsible for his death?"

"Don't ever blame yourself for any of this," he said firmly, getting up. He pulled me into his arms. "Whether or not your dad is involved, this isn't your fault. Okay?"

I wished I felt the same way.

"Who knows? Maybe he actually did kill himself?" Maddox added.

I didn't believe it. Cody had loved himself too much to end everything. His father was right. Someone had him killed and my father had every motive.

FORTY-THREE

MADDOX

CHUCK WAS CLEARLY tormented by the idea of Tony ordering a hit on Cody. Even after the shit he'd pulled, she still didn't want to believe he was that corrupt.

"It's late. Let's get ready for bed," I said, trying to change the subject.

Chuck nodded.

We turned off the television.

"What do you think Bruce is going to do?" she whispered later, as I held her in my arms.

"Try to find some evidence to back up his story, I guess."

"You don't think he'll try and kill my father?"

"Not everyone is a murderer," I replied, closing my eyes. "Try to get some sleep. We'll talk about it tomorrow."

"Okay."

THE NEXT MORNING we didn't get much time to talk. After making myself a quick bite to eat and filling a canister with coffee, I promised to send someone over later to take Chuck for her interview.

"Okay."

I kissed her goodbye and headed to the shop. I could tell that she was still upset about Cody's death, and wondering about her father's involvement. I wasn't sure how to handle it. The guy was a criminal, plain and simple. I just hoped she didn't continue to blame herself for what had happened.

THE DAY MOVED by pretty quickly. Fortunately, I was able to find Chuck a ride to her interview and afterward, she texted me the good news.

Chuck: *I got the job! I start Thursday.*

Me: *Sweet! I knew you'd get it.*

Chuck: *Why, you bribe him? LMFAO.*

Me: *I knew once he saw you he couldn't say no.*

Chuck: *You thought he'd find me attractive?*

Me: *Hell yeah.*

Chuck: *That explains why he asked me to dinner.*

Me: *WTF???*

Chuck: *Ha. Just kidding.*

I grinned and then told her to meet me in the back parking lot by my bike. Fortunately, I was already done for the day.

"Jesus, no wonder why he hired you," I said, walking outside a few minutes later and seeing her. She was dressed to kill in a black pinstriped pantsuit outfit that hugged her curves. Professional and yet very sexy. I whistled.

She smiled. "I'm glad I brought this suit with. I guess in the back of my mind, I knew I'd be trying to find a job out here."

"Smart. So, how much they paying you?" I asked.

"Twelve bucks an hour."

"Well, it's a start. You should still think about working at that French restaurant. I'll talk to Tank about it when I see him tonight."

"You have a club meeting?" she asked.

"No. I just figured you and Jackie would want some alone time. You know, talk about chick stuff. Boast about how great I am in bed."

She snorted. "Is *that* how you think the conversation is going to go?"

"You probably don't want to tell her too much. She might come knocking at our door in the middle of the night. I can barely handle you as it is, you little wildcat."

Chuck hit me playfully. "Her plane comes in at seven. She rented a car, so if you can just drop me off there around that time, I'd be very grateful."

I raised my eyebrow. "How grateful?"

She squeezed my ass. "You'll just have to wait and find out."

Chuck definitely made it worth my time when we got home. We made love in the shower and then had dinner together, before I dropped her off at the airport.

"Call me if you need anything," I said as she got off my bike.

"I will. Thanks for the ride, Maddy."

"Anytime."

We kissed and then I watched her walk into the terminal before heading to the clubhouse.

FORTY-FOUR

CHARLIE

J ACKIE'S PLANE WAS right on time. As soon as I saw her, I could tell that something was wrong. I just couldn't put my finger on it.

"I've missed you so much and you've only been gone for a couple of days," she said as we hugged.

"I know. I've missed you, too."

She stepped back and then we headed toward the luggage claim area.

"Are you okay?" I asked, noticing how quiet she was and how she smelled like alcohol. Although she wasn't drunk, it was obvious that she'd had a few on the plane.

She gave me a wan smile. "Yeah, I'm fine. Mom's having some issues and I'm just a little worried about her."

"Why, what's going on?" I asked, concerned.

"We're not really sure. She's been having some stomach pains. It could be an ulcer. We don't know."

"I'm so sorry to hear that."

She shrugged. "She'll probably be fine. They're running some tests in the morning."

"Is she at home or in the hospital?"

"At home. My stepdad is going to drive her to St. John's tomorrow."

"Why didn't you stay home?" I asked, shocked. Jackie and her mother were so close. She was obviously worried about the woman.

"I wanted to see you," she replied. "And I had some time off. So I figured I'd jump on a plane and come see my best friend."

I felt like there was more to it than that. I didn't want to press her on it, though. She'd tell me eventually. I had a feeling it had to do with Brian.

We picked up her luggage and then the rental car. We decided that I would drive, considering she'd had a couple of drinks and I was a little more familiar with the area.

"So, are you liking it here?" she asked as we headed to her hotel.

"Yeah. I do. I got that job, by the way."

"The one at Maddox's auto shop?"

"Yep. I start on Thursday."

"Wow. That was fast."

"I know. I'm happy, though. Lord knows I need the money."

"You should ask your dad for some. Mr. Money Bags," she replied dryly.

"We're not even on speaking terms right now." I was actually surprised he hadn't tried calling me again. Or worse, showed his face in Jensen. I knew it was just a matter of time, though. I was just waiting for the other shoe to drop.

"So, you two had it out on the phone?"

"Yeah. I talked to him yesterday and told him what I'd found."

"Let me guess. He denied it, right?"

"Oh, of course." I told her what his explanation had been about the donation to the college.

She snorted. "He's so full of it."

I agreed. It hurt to think that my father was so devious. He'd always been my hero growing up. Now I saw him in such a different light and it hurt like hell.

And what if he actually was responsible for Cody's death?

I asked Jackie if she'd heard the news about him.

"No. What's going on?"

I told her about the report on television.

Her jaw dropped. "So, he actually *killed* himself? Maybe he regretted losing you."

"I doubt it. You saw him at the strip joint."

She sighed. True."

"His dad, Bruce, claims that it was murder."

"Really?"

I nodded. "You should have seen him on the interview. He didn't actually say my father's name, but he may as well have."

"What do you think?" she asked, not sounding particularly surprised.

"I know he's done some shitty things, but… killing someone? Or arranging it?" I'd been thinking about it all day. Bribery was one thing. Murder was a totally different ballgame. I also knew that Cody did business with a lot of sketchy people. It was always possible that he'd pissed someone else off. "I mean, the guy goes to church on Sundays. Who does that and orders hits on people the other days of the week?"

"Someone trying to repent for their sins," she mused. "His skin probably starts to smoke when he walks through the door every Sunday."

Normally, I'd find that amusing. But with everything going on, it didn't seem as funny. I decided to change the subject. "So, um, how long are you staying?"

"Just overnight. I was going to try and stay longer, but now with Mom not feeling well, I'm heading back tomorrow at four."

"So, that doesn't give us much time," I said, disappointed.

281

"We'll just have to make the best of it tonight." She yawned.

"After you nap by the pool?" I said, smiling.

"I *am* pretty beat. Too bad they didn't have Red Bull on the plane." She opened up her purse and pulled out a small bottle of pills.

"What's that?" I asked as she removed the cap.

"Speed. Want some?"

"No." I stared at her in shock. "When did you start that?"

"I've been taking Speed on and off throughout the years. Hell, these are so old now. They probably won't even do the trick," she replied before swallowing two of the tiny pills.

The pills actually worked very well, because fifteen minutes later, she was babbling about everything.

"So, what should we do when we get to the hotel? Hang out by the pool? Did you bring your bathing suit?"

"No. I didn't even think about it."

"I bet they have some at the hotel. I know you're broke so I'll get you one. I wonder if it's even worth it?"

"What?"

"The pool. We could always just go and hang out at the bar…"

By the time we made it to her hotel, I was exhausted from listening to her ramble on about pools, bathing suits, and everything else under the sun.

We checked in at the front desk and then found her hotel room. It was a suite that overlooked the pool.

"Wow, you went all out," I said, looking around. There was a kitchen, a fully stocked bar, and a bathroom with a Jacuzzi.

"I figured it was for only one night, so what the hell," she replied, walking over to the bar. "You want a drink?"

"Sure. Do they have any vodka?"

"Yes ma'am," she replied. "They also have tequila, whiskey, and Malibu."

"Any pineapple juice?"

She looked around. "Yes. You're staying until tomorrow, right?

As much as I wanted to sleep in Maddox's arms that night, I owed it to Jackie. Not to mention, it was already eight. We didn't have much time to hang out.

"Yeah, I'm staying."

She smiled. "Let's party then."

"You're on."

AS SHE MIXED our cocktails, I sent Maddox a text and told him about our plans. He replied that he would miss me, but was happy that I'd be having fun.

Sighing happily, I put my phone away.

"What did he say?" she asked, handing me a drink.

"He wants us to have fun."

Jackie raised her glass. "To fun."

I raised mine, too. "To fun *and* to best friends."

"To best friends."

FORTY-FIVE

JACKIE

I hated myself. Not as much as I hated Tony, but pretty damn close. I was supposed to be Charlie's best friend and I was really only there to try and fuck up her relationship with Maddox. And, if I didn't, Cody wouldn't be the only one "committing suicide."

"Are there any clubs close by?" I asked, already setting the stage for what was supposed to unfold that night.

"I don't know. We could look. Why? Don't you just want to stay here?"

"Nah, that's boring. Let's hit the town and go dancing."

"Okay. Sure, why not?" Charlie pulled out her phone. "Let me ask Maddox if he knows of any good dance clubs nearby."

"Wait. If he finds out he might get all weird about it. You know how guys are. Especially when they have as much testosterone as someone named Mad Dog, right?"

"He's pretty low-key, actually. He's mellowed out since Aubrey, he told me. I don't think he'd flip out."

"I just want this night to be for us," I pouted. "Please?"

Charlie smiled. "Okay."

I hugged her and pretended to be happy, when I really just felt like crying.

"How's your drink?" I asked, taking another gulp of mine.

"It's great," she said, scrolling through the Internet. "I'll find us somewhere to go and we'll take an Uber. Just to be safe."

"Good idea. Let's get our buzz on first, too, and then we'll head out."

"Okay."

A COUPLE OF hours later, we were at a club in Iowa City called *Rumors*. Fortunately, it was ladies' night and the place was packed.

Charlie and I were already buzzed, so it didn't take us much to get onto the dance floor. Of course, as we were getting our groove on, guys were checking us out. Mainly, her, of course. I was used to it, though. Charlie had always turned heads.

After a couple of songs, we grabbed another drink and tried to find a place to sit. Unfortunately, it was so busy that there weren't any open tables. That was when we met Lance and Roger. They offered to share their spot with us.

"It's okay," Charlie said. "Thanks, anyway."

"Sit down," Lance said, patting the seat closest to him. "We won't bite. We're together anyway." He blew Roger a kiss. "Right, babe?"

Roger smiled and nodded.

So, we sat down and spent the rest of the night dancing, drinking, and getting to know Lance and Roger. They claimed to be in town for some kind of convention.

"We're going back to our hotel to swim," Lance said, around midnight. "Can we give you a lift anywhere?"

"Hotel? Where are you staying?" Charlie asked.

They gave the name of my hotel.

"That's where I'm staying. What a coincidence," I replied.

Not.

"We'll give you a ride back, and you can come up and party some more with us," Lance suggested. "We have a rooftop swimming pool. You're going to love it!"

Of course, Charlie was ecstatic about the idea. When she was in a good mood and had a few in her, she was up for almost anything. She was also too trusting at times. This was one of them.

We took them up on the offer and they gave us a ride in their rented limo. Once we arrived back at the hotel, we followed the two men up to the top floor.

"Who wants Cristal?" Roger called out, holding up a huge bottle of champagne.

"You have *Cristal?*" Charlie gushed. "I haven't had that in forever. I'll have a little glass. Thank you."

"No problem. What about you, Jackie?" he asked.

Our eyes met. I knew what was going to happen next. Roger would slip something into Charlie's champagne, a roofie, compliments of her asshole father. As much as I didn't want it to happen, I was as helpless as her. "Sure. Thanks."

Roger poured four glasses of champagne and them out.

"To new friends," Charlie said, raising her glass. "And old. One is sliver and the other's gold. Or, something like that."

We toasted and took our sips.

"Isn't this delicious?" Charlie asked. "I could drink this stuff all night. Thank you for treating us like this."

"You're welcome. There's plenty more, too, so indulge as much as you want," Lance said.

Her face lit up.

"So, who's ready to swim?" Roger asked.

"We forgot our swimsuits," Charlie replied with a little pout.

"Just go in your underwear," Lance suggested.

"Hell, you could go naked. It wouldn't matter to us," Roger added. "We're used to nakedness."

"We're massage therapists," Lance explained.

"Ah." Charlie took another sip of her champagne and looked at me. "Did I tell you that Maddy and I went skinny-dipping at the Holiday Inn? It's finally off of my bucket list."

"You mentioned it," I replied.

She started talking about it again, although I'd heard the story before.

"It was so fun, although for different reasons." Charlie giggled. "Let's check out the pool."

The four of us went outside and decided to swim. Charlie and I kept our bra and panties on. Lance and Roger went completely nude.

"How's your champagne, Charlie?" Lance asked, swimming away from the edge.

Charlie, who was in shallow water, smiled. "I'm getting pretty tipsy. I'd better be careful."

"Don't worry. You're with friends. We won't let you drown," Roger said.

She smiled and took another sip of the bubbly.

Ten minutes later, Charlie was so out of it, she even removed her bra and panties.

"Now I can scratch it off twice," she slurred with a loopy grin.

"What's that, dear?" Roger said.

Charlie raised her glass in the air. "Skinny-dipping!"

I cringed inwardly. She was so bombed.

And I was allowing it.

I was despicable.

"It's different when you're alone with a date. Totally," I said, forcing a smile to my face. "So, actually, it's a new one to scratch off. Skinny-dipping with friends."

She giggled. "You're right. Oh, my God, isn't it a beautiful night? I'm so happy you're here. I'm happy we met you guys, too."

I listened as she babbled on, feeling sicker by the moment.

Eventually, the two guys steered the conversation toward their careers, although Charlie was so out of it she could barely focus. She even allowed Roger to give her a shoulder massage.

"Don't worry. This is purely therapeutic," he said, pushing her hair to the side.

I looked over at Lance, who discreetly started taking pictures. Although, there wasn't anything sexual about the incident, I knew it would look incredibly bad in the photos. Especially, since Charlie was topless and smiling dreamily.

"This feels great. You must make a lot of money," she said, closing her eyes.

Roger smiled for the camera. "You could say that."

I didn't know if he was really gay or not, but at the moment, he looked like a heterosexual male turned on by the bombshell in front of him.

"I think that's enough. Don't you?" I said, glaring at him.

He frowned and let go of her.

"You know, I don't feel so good," Charlie murmured. She quickly got out of the pool, threw up in a large potted plant, and ended up passing out on a lawn chair.

"You got what you needed?" I asked Lance coldly.

"What's with the attitude? You were involved in this just as much as we were," he whispered.

I also knew that they'd been paid very well for their part.

"I was forced into it," I replied, taking another drink of champagne and staring toward the pool. If it weren't for my mother, I would have tried drowning myself right then and there.

"There's always a choice. You took yours," he replied. "So, don't act all high-and-mighty around us."

I didn't reply.

FORTY-SIX

CHARLIE

WHEN I WOKE up the next day, it was almost eleven a.m. and I had the kind of hangover that made one want to stop drinking for good. Moaning, I sat up and rubbed my temples. My head throbbed. My stomach was queasy. The night before was a blur of dancing and drinking.

"You're awake."

I looked up and saw Jackie standing by the door with a cup of coffee.

"I wish I wasn't. What the hell happened last night?"

She smiled. "We partied like animals."

"I don't remember much after we got to Lance and Roger's hotel room. Did we ever go swimming?"

"Yeah. Then you threw up and they helped carry you back to my room."

I put my head in my hands. "I feel like shit."

"I'll get you some Advil." Jackie disappeared and then came back a few seconds later.

"Thanks." I took the pills from her and then waited for my headache to go away. Unfortunately, it did nothing for my queasy stomach.

"I'm going to be checking out of here soon," she said. "Do you want me to give you a ride to Maddox's?"

"Yes. Please."

"Okay. If you want, I can also give you something else to wear."

"Thanks." I caught a whiff of my hair. It smelled like rancid. Like vomit. "Oh, God." I felt the bile rise to the back of my throat. "Do I have time for a shower?"

"Of course."

AFTERWARD, I FELT a little better but wanted nothing more than to crawl back into bed.

"Here. Drink this," Jackie said, handing me a bottle of ginger ale. "I went down to the shop and got it for you."

"Thanks."

I took it from her and then sent Maddox a text. Unfortunately, he didn't respond. Knowing he was probably too busy with work, I didn't think much of it.

"I can't reach him. I don't know if I can even get into the house he's staying at," I told her.

"Why don't we get you a room here at the hotel, so you can rest some more and not worry about it?"

Under the circumstances, I thought it was a great idea. Especially feeling the way that I did

FORTY-SEVEN

MADDOX

I STARED DOWN at the images on my phone and could barely breathe. I wanted to kill someone. I still couldn't believe what I was seeing.

Chuck.

She was naked and some guy had his hands on her. Not only that, she was smiling and obviously enjoying herself.

Growling, I looked at the other pictures, which were basically the same. She appeared to be in some pool. I couldn't make out the prick's face very well, but it didn't matter. She'd obviously fucked around on me last night and someone wanted me to see it. That someone had to have been Jackie. I just couldn't figure out why she'd squeal on her friend.

I sent a text back to the number that had sent me the photos.

Me: *Who is this?*

They ignored me.

Me: *Jackie?*

Still nothing.

I was about to send another text when my phone began to ring. It was a number I didn't recognize and different from the person who'd sent me the pictures.

"Hello?"

"It's Jackie," said a soft voice. "Did you get the photos?"

My blood boiled. "Yeah. Who in the fuck is that guy with her?" I growled.

"Nobody special. Look, I know you're pissed, but I wanted you to know what happened last night."

"Thanks a-fucking-lot," I snapped. "How kind of you. Is there anything else?"

"There will always be something else."

"What's that supposed to mean? She's a whore?"

Jackie sighed. "She's a product of her father's wicked ways. The apple really doesn't fall far from the tree, if you want to know the truth."

I began to pace.

"She's been pampered her entire life. She takes whatever she wants. Up until last night, it was you. But, that was mainly to piss off her father."

Fuck.

I knew it.

"When she's bored with you, she'll move on."

"Apparently, she already has," I replied.

"Almost," Jackie said. "She has nowhere to go right now. She still needs you."

Too. Fucking. Bad. As far as I was concerned, she was on her own.

"Who took the pictures?" I asked.

"It wasn't me, but... I wanted you to see them. So, you'd know what she's like."

I grunted. "Why did you squeal on her?"

"Because, she kept telling me what a nice guy you were. I just didn't think it was fair. You deserve better."

I softened toward Jackie. "Thanks."

"Just... you can't tell her that I called to warn you, though. Please. Just, leave me out of it."

I sighed.

"Just remember, you would have never known if it weren't for me."

She was right. "Fine."

"I'm sorry, Maddox," she said sadly. "You'll never know just how much."

She hung up.

FORTY-EIGHT

CHARLIE

AFTER CHECKING INTO my own room, I sent Maddox a text to let him know what was going on and then crashed for several hours. At around four o'clock, I woke up parched but feeling much better.

Realizing how late it was in the day, I grabbed a bottle of water from the refrigerator, drank some of it, and left another text for Maddox. This time, he replied back.

Maddox: *I'm sending someone with your stuff.*

His words confused me.

Me: *What? Why?*

Maddox: *It's over.*

Me: *What do you mean, it's over?*

Maddox: *WE are over.*

I stared at my phone in horror. Had he found someone else? What in the hell was going on?

Me: *I don't understand. What happened?*

He didn't answer, but sent me three photos. When I saw them, I gasped.

"What the *fuck*?!" I hollered, staring at the images of myself and Roger. I didn't remember taking my bra off. I certainly didn't remember Roger caressing me.

Panicking, I tried calling Maddox but he didn't answer.

"What in the hell is going on?" I cried, my hands now shaking. I quickly called Jackie. Unfortunately, she didn't answer and I realized that she was probably on the plane or getting ready to fly.

"Oh, my God, how did this happen?" I said, staring at the photo again. I remembered nothing.

NOTHING.

I tried calling Maddox again. When it went to his voicemail, I left him a message.

"Maddy, I don't know where that photo came from. I don't remember that happening. I was really drunk last night," I said, now crying. "Please, believe me. I swear to God I'm telling you the truth."

MADDOX

I LISTENED TO my voicemail and felt sick to my stomach. Whether she remembered, or not, it happened. Drunk or not, she *let* it happen. I didn't need someone like that in my life. I refused to even listen to her excuses.

Jackie's warnings rang through my head. *She's using you…*

I rubbed my face with my hands and then stood up. I wasn't going lie to myself. This hurt. *Badly*. But, I had to let it go. I had to let her go.

Fuck…

FORTY-NINE

CHARLIE

ONE OF THE prospects dropped my things off at the hotel service desk. Once I picked them up, I tried calling Maddox again and again, but he refused to answer. Soon my calls wouldn't go through and I realized that he must have blocked my number.

Heartbroken and confused, I tried calling Jackie again, but couldn't reach her for several hours. It wasn't until about nine o'clock that I finally got through to her.

"Hi, what's up?" she said, sounding tired.

"What in the fuck happened last night?" I asked, shaking again.

There was a long pause. "What do you mean?"

"Did I have sex with Roger?"

"Wait. Roger is gay, right?"

I told her about the photo and how Maddox had sent it to me.

"Wait a second, Roger and Lance took naked photos of you and sent them to Maddox?" she said angrily. "How?"

"I don't know."

"That's crazy. Why would they even do that?"

"I don't know. Maybe they looked through my phone and got his number?"

"So, they sent them to Maddox to try and break you up? Who does that shit?"

"I don't know. Nothing is making any sense." My head was reeling. A horrible thought crossed my mind.

Did Jackie know about this and let it happen?

I refused to believe it. She was my best friend. She would never hurt me like that. Not ever.

"You didn't see them do any of this?" I asked.

"I passed out on the lawn chair until they woke me up later. If you guys were fooling around, or if they were taking photos, I didn't see any of it."

I closed my eyes and moaned. "Maddox hates me now. I can't believe this is happening."

"Did you talk to him?"

"No. He refuses to call me back and I think I'm blocked now."

"I'm so sorry, Charlie. Is there anything I can do?"

"I don't know," I replied, tearing up again. "The photos look pretty bad. He must think I'm a slut."

"We both know you're not."

"I don't even remember taking my bra off. I don't remember anything after drinking the Cristal. Maybe they slipped us something?"

"I guess it's possible."

"Maybe I should call the police?"

"You could. How would we prove anything, though?"

"I don't know."

"We did drink a lot before we ended up back here. Someone could have even slipped us something at the nightclub."

I sighed. I hadn't thought about that. "Still, Roger and Lance took those pictures and sent them to Maddy." I gasped. "What if my father is involved?"

She laughed harshly. "Even he isn't that despicable."

Jackie was right. My father would never allow this to happen. He'd go after Lance and Roger himself if he found out what had happened. The problem was, I didn't really know myself.

"What am I going to do?" I asked, feeling hopeless.

"I don't know. Come home?"

"Hell no. If I come home, it's admitting defeat. I will not let Tony gloat and tell me how he was right and that I was wrong. I'd rather stay out here and try to fix this."

There was a long pause. "What if you can't?" she asked softly.

"I have to."

Not knowing what else to do, I booked a couple more nights at the hotel and rented myself a car. I also decided that on Thursday morning, I'd show up at the body shop, like I'd committed to. Not just to work, but sort things out with Maddox. I wasn't ready to give him up.

FIFTY

MADDOX

T HE NEXT COUPLE of days were tough, especially at night. I had never felt so utterly fucked over by someone I cared about. The only way that I could sleep was with alcohol, which was dangerous in my current mind-set. Many times I had to stop myself from calling her by looking at the photos again. I had to remind myself of what she was really about and it hurt like hell. But, I was determined to put her behind me and move forward.

I had to.

And then Thursday morning came.

I'd forgotten that Chuck had accepted a job at the shop, so when I walked into the office and saw her with the manager, everything came rushing back. Including my rage.

"Hi, Maddox," Rob said, noticing me.

"Hi, Rob," I replied, avoiding all eye-contact with Chuck, although I'd gotten a good look at her when I first walked in. Today she had on white slacks and a light blue silk shirt. Her hair was in some kind of soft, curly, up-do. She was as hot as ever and it burned me even more.

"We hired your friend here, Charlotte. Thanks for the reference," he said to me. "I think she's going to work out very well here."

My eye twitched. "Good."

"Hello, Maddox," Chuck said.

Our eyes locked for a moment before I nodded curtly and headed back to the service area.

CHARLIE

SEEING MADDOX AGAIN made my heart ache. I wanted to pull him aside and plead and beg for his forgiveness. But, it was obvious from the hateful look in his eyes, that he wanted nothing more to do with me.

And, man… did it hurt.

After he stormed out of the office, it took me a few seconds to compose myself.

"Someone must have woke up on the wrong side of the bed," Rob said, noticing Maddox's mood as well.

"Well, they don't call him Mad Dog for nothing, right?"

He smiled. "True. He's usually a lot chipper, though."

I nodded.

"Someone must have stolen his bone," Rob joked.

I laughed nervously. "Yeah."

Brushing it off, Rob took me to the back, where I filled out some paperwork and watched a brief video about the company. Afterward, he introduced me to Janet, who was I was replacing. Apparently, she was retiring.

"She'll train you in and introduce you to all of the service technicians. You'll also be in charge of printing out Friday paychecks and passing them out to the staff."

"Okay," I said, thinking about Maddox again. He wasn't going to be happy when Janet brought me back.

Rob looked at his watch. "I have a meeting soon. If you have any more questions, I'll be around later. Otherwise, you're in good hands with Janet."

"Thanks, Rob," I replied.

He smiled. "No problem. Welcome aboard."

"Thank you."

He left me alone with Janet, who seemed very nice.

"So, you're from New York?" she asked.

"Yes. Buffalo."

She looked at my left ring finger. "Oh, you're not married either. Watch out for some of those boys back there. I have a feeling once they get a look at you, they're going to have a hard time concentrating on cars," she said with a twinkle in her eyes.

The only guy I was interested in despised me. I couldn't let that deter me, though. I couldn't walk away without a fight. I was going to make him listen to me. I knew the pictures looked bad, but in my heart, I knew nothing had really happened between Roger and myself. I'd just have to make him believe me.

THE REST OF the day was crazy busy. Customers came and went. The phones rang off the hook. Fortunately, I picked up on their computer system pretty easily, and soon, I was handling calls and clients almost as well as her.

"You're doing great," Janet said around three p.m. "Since we're not terribly busy right now, we should go back into the service area so that I can show you around."

Anxious about seeing Maddox, I quietly followed her to the back, where it was noisy and just as busy as the reception area. One-by-one, Janet introduced me to the service advisors, auto technicians, welders, and finally the guys in the Paint Shop. As we stepped through the doorway, I saw Maddox talking to one of the other technicians. They were laughing about something and he looked so relaxed; it made my heart warm to see him smiling. When he noticed me, however, his face turned to stone. I watched as he quickly turned away and disappeared out the back door.

Trying to stay positive, I pasted a smile on my face and let Janet introduce me to the other technicians.

FIFTY-ONE

MADDOX

S EEING HER AT the shop was making me livid. I wanted to throttle her and yet I also felt like tearing her clothes off and fucking the shit out of her. I wanted to show her exactly what she'd be missing, make her beg for more, and then leave her high and dry.

But I knew it was never going to happen. I'd rather die than stick my dick into a woman who'd cheated on me. No matter how beautiful she was. I'd be lost forever if I gave in to the hunger I still had for her. She was an addiction and I needed to get clean, plain and simple.

I waited until she left the Paint Shop and then returned to work.

"Did you see the new receptionist?" Benny, one of the paint techs asked. "Damn, was she hot. I'd love to get a piece of that."

Trying to ignore the pangs of jealousy eating away at me, I told him to be careful with chicks who looked like her. "They're usually selfish and fucked in the head."

He grinned wickedly. "I don't want to marry her. I'd just like to bend her over and—"

"I get it," I snapped.

His eyebrows shot up.

"Sorry," I mumbled, relaxing. "Late night."

"No worries," he replied.

I CLOCKED OUT at five. Unfortunately, I had to go into the office to do it and ran into Chuck again. Luck for me, she was busy with a customer and I was able to slip out without having to interact with her.

At least I thought that would be the case.

As I was getting onto my motorcycle, I saw her walk out of the building and head straight toward me.

Fuck.

She was persistent. I'd had to block her number after she'd sent me several messages and texts the other day. I'd half expected her to show up at Frannie's. Thankfully, she hadn't.

Watching her approach, I thought about just taking off and leaving her in my dust. But, there were a couple of other guys in the parking lot and I didn't want to make a scene.

"Maddox, I need to talk to you," she said, with a determined look on her face.

"Aren't you supposed to be answering phones or some shit?"

"Yeah, but it'll have to wait." She moved closer to me. "Listen to me, I don't remember those pictures being taken. I was wasted." She began rambling on about the same bullshit. All lies, I'd determined.

"Who was the guy?" I asked, curious.

"Roger. He's gay. There was nothing between us."

I smiled coldly and shook my head.

What kind of a fool did she take me for?

I clenched my jaw. "Do you really think I'm that much of an idiot? He had his hands on you and you were *naked*. And looking pretty fucking happy, if I might add."

"I was drunk. I don't remember anything," she replied, her eyes filling with tears. "Why can't you believe me?"

"Oh, I believe you were drunk. That's not the point. I do a lot of shit when I'm drunk, but I own up to it. You took your clothes off. You let that asshole touch you. You even smiled and enjoyed it. Now, my only question is what the fuck are you still doing in town? *My* town."

FIFTY-TWO

CHARLIE

HIS WORDS CUT like a knife.

"Did you ever think that maybe, just maybe, someone drugged me?"

He rolled his eyes and laughed coldly. "Really? And what about Jackie?"

I remembered what she'd told me about passing out on the lawn chair. "I don't know. She fell asleep, so it's possible."

"Who took the fucking pictures?" Maddox asked.

"I think it was Roger's boyfriend, Lance."

"Was he naked too?" he asked wryly.

"I don't know."

"How convenient. Must have been some night."

"It was all innocent. There was just the four of us and they were a couple. I swear to God, nothing sexual happened."

Something flashed in his eyes and I almost thought I had him. But then he scowled. "Look, I don't have time for your bullshit stories and lame explanations. You're not using me to get back at daddy anymore, either, princess."

"I was doing no such thing," I protested.

"Right. Let me put it to you straight—I don't have time for two-bit whores. Especially the kind who spreads her legs for anyone after a couple of drinks."

I gasped. "Fuck you."

"Been there. Done that. Apparently, a lot of others have, too." He put his helmet on and started the engine.

"I can't believe you're acting like this!" I said loudly. "You're not even giving me the benefit of the doubt?"

He revved his engine.

Glaring at him, I turned around and stormed back to the office.

ALTHOUGH I WAS angry and upset, I finished up the day and then headed back to the hotel. Once I arrived in my room, I started packing.

He was right.

Why *was* I still there?

Maddox hated me.

I was alone.

I didn't even have a place to live.

I really had nothing to keep me in Jensen. Just a new job that paid hardly anything.

And yet…

I stopped what I was doing and sat down on the bed. I knew I couldn't leave him. Even after the harsh words between us. My heart belonged to Maddox. We barely knew each other and yet, I was obsessed with him. I couldn't leave Jensen until I *made* him believe me.

Whatever it took.

My thoughts suddenly returned to Roger and Lance. I recalled them saying something about staying at the hotel for a few more days. I needed to get my hands on them. I'd make them tell me why they'd sent those photos to Maddox. Whether it was because they were crazy assholes, or it was something else. I needed to know what the hell they'd been thinking.

Determined, and ready to go off on the two jackasses, I took the elevator up to the top floor and located their room number. Unfortunately, after I knocked a stranger answered the door. It was a woman. Apparently, she'd just checked in.

I apologized and then went back to my room to call the front desk. Of course, they wouldn't give me any information about the two men.

"Can you at least tell me when they checked out?"

I learned it was the same morning they'd sent the pictures to Maddy.

Frustrated, I knew I was hitting some dead ends, but I couldn't let it stop me from trying. I decided that I would remain in Jensen and work on Maddox. He'd eventually cool down and maybe even listen to me. I wasn't about to let him go that easily. In my heart I knew he was a good man and worth the trouble.

Hungry, I decided to leave the hotel, grab a bite to eat, and do some shopping to get my mind off of everything.

FIFTY-THREE

MADDOX

AFTER GRABBING SOME Chipotle, I headed to the clubhouse and waited for the other members. We had church at six and I was relieved that I'd have something to keep my mind off of Chuck. After bitching her out in the parking lot and leaving, I almost headed back there. She'd seemed so desperate and determined to set things right between us.

Had she been drugged?

I reminded myself of Jackie's phone call and her warnings. I had to admit, outing her friend to a stranger was still a little odd. No matter how nice she believed me to be. I thought about all of this as Tank called the meeting to order.

"First things first," he said, after pounding the gavel. "I don't know if you all have heard, but Buster has been charged with murdering the college student."

"No shit?" Hoss said, looking surprised.

I'd heard about it already from Tank. We'd killed two birds with one stone. Not only did we get rid of Buster, but we managed to keep a rapist off of the streets.

"He's also been charged with killing the manager at the sandwich place on Seventh Street," added Cole.

"Yeah, apparently, they found some items belonging to the two girls in his pocket the night the cops pulled him over." Tank grinned. "Thanks to us."

"Yeah, we're fucking heroes, man. Good thing we planted that kilo," Dover said, looking pleased. "Who says that drugs can't save lives?"

Tank snorted. "I don't know about that, but it was money well spent. I'm just glad we were able to get our hands on some so quickly."

"Especially that large of an amount," Cole said.

We all agreed.

"You didn't tell Lauren, did you?" Tank said to Cole.

"About our part in it? Hell, no. She's flying high knowing that dirtball is locked up. I don't want to throw a wrench in anything. I mean, we did set him up. I don't want it blowing up in our faces," Cole answered.

"Exactly," Tank replied.

"Whatever happened with Cherry?" Dover asked.

Tank smiled again. "Let's just say that we managed to help her get her son back."

"The Judge help with that?" Cole asked.

"Just with the new IDs," Tank replied. "Graham and Raptor drove out to Chicago with Cherry. They were able to snatch the baby while Rusty was at work."

"Yeah, good thing, too, because the bitch watching him was passed out and unaware of what was going on. Easiest heist we've ever done," Raptor said with a grim look on his face.

"That's a relief," I said, thinking about my own daughter. As frustrating as Kathy could be, at least her vice was gambling and not drugs. I was happy for Cherry and hoped that wherever she was now, things would work out.

"So, what are we going to do about the Devil's Rangers?" Hoss asked.

"I'm hoping that after what happened with Buster, they'll take that as a warning and stop fucking with us. In the meantime, we just gotta keep our eyes peeled and stay alert," he replied.

"You have anyone else spying on them?" Dover asked.

Tank's eyes danced. "Always."

AFTER THE MEETING, I headed back to Frannie's place and began searching online for a house of my own. She'd be back soon and I really wanted more space. Not mention, a bedroom for Aubrey. There were a couple of homes that looked interesting, so I decided to contact a real estate agent in the next couple of days. As I was searching for one, I received a phone call. It wasn't a phone number I recognized, but I answered it anyway.

"Is this Mad Dog?" a voice asked on the other end.

"Yeah. Who's asking?"

"It's Tony Armati," he replied.

Christ. Just what I needed.

I rubbed my face. "Yeah, what can I do for you, Tony Armati."

"I'm in town and was wondering if I could buy you a drink."

I wanted to tell him to go fuck himself but my curiosity got the best of me. I wondered if he knew that Chuck and I were no longer seeing each other. I decided he probably didn't, which was why he was looking to meet with me.

"Sure. Where?" I said.

"This is your town. You tell me where to meet you and I'll be there."

My mind went to the dive bar not too far from Frannie's. It was a hole-in-the-wall, but I didn't feel like driving all over town to meet with Chuck's old man. "There's a bar called Floyd's on Tenth Street. I can meet you there in an hour."

"Sounds good. By the way, if you could keep this between us, I'd appreciate it."

"I'll meet you there in an hour," I repeated, not answering him.

He paused. "Fine."
I hung up.

TONY WAS ALREADY at Floyd's when I arrived. He was in a back booth with a fresh drink in front of him. I sat down across from the guy just as the waitress appeared.

"Can I get you anything?" she asked me.

I ordered a Michelob Ultra. She nodded and left us alone.

"So, what's this about?" I asked, leaning back.

"Come on. You're not stupid. You know." Tony took a drink of his cocktail. "

"Not really."

He studied my face. "Charlotte."

"You're wasting your time talking to me about your daughter. We're not together."

Oddly enough, he didn't look too surprised. I mentioned that.

Tony shrugged. "She's a rebellious girl who is always moving from one man to another. I once thought it was to get back at her mother and me."

"You think she's trying to prove something?" I said, feeling pissed off again.

"Mostly to me. I sheltered her too much when she was growing up."

"She mentioned that you were always trying to run her life. Anyway, like I said—we're not together, so you can save your breath."

"Is it true that she's working at the same company you are?"

"Yeah."

321

The waitress returned with my beer and then left.

"I'm a little curious as to why she's staying in Jensen if you two aren't an item," he replied.

"Why don't you ask her yourself?"

"She won't talk to me."

"Lucky you."

His eyes burned into mine. "Somehow I don't feel as if you're happy about the current situation."

"Look, I'll be frank… I don't give two shits about your daughter or what she's doing," I lied. "She can work or live wherever she wants."

"But, you'd prefer it not be in Jensen."

I grunted. "Maybe."

"She got under your skin," he replied with a smirk.

"No." Another lie. "We barely even knew each other."

"Charlotte is a beautiful young woman. She's also spoiled and reckless. I suspect that she's working at your company to try and win you back. Why else would she stay here?" he said, playing with his stir straw.

I'd been mulling about that myself.

"Maybe. I don't have time for games, so it's not going to happen." I wasn't even sure as to why I was having a discussion with Tony Armati anyway. He didn't deserve my attention.

I took a long swig of my beer, determined to get out of there as quickly as possible.

"Wise choice."

I didn't reply.

"So, where is she staying?"

"I have no idea. I'm sure you can figure that out on your own," I replied.

He nodded.

I finished the rest of my beer quickly. "Not to be rude, but I have better shit to do right now then talk about this."

Tony looked amused. "I'm sure you do."

"We through here?"

He nodded. "Unless… you'd be interested in helping me get her back to New York?"

I wasn't interested in helping him with anything, but once again, my curiosity got the best of me. "I'm listening."

He looked around and lowered his voice. "I'm sure you're tired of seeing her at your place of business anyway, so this could be a win-win situation."

"Yeah? How so?"

"If you can persuade her to come home, I'll make it worth your while."

I grunted. "Still manipulating your daughter's life with bribes, huh?"

His eyes hardened.

I stood up. "A word of advice from one father to another—let her learn from her own mistakes and pick your battles wisely."

"Says a man with a five-year-old," he scoffed.

It didn't surprise me that he knew about Aubrey. It still pissed me off, though.

I leaned down and stared into his eyes. "If there's one thing I do know, it's that being a father isn't just about protecting your child. It's about letting them experience the world and being there for them when they need it."

"The world is—"

I cut him off. "Fucked up. Sheltering them only makes weak snowflakes."

"You think my daughter is a weak snowflake?" he asked, almost amused.

I pictured Chuck hammering Cody's car with the bat. I then imagined her drunk and fucking around on me and the other schmucks who'd bought in to her gorgeous smile. "She's weak in the places that count."

FIFTY-FOUR

CHARLIE

I RETURNED TO work the following morning and found out that it was "Potluck Day."

"Oh, I'm sorry. I think someone mentioned it yesterday, but I forgot. I can go and pick something up from the grocery store quickly," I told Janet.

"Nonsense. It's only your second day here. We hold these once a month. There's usually a signup sheet in the breakroom. Just bring something next time."

"Okay."

Of course, Maddox and I ended up bumping into each other at lunchtime. He gave me a dirty look and the same cold attitude. Janet, not picking up on the awkwardness between us, asked him if he'd brought anything.

"Chicken wings," he said, nodding toward a red crockpot.

"Oh, what kind?" I lifted the lid. "They smell delicious."

"Jamaican," he said gruffly.

One of the other techs, a guy named Art, started ribbing him. "I thought maybe you were the one who brought the little weenies."

"I didn't want you to be intimidated by them," he joked, watching me take one of the wings. I bit into it and my mouth was immediately on fire.

Janet, not noticing my misery, put a wing on her plate. "Are they spicy?"

"Hell yeah. Don't eat it. The guys asked me to bring the wings in to test them out. I used ghost peppers. I was just about to put this sign up warning people," Maddox said, placing a card next to the crock pot that said INSANE WINGS – GHOST PEPPERS.

"Thanks for warning me," I said hoarsely.

He smirked.

I rushed over to the water dispenser and filled myself a cup of water.

"Ghost peppers. Aren't those a million Scoville units or something?" Janet asked.

"Something like that," Maddox replied.

"What's Scoville units?" I asked. My eyes were watering and I was sweating, the wings were so damn hot.

"A measurement of pepper heat. Ghost peppers are one of the hottest ones out there. It's like eating acid," Art said.

I looked over at Maddox who was still enjoying my pain. I gave him a dirty look and he chuckled.

"He should have warned you," Art said, after Maddox left the breakroom with a pile of food on his plate.

I agreed.

Fine.

He wants to play?

Game on.

I DIDN'T BUMP into Maddox for the rest of the day and when I left the building, I noticed his bike was gone. I knew I probably wouldn't see him until Monday, so I was a little disappointed.

I got into my rental and drove back to the hotel and changed into some shorts and a T-shirt. I then headed to the mall. Still determined to get Maddox's attention, I decided I would splurge a little. After purchasing several eye-catching outfits, four pairs of heels, and bottle of perfume, I had my nails and eyebrows done as well. Afterward, I picked up something to eat and headed back to the hotel.

The next couple of days were spent working on my tan and using the fitness room. Of course, I constantly kept checking my phone to see if Maddox had suddenly found a change of heart. There was nothing, though.

When Monday morning came, I put on a new white blouse, which complimented my tan, a pair of black pants, and stilettos. I carefully did my hair and makeup, and then added a spritz of perfume. When I finally walked out the door, it was with more confidence than the week before. I was hoping Maddox had cooled down and would realize how much he wanted me. In case he hadn't, I was determined to remind him.

MADDOX

I'D BEEN HOPING I'd return to work on Monday and find out that Chuck had quit. Unfortunately, it wasn't the case. Not only that, but she seemed to be glowing and looked better than ever.

"Hi, Maddox," said Janet, who was standing next to her at the front counter. "You're in a little late today. Rough weekend?"

I'd spent most of it at the clubhouse, drinking and watching sports with the guys. It had actually been pretty boring, but I wanted Chuck to think differently. I wanted her to give up whatever it was she was doing, so I lied.

"Oh, hell, yeah. We had a huge bash this weekend. I'm still recovering," I replied noticing, with pleasure, the irritated look in Chuck's eyes.

"And you didn't invite me?" Janet joked.

"I already had a date, otherwise… I would have," I replied.

Of course, none of it was true, but the scathing look Chuck gave me was a homerun.

"You have my number," Janet said, winking and smiling.

I chuckled and headed to the back.

A COUPLE HOURS later, I headed outside to eat lunch outside when I found Chuck sunbathing at one of the picnic tables. She'd taken off her white blouse, revealing only a white camisole that barely contained her gorgeous rack. Nestled between her breasts was a thin, gold necklace I'd never seen before, which was also sexy as hell. She had her eyes closed and was leaning back against the table. Talk about a wet dream.

Fuck me.

At the next picnic table over were two techs smoking and gawking at her.

Seething inside, I wanted to tell her to put some clothes on, but remembered that she wasn't my business anymore. Instead, I turned on my heel and went back into the shop.

CHUCK

I OPENED MY eyes just as Maddox was turning around. He headed back into the building so quickly, I almost missed him. Of course, I knew he'd seen me and was determined to make sure he *kept* seeing me. As angry as he was, I knew I had only one thing in my arsenal that could win him back—my body and my looks. It was a cheap play, but I was desperate.

THE REST OF the week went pretty much the same way with Maddox trying to avoid me and me making sure that he couldn't. Every outfit I wore was appropriate for when I wanted it to be and revealing when I *needed* it to be—which was usually around lunchtime or in the parking lot.

A couple of instances, I could tell that he was furious enough to spit bullets and thought he'd live up to his road name. But, he kept his cool. Then, on Thursday night, I thought I'd almost had him. After clocking out, I changed into some super short-shorts and timed it so that we walked out to the parking lot at the same time, with him following. I dropped my keys and leaned down to pick them up, knowing he was getting an eyeful of my new black thong.

"Classy," he mumbled, walking around me. "There's a dress code, you know."

"I'm done working," I replied, standing up.

He looked back and scowled. "Dressing like that around here could get you into trouble."

"With who?"

He grunted and turned around.

"Maybe I'm looking for some trouble."

Maddox stopped for a second and then picked up his pace.

I hid my smile.

FIFTY-FIVE

JACKIE

"**I**'M SORRY. WE did everything we could," the doctor said to me and Tom.

I stared at him in horror.

Had we heard him right?

"Wait a second. What are you saying? She's gone?" Tom asked in disbelief.

The doctor nodded. "I'm so sorry for your loss. I know it was sudden and unexpected."

Tom had just brought my mother into the ER and I'd met them there. Apparently, she'd been having severe head and stomach pains, worse than before. I thought they'd just give her some pills or keep her overnight for observation.

But not this.

I hadn't even gotten to say goodbye to her…

"I don't understand. How did she… what killed her?" I asked, barely able to get the words out.

"Metabolic Encephalopathy." He began to describe it and all I heard was something about an infection and organ failure.

"We have a chaplain here, if either of you would like to talk with someone," he said softly.

"I'd like to see my mother," I said, openly crying now. I couldn't believe this was happening. It felt like a horrible, horrible dream.

"We both would," Tom added tearfully, putting his arm around my shoulders.

"Yes. Of course," the doctor replied.

TWO HOURS LATER, I was back at home and feeling completely overwhelmed by the loss of my mother. Sitting at the kitchen table, I stared blindly at the refrigerator, feeling as if nothing else mattered anymore.

She was gone.

Forever.

I had nobody else. Tom and I weren't really close, although he was a nice guy. There wasn't anyone else in our family to share this kind of grief. Of course, there was Charlie, but I didn't deserve her sympathy.

Not after everything I'd done.

Feeling utterly heartbroken, I covered my face and wept.

I SPENT THE next forty-eight hours shut up in my apartment, either crying or contemplating suicide. I didn't care anymore. I just wanted the heart-wrenching pain to stop. As I stared at the bottle of Ambien, wondering how many it would take to put me out of my misery, my phone rang. When I saw who it was, hate and disgust burned in the pit of my stomach. Of course, he would be the one to call me at my darkest hour. No doubt to make more demands.

"Have you talked to Charlie recently?" Tony asked when I answered. "Is she coming home?"

I doubted he'd heard about my mother's death. Or, maybe he had and was just that cruel and insensitive.

"I don't know," I replied hoarsely.

"Strange."

I couldn't believe how evil and ruthless the man was. He'd set everything up. Including having his own daughter drugged enough to pose for pictures. And I'd let it happen. I didn't know who I was more ashamed of—me or him.

"I just got back from the airport."

Not caring, I didn't reply.

Tony then told me about his trip to Jensen.

335

"I talked with Mad Dog and they're not together anymore, which is a relief. I guess our plans paid off."

Our plans?

I bit my tongue so hard, it started to bleed.

He went on. "I don't understand why she's staying in Jensen, though. There's nothing there of interest, as far as I can see. Not even for her. Do you have any ideas?"

"No."

"Are you okay? You sound weird."

"My mother died."

There was a long pause. "I'm sorry for your loss, Jackie."

Like *hell* he was.

"Do you want some company?"

I was about to tell him that I wanted to be alone, but then changed my mind. "Yeah. I could use some."

"I'll be there in an hour," he replied, a smile in his voice.

"Okay."

I hung up the phone. I knew what I had to do. For me. For Charlie. Even for Cody, the lousy, greedy bastard.

I TOOK A shower. As I stood under the water, I felt calm and almost relieved. I knew I was making the right decision.

A short time later, Tony knocked on the door. I let him into my apartment. He pulled me into his arms and I stiffened up.

"I'm very sorry. I know how much she meant to you," he murmured in my ear.

"Thank you," I replied, pulling away from him. I'd always hated physical contact with Tony. His touch made my skin crawl.

He held up the bag he was holding and smiled. "I know how to make things better. I brought some wine and your favorite chocolate."

Make things better?

There was only one way and I was determined to make it happen.

"Thanks," I replied.

"It smells great in here. What are you cooking?" he said, following me into the living room.

"I made lasagna."

It was just the frozen kind from the grocery store. I knew he'd hate it, but didn't care.

"That sounds good."

I asked him to join me.

"I will. Thank you," he said with a grin.

We walked into the kitchen and Tony began rifling through my drawers for a corkscrew. I pictured stabbing him in the eye with it, and it brought a smile to my face. "I'll take care of this. Why don't you relax?"

He sighed. "I should be taking care of you right now. After everything you've been through."

I knew he was only showing compassion for his own best interests. He would grill me about Charlie again. Then try to have sex with me.

Not tonight.

"I'm fine. The food is probably ready, so just take a seat at the table."

He grinned happily. "Perfect timing on my part."

I agreed.

He sat down and I poured each of us a glass of wine. I then fixed two plates of lasagna and set them on the table.

Tony looked down at his food and frowned. "This is frozen?"

"Yes. With everything that's happened, I haven't had time to prepare any gourmet meals," I said dryly."

"I understand." He looked at me and smiled. "Have you tried the lasagna at my brother's restaurant? It's the best..."

I listened as he bragged about the restaurant and how wonderful the food was.

"It sounds great. You know, we should have a toast," I said, raising my glass. "To *Wine Garden's* culinary delights."

We clinked glasses and both took a sip.

"Speaking of *Wine Garden*, I hope that Charlie returns soon. They miss her there. Do you think I should return to Jensen and plead with her to come home?"

I laughed harshly. "No. You're the last person she's going to want to see."

He didn't like my response. "She's my daughter. I have only done, what I've done, for her own good."

"Right," I said dryly.

"You know, I understand you're upset about your mother, but you don't need to be rude," he replied with a disapproving look.

I forced a smile to my face. I had to quit being so flippant or things wouldn't work out the way I needed them to. "You're right. I'm sorry."

He took another sip of wine. "This tastes funny. Does yours?"

"Like how so?"

"I don't know. Just bitter."

"Mine is fine.

"Maybe it's because of the lasagna."

"That's probably it."

We ultimately finished the bottle of wine and he choked down the food. Afterward, Tony stood up and began to sway.

"Are you okay?"

"I'm tired. I think I'll go and lie down for a while," he said, looking disoriented. "It's probably just jet-lag."

"Yeah, I'm sure," I replied.

"I never did like flying." He began walking away. "Would you like to join me? We can watch a movie or something."

Normally, *something* was sex.

I smiled. Not tonight. Not ever.

"Sure. I'll be there in a minute."

Nodding, he left the kitchen.

I waited for a few minutes, until I knew he'd be asleep, and entered the bedroom. I found him lying on my mattress, snoring. The Ambien I'd crushed and put in his wine had worked perfectly.

I sat down at my laptop and typed a letter to Charlie, confessing everything. I told her about the relationship I'd had with her father and all of the things he'd made me do. Even about my part in Jensen. I apologized and asked for her forgiveness, although I didn't deserve it. Afterward, I printed out the letter and signed it.

Sighing, I walked over to my nightstand and pulled out the gun I had hidden. Tony had given it to me for protection. In a sense, that's what I would be using it for. Protection for me, Charlie, and all the other faceless people who stood in his way.

I loaded the gun and pointed it at Tony. My hand shook as I pulled the trigger. I unloaded every bullet into him, but one.

"Please forgive me, Charlie," I whispered, before turning it onto myself.

FIFTY-SIX

CHARLIE

I WENT BACK to work on Friday, this time wearing a black skirt and green blouse. It showed a little cleavage, but wasn't too revealing.

"Some of the guys have been asking about you," Janet said.

I raised my eyebrow. It certainly wasn't Maddox. "Really?"

"I knew that would be the case. You're a pretty girl."

I smiled. "Thank you. That's very sweet of you to say."

She sighed. "I was a looker back in my twenties," she said with a wistful look on her face. "Then I had three kids and everything went to hell." Janet chuckled. "It made me a grandmother though, too. Definitely worth it"

I was about to ask her about them when Maddox walked through the door. Our eyes met for a minute and then he looked away again.

"Hi, Janet," he said, ignoring me. "When is your last day again?"

"Next week," she replied.

"You're definitely going to be missed. I don't know what this place is going to do without you," he said.

She looked pleased. "I'm sure Charlie here will hold it together."

"Right," he replied bitterly before disappearing into the back.

"I wish I was thirty years younger, I'd show that hunk a thing or two. You know, you two would make a good looking couple," Janet said.

"You think?" I asked softly.

She gave me a puzzled look. "I thought Rob said you two knew each other."

"A little."

"Do yourself a favor, get to know him more than 'a lot'. I have a feeling it's worth it. Even though he wears one of those biker vests, he's one of the sweetest guys in the shop."

"Interesting."

"Very. Anyway, let's get started," she said. "We need to get the paychecks printed for our employees before noon."

"Okay."

For the next couple of hours, we worked on payroll. Afterward, she showed me how to use the printer. When the checks were finally ready, she asked if I needed help distributing them.

"No, I'll be fine."

"Okay. When you're done, you may as well go to lunch, too."

"Thanks."

FIFTY-SEVEN

MADDOX

I WAS ON my knees, and in the middle of pin-striping a GTO when I heard the sound of heels moving toward me. Knowing who it had to be, I groaned inwardly and turned my head and got a close view of her legs. The last time I'd been that close to her thighs, they'd been around my waist.

"What?" I asked sharply, looking up at her.

Chuck handed me an envelope. "You want to get paid, don't you?"

"Can you put it over on the shelf?" I nodded to my work station. "My hands are a little busy right now."

"Okay."

I watched her walk away and scowled. She'd been driving me wild all fucking week. Especially last night, when she'd bent over and I saw her thong riding up her ass. It took everything I had to walk by without sliding my hand down her shorts. It was all I could think about that night and had to jerk off to calm myself down.

Today, she had on a pair of black heels that showed off her sexy calf muscles and heart-shaped ass. If that wasn't irritating enough, she dropped the check and bent down to pick up the envelope. She'd turned into a klutz, but I wasn't stupid. I knew Chuck was secretly messing with me. She was doing a good job of it, too.

"Damn," whispered Jeffrey, one of the other paint techs, who was now standing next to me. "What an ass, huh?"

I gave him a dirty look. "You know, if HR heard you right now, you'd be in deep shit."

345

"It would be worth it. I wonder if she's single?" he said, still admiring her.

"If she is… it's because she has baggage," I growled, looking back at the pin-stripe I was working on. "Hot chicks are trouble. I keep telling you guys that, but nobody seems to listen."

"They're also rare. Especially, here. Mm… So are tits that perfect. I wonder if they're real."

My eye twitched.

They were one-hundred-percent real. The same with her dusky, pink nipples…

Chuck walked back over and smiled at Jeffrey. "I bet you want your check. Sorry, what was your name again?"

"Jeffrey Anderson. You can call me Jeff," he replied, his voice a couple octaves lower now.

"Okay, Jeff. Here you go," she said, handing him an envelope.

"Perfect. So, where are you from?"

"New York," Chuck replied.

The two of them kept talking and I had to bite back from telling them to move the fuck along. Just listening to the exchange was irritating. Especially knowing where all of this was going.

"So, you don't know a lot of people in town, huh?" Jeff asked, as their conversation wound down.

"Not really," she replied.

"I could help you with that. There's an outdoor concert tonight, downtown. If you want to go, I'll introduce you to some of the locals. A lot of people will be there. It'll be a blast."

"It's nice of you to offer, but… I don't know." She sighed. "I mean, we work together… people might get the wrong impression."

"It doesn't have to be a date. We'll go as friends and nothing more."

"Oh. Well, in that case…" she replied, smiling. "Sure, why not?"

I growled under my breath and stood up. "You'd better get those checks delivered. Some guys leave early around here," I said to her sharply.

"They'll be fine," Jeff replied. "There are times when Janet doesn't get them to us until two anyway. By the way, Charlie, have you lunch yet?"

"No, but I'm hungry," she replied.

"Did you bring anything? I was thinking about grabbing a bite to eat from the deli down the street."

"Do you mind having this conversation somewhere else? I'm trying to concentrate on this paint job," I snapped.

"Sorry. I should get these checks over to the others," Chuck mumbled, walking away.

"Man, did you wake up on the wrong side of the bed or what?" Jeff asked when she was gone.

"I've got a lot of work to do. I don't need distractions."

"Or friends, apparently." He turned and walked away.

I sighed. Her working at the shop was *not* going to work for me. Not if I was going to stick around. Just listening to her talk about hanging out with another guy made me livid. Hangry and jealous, I decided to go and grab some food before I murdered someone.

I cleaned up and headed out the back of the shop. Of course, I ran into *her* again. She was standing in the parking lot and looking under the hood of the Chevy Malibu she'd been driving all week.

I tried ignoring her, but my curiosity got the best of me. I doubted she knew anything about cars, for one thing. For another, I wondered whose vehicle it was.

FIFTY-EIGHT

CHARLIE

"WHAT ARE YOU doing?" Maddox asked in a grumpy voice.

I looked up. "I have no idea. The Check Engine light came on and I just thought I should see if something was steaming under the hood."

I grunted. "And what would you do if it was?"

"I don't know. I guess I'd figure it out from there."

"Whose vehicle this?"

"I rented it."

"Let me have a look. Why don't you start the engine?"

I did what he asked. Of course, the Check Engine light didn't come on. It never had.

"Good," he said, closing the hood. "I'd still tell the rental agency about it."

"I'm going to."

Not saying anything else, he began walking toward his bike.

I was about to get back into the car when I saw Jeff jogging toward me.

"Going out to lunch?" he asked, smiling.

"Actually, yeah. I was going to check out the deli you mentioned."

"Mind if I join you?"

Before I could answer, Maddox stormed back over, clearly ticked off again.

"She and I already have plans," he muttered.

Jeff's eyes widened. "Oh, really?" He looked at me. "Is that true?"

I laughed nervously. "Uh, I guess so."

Jeff smiled. "Okay. Have fun."

After he walked away, I looked at Maddox and frowned. "You and I are having lunch? *Really?*"

"Get in the car," he ordered.

As much as I hated being told what to do, I was secretly thrilled at what was happening. And, I had Jeff to thank for it. Little did Maddox know that he and I'd run into each other at Panera a couple of nights ago. Recognizing each other, we sat down and got to talking. Eventually, the conversation turned to Maddox and I told him that we'd recently broken up.

"I can help you get him back if you want," he'd said.

"How?"

"Make him jealous."

I'd been trying to attract him, but Jeff suggested we take it to a whole new level.

"If he still wants you, he'll be possessive and angry as hell," Jeff said.

"He's already angry, why not?"

And now, here we were. Maddox was furiously jealous. It was obvious. I just had no idea what he was going to do with me.

"Where are we going?" I asked Maddox as we left the parking lot.

"I don't know yet," he growled. "I just need some time to think."

"Well, I'm hungry."

"So am I," he snapped.

"Obviously. Why don't we do something about it then?"

He gave me a sideways glance and then sped up. A few minutes later, we arrived at the clubhouse.

"What are we doing here?" I asked, confused.

Ignoring me, he got out of the car, opened up the gate, and then returned to the driver's seat.

"Maddox?"

"Are you seriously thinking about going out with Jeff?" he asked as we pulled into the parking lot.

"Yeah. But, just as friends."

He grunted.

"What are we doing here?"

"Having lunch and making plans."

"For what?"

"Your trip back home."

I crossed my arms under my chest. "I'm *not* going back to New York."

"We'll see."

He parked the car and we headed into the clubhouse. He unlocked the door and we stepped inside.

The place looked deserted. "Nobody is here."

"I know." He locked the deadbolt behind us, which was a little alarming. I thought I knew Maddox, but what if I was wrong? What if he turned violent on me?

"What are you doing?" I asked nervously.

He walked toward me with a scowl on his face. "The real question here is—what are *you* doing?"

This wasn't going the way I'd thought. He looked like he wanted to murder me. I backed away. "In regards to…?"

"Don't play coy with me," he snapped, coming at me until my back hit the wall. "Why are you still in town?"

FIFTY-NINE

MADDOX

S HE WAS FRIGHTENED. I could see it in her big green eyes.

Good.

The plan was to scare the fuck out of her so she'd go back to New York and get out of my life, once and for all.

"To work," she answered.

"Bullshit. You could get a job anywhere. Especially as a receptionist. You're here to fuck with me, aren't you?"

Her eyes hardened. "I'm not the one who brought me here. You could just keep ignoring me in the shop and we'd both be fine."

I looked down at her cleavage and the tight little skirt she had on. Even now I wanted to rip everything off, bury my face in her breasts, hike up her skirt, and jam my cock deep inside of her. "Ignore you? How am I supposed to ignore you when you're flaunting yourself in front of me at work?"

"I'm not doing any such thing," she said, lowering her lashes.

"Really? Look at me," I ordered.

Our eyes met. Hers were smoldering.

Fuck.

"What's going on, princess?" I growled, putting both hands against the wall and trapping her. "What exactly is it you want from me?"

Charlie swallowed.

I slammed my hand against the wall, startling her. "Tell me!"

"You," she whispered.

I glared at her. "You. Had. Me."

Charlie grabbed my belt and pulled me closer. "But not anymore?"

Lust, and a raging hard-on, drove me over the edge.

Our lips crashed together in a fiery kiss. She moaned into my mouth as I tore at the buttons of her top and yanked her blouse open. I unclasped the peach bra she wore and nuzzled her breasts, savagely licking and sucking the tips.

Gasping, she unbuckled my belt and opened my jeans.

CHARLIE

I WANTED HIM so badly, my legs were shaking.

His cock sprang free and I grabbed it hungrily. As I stroked his shaft, he reached down and hiked my skirt up. His fingers reached for my panties and he groaned when he felt how wet I was. He slid his fingers under the fabric and rubbed my clit.

"Oh, God," I moaned.

Pushing my hand away from his cock, he got down on his knees and buried his face between my thighs. His tongue lashed inside of me, working me open and driving me wild. I arched into him as he drove me crazy with his mouth and fingers. My body shook and my brain reeled as he worked me into a frenzy until a violent orgasm hit me full-force. I heard myself shrieking like a madwoman as the waves rippled through me.

Maddox

AS SOON AS I heard her scream in pleasure, I stood up and turned her around. Spreading her hips apart, I entered her tight, hot wetness and growled in pleasure. I pulled out and slammed into her again and again until I was moving hard and fast, like a jackhammer. The need to explode built within me, a rising crescendo as my pulsing cock raced to climax. My balls tightened and suddenly I was blowing into her like a hurricane. Gasping in pleasure, I could feel her pussy clenching around my cock, milking every last drop out of me.

When it was over, and my senses returned, I felt like I'd betrayed myself and my integrity.

I was a horny asshole.

A fool.

Angry, I pulled away from her and we started getting dressed. Both of us were silent and the tension in the air was awkward.

"Um, so what now?" she asked, as I buckled my belt.

"You hungry?" I asked, not looking her in the eyes. I was starving now more than ever. It wasn't just about the food either. I felt empty inside.

"Maddox," she said firmly.

I looked at her.

"Do you really believe that I fucked that guy?"

"I don't know what to believe anymore."

"I came out here to be with you. Not because of my father. But, because I thought we had something going. I thought you really cared."

"And I thought—"

"Hold on. I have the floor right now," she snapped. "Now, I don't care what those pictures show. That was not me. I don't remember anything. Mentally, I wasn't there.

Those guys *must* have drugged me. I wish I would have known to go in and get tested the next morning. I had no idea, however, that things would turn out like this. That you wouldn't believe me."

I frowned.

"Listen to me, dammit. I would have *never* had sex willingly with anyone else but you. Or fucked around on you." Her eyes bored into mine. "For God sakes, Maddox," Chuck said, her voice breaking. "I'm not here to punish you. I'm here because I fucking *love* you."

SIXTY

CHARLIE

HIS EYES WIDENED. "Why would Jackie call me and tell me that you were using me then?"

My jaw dropped. "What?"

Maddox told me about their conversation and how she'd begged him not to say anything.

"Oh, my God, why would she do that?" I said, horrified.

"You don't believe me?"

"Yes, I believe you," I said. There was no reason for him to lie. "I just don't understand… unless…"

"What?"

"My father is really behind all of this," I replied, getting angry.

His jaw clenched.

"I mean, why would she come and see me when her mother was having major health issues, anyway?" I began to pace back and forth. "And, what if this was all a setup to begin with?"

"That would really be fucked up. Two people who are supposed to care about you? I hope to hell it's not true. For your sake."

I hoped not, too, but the more I thought about it, the more plausible it was becoming.

"If it's true, does that mean my father knew that I would be drugged?" I said, feeling sick to my stomach.

Maddox sighed and told me about the visit from my father.

"So, he didn't know we were broken up?"

"Apparently, not." Maddox told me how Tony had tried bribing him.

Before I could respond, my phone began to ring. I grabbed my purse and took it out. The phone number was from New York. I answered.

"Charlie?" a male voice said on the other end.

"Yes."

"This is Jackie's stepdad, Tom. There's been an incident. I'm… so sorry."

A lump formed in my throat. "What kind of an incident? Is her mother okay?"

"Oh, God. You didn't know about that, either?" he asked, his voice filled with emotion.

"What's going on?"

He told me that Jackie's mother had passed away, and then shortly after, my father and Jackie were found dead in her apartment.

"It looks like a murder-suicide," he added.

I gasped in horror.

"What's wrong?" Maddox murmured, moving closer to me.

I looked at him, but couldn't speak.

Tom began to cry. "I'm so sorry."

The room began to spin and then everything went dark.

SIXTY-ONE

CHARLIE

Four Weeks Later

New York

"**A**RE YOU SURE you don't want to come and live with me for a while?" my mother, Bianca, asked as the limo drove us to the airport. She'd just finished signing the paperwork to sell Dad's home in Buffalo and was flying back to Paris. Fortunately, for me, she'd been able to stick around for the last three weeks. It had been the longest time she'd stayed in the States since I'd graduated from high school.

I reached into the new black purse mom had given me and pulled out a mirror. It was one of her newest designs and named "Charlie." It was gorgeous and I'd been honored when she'd presented it to me.

"I'm starting at Fremont next week, remember?" I said.

"That's right. The culinary school. You mentioned that it was in Iowa, right?"

I nodded.

It was only an hour away from Jensen, so Maddox and I could still see each other. Unfortunately, I'd been forced to give up my job at the body shop. My father had left me almost everything in his will, although I was planning on donating most of the inheritance to charity. Along with the fortune I was supposed to receive when I turned twenty-five. From my grandfather. I'd learned that he'd also been part of the mafia and I didn't want any part of it.

"Are you going to continue to see Maddox?" she asked, studying my face.

"Yes. Why? You don't approve of him?" I replied, wondering how she really felt. They'd met at Dad's funeral, and appeared to have gotten along very well. Of course, she'd always been good at pretending. She'd even played the perfect, grieving widow, although I suspected being rid of my father was a relief. Especially after reading the letter Jackie had written. I was certain that he'd manipulated Mom throughout the years, although she hadn't admitted anything to me.

"I liked him. He's just from such a different world," she replied, her eyebrows knitting together. "Are you certain you really want to get involved with that lifestyle?"

"You're talking about the biker club?"

"Yes. I've read a lot of frightening articles about the Gold Vipers. Danger seems to follow them everywhere."

"Apparently, I've been surrounded by *that* my entire life. At least I know what I'm getting myself into with Maddox."

"I guess I can't argue that," she said with a sigh.

"Anyway, Maddox claims the media has it out for them and to ignore the gossip."

"Weren't they involved with some murders?"

"That was a few years back. Anyway, they were the ones targeted by a rival club. Tank lost his girlfriend to the Devil's Rangers. Not to mention his father," I replied.

"That's what I read," Bianca replied. "He's the president of Maddox's club?"

"The Jensen chapter. Anyway, things have died down and they've made peace with their enemies."

That was what I'd been told, at least.

"Good."

"As for the rest of the club, they're all very nice people," I added.

In fact, I'd flown to Jensen the week before to visit for three days while Mom stayed in New York. Before returning to Buffalo, he brought me to a club barbecue. Admittedly, I'd been a little anxious at first, but most of his friends had accepted me with open arms. Of course, we'd gotten some ribbing when he'd called me Chuck and I'd called him Maddy. But, all-in-all, I'd enjoyed the get-together and was looking forward to seeing them again. Not to mention, returning to Maddox. I was missing him like crazy. I didn't know for sure what tomorrow held, but he'd admitted that he loved me, too, and wanted a future together. I didn't know if he meant marriage and kids or what. But, I was willing to go all the way if that was where it led us.

"That's good," she replied. "It's just so odd for me. I would have never expected you learn how to ride a motorcycle or get a tattoo."

I looked down at the trail of hibiscus and tropical leaves on my wrist. I'd had it done before returning to New York by a guy named Hollywood. He'd been visiting from Minnesota and belonged to the Gold Viper Chapter in that area. We'd left it uncolored, although I was trying to decide whether I wanted it filled in or not.

"You don't like it?"

"Actually, I do. It's just hard seeing these changes. It reminds me of how little we see of each other."

"We'll just have to change that, won't we? Especially now."

She nodded and smiled sadly. "You know, I wanted to take you with me to Paris when I first moved back there. Tony wouldn't hear of it, though."

"I realize that. You never made me feel as if I'd been abandoned," I said, knowing she needed to hear it. In all honesty, I might not have followed her anyway. Not at eighteen. I'd been clueless as to what had been going on around me. I still couldn't believe that Jackie had been involved with my father or how he'd manipulated her. I understood why she'd needed the money, but her deception still felt painfully fresh. Not to mention her involvement at the hotel and lying to Maddox.

"I'm glad you feel that way. Many times, I felt like such a failure. But… your father wasn't an easy man to live with."

"Why did you two even get married?" I asked bluntly.

Bianca opened up about their "arrangement." Apparently, she'd been pressured into marrying him by her own father.

"I wanted to say 'no', but I knew it would have killed Papa."

I stared at Bianca in shock. "Why?"

"Your grandfather borrowed a large sum of money from Tony and couldn't pay him back. It was for some investment that failed miserably. He owed so much that even I couldn't gather what was needed. Not even with my modeling career. Anyway, Tony agreed to settle but only if I became his wife."

A familiar story.

"So, you never loved him?" I asked.

She looked down and shook her head in shame.

I couldn't blame her, however, it was tough finding out that my mother had been forced into marriage. Not to mention that I clearly hadn't been conceived out of love.

"You're upset," she said, reaching for my hand. "I'm sorry, Charlotte. I didn't mean to hurt you."

"Don't apologize, Mom. You were a victim. One of many," I replied softly.

She nodded and then leaned forward to hug me. "You were the only good thing to come out of all of this. I hope you know that I love you with all of my heart."

"I love you, too, Mom."

She sat back in the seat and I could see there were tears in her eyes.

"Honestly, I feel like I'm abandoning you all over again. I wish I could stay longer…" she said.

I knew Bianca had a new line of purses dropping next week and had been stressing out about it.

"You're not abandoning me. You have to get back to work. I understand, and would never hold it against you. I'm just happy you were able to stay these last few weeks and help with everything."

"Me, too." She pulled out a tissue from her purse and dabbed at some tears. "You know, as horrible as your father was, we created a pretty incredible young woman. I'm proud of you for following this dream of yours to become a chef. I know you're going to be very successful one day."

"Thanks."

"Maybe you'll even open up your own restaurant in Paris?"

I smiled. She was never going to give up on trying to get me to move out there. "Maybe."

"That's not a 'no'," she replied, looking pleased. "I'll take what I can get."

I chuckled.

We arrived at the airport and said our bittersweet goodbyes. Afterward, watching her walk away from the limo made my heart heavy, but… I felt closer to her than ever and knew she felt the same.

"Where to next, Ms. Armati?" the limo driver asked.

"Beresford Cemetery," I replied

THIRTY MINUTES LATER, I stood over Jackie's gravesite and let out a shaky breath. I'd been too upset to attend her funeral, but knew I couldn't leave New York without closure. Deep down, I knew the things she'd been forced to do had brought her so much misery. If anything, she'd been my father's worst victim.

My eyes filled with tears as I remembered our childhood and the fun times we'd had growing up together. Our lives had been filled with laughter and innocence. Our friendship had been real. There'd been no secrets. Only joy and excitement.

"I'm sorry about my father," I whispered, thinking again of the letter and multiple confessions.

She'd even been responsible for the anonymous caller. Jackie had explained that she'd paid someone to warn me about Cody and Dad.

"I forgive you, Jackie. I'm still angry, but I know you didn't mean any harm. I just hope that you've forgiven yourself."

A sudden gust of wind blew my hair around. Knowing it was supposed to rain soon, I looked up at the gray clouds moving across the sky. I watched as two broke apart and the sun peeked through.

Smiling, I wiped the tears from my cheeks. In my heart, I knew it was a sign from her.

I kissed my second two fingers and touched her gravestone. "I love you, girl. See you later, Gater."

I could almost see her smiling back at me.

I turned around and walked toward the limo. Before I made it back, my phone rang.

It was Maddox.

"I was just calling to see how you're doing," he murmured in my ear. "I know your mom is heading back today."

"Yeah. I already dropped her off at the airport."

"Ah. So, you sold the house, huh?"

I'd forgotten to tell him. "Yeah, how did you know?"

"There's a SOLD sign in front of it."

I froze. "Wait, are you there?"

He chuckled. "Yeah, babe. I followed a moving truck through the gates. You should have seen the looks on the new tenants faces when they saw me."

I squealed in joy.

"Where should we meet?" he asked. "I managed to get some extra time off and want to spend it with you."

My heart melted. "I'm staying at a hotel." I told him which one. "I just checked in last night."

"Okay, sounds good. I'll meet you there."

"Perfect."

"I love you, Chuck."

"I love you, too, Maddy."

SIXTY-TWO

MADDOX

I PUT MY helmet back on and touched my pocket to make sure the ring was still there. Of course, I'd been checking for the last several hours. I was nervous as all hell, but excited at the same time.

I fucking loved that woman.

My old man always told me that when I fell in love it would hit me like a cement truck. And he was right.

"Beautiful women will turn your head all the time. It's the ones who turn your head to mush that are the real keepers, though."

And he was right. I couldn't concentrate on anything other than the girl I was about to see. It was now even starting to affect my creativity at work. I had to make her mine completely. Seal the deal in every way.

I wanted her heart and soul.

I wanted her future.

Hell, I wanted to *be* her future.

She could go to college and pursue whatever career she wanted. I didn't care.

I just needed her to say 'yes.'

Because of the lengths she went through to try and get me back, I had a feeling she'd give me what I wanted, too.

Revving my engine, I headed away from Chuck's past, toward our future, smiling like an idiot.